Other books by **Robert J. Morrow:**

FICTION

New York Fried, an Artichoke Hart adventure

with *Toni Carrera*
Highland Hiatus, Menu for Passion, Book 1
Trinidad Tryst, Menu for Passion, Book 2
Detroit Dalliance, Menu for Passion, Book 3

with *Natalie Tang*
Sympathy for a Devil, Devil's Run Book 1
Devil in Disguise, Devil's Run Book 2
Devilish Behavior, Devil's Run Book 3

NON-FICTION
Investing in Student Housing
How to Sell your Home Privately in Canada

Sold Strategies *(US & Canada Edition)*
The Cheapest, Safest, and Smartest Ways to Sell Your Home!

Buck Tradition
The Smartest Way to SELL YOUR HOME in Canada

The Barre Chord Approach
Learn Rhythm Guitar without Theory

Twenty-Five Years of Magic
History of Panasonic Canada Ltd.
remo
available at www.amazon.ca and www.amazon.com
in paperback and/or Kindle version,
or for other e-formats: www.robertjmorrow.com

Prologue

The Dutchman watched the waves as they pounded the shore, curious as always with the destructive power wielded by something that appeared so soothing and beautiful. Controversies in nature intrigued him, as did all things he couldn't control; there were so few of them.

The tropical sun beat down as he shifted his gaze to the rocks below the cliff he was standing on. The Caribbean Sea and its endless need to pound his island and reshape the contour of the shoreline brought a smile to his weathered face.

His thoughts wandered to images of how, in the movies, a body falling from a cliff top would unceremoniously bounce on the rocks and spin a couple of times in the air before disappearing into the sea.

The Dutchman knew that Hollywood didn't quite have it right, of course, having experimented with the concept a few times now. He leaned forward a little more, catching a glimpse of where the last body had landed. No bounce, just an insignificant thud. And the mangled corpse hadn't disappeared for several hours while the undercurrents and lapping waves licked at its prey in a monotonous courtship until finally drawing the prize into its depths. It had taken yet another hour before all the blood and body parts had slithered into the deep water for the sharks to feast upon. The Dutchman had sat in this very spot watching, just three months before, not sure what he was waiting for but confident that he was in the presence of something he simply had no control over. And yet he was enthralled. He was anxious to see it again.

Despite being fair haired and ruddy in complexion, the sun didn't bother him now. He spent a lot of time outdoors, ever since purchasing the island a few years ago. In fact, he rarely left now that there was no need.

A distant relative of one of the founding families of Shell Oil, the Dutchman had taken his nominal inheritance at age twenty-one and turned it into a multi-million-dollar enterprise by investing in start-up technology companies back when investing in internet projects was considered reckless and foolhardy. While attending a conference at Harvard, he'd met two bright young men who had what the Dutchman thought was an innovative plan. He invested a large portion of his portfolio with them on a hunch that they were on to something big. When Microsoft was finally allowed to purchase the company some years later, his YAHOO! friends had, indeed, created something quintessential to the emerging masses. But they had relinquished control and so the Dutchman was no longer interested. The sale, however, had made him a multi-millionaire overnight. Seclusion had been imperative, and Shell Island had become his haven.

He felt a vibration in his pocket and took out his satellite cell phone, another wonder of technology that he wasn't able to control…unless he turned it off. He had been waiting for this call, however, and answered it quickly.

"Is she here?" he asked

A female voice replied. "The team is ready and in place. She will arrive in three days."

He smiled and stared out into the deep blue ocean, slow moving clouds etching their way across the near horizon. "That's wonderful," he said gleefully. "I'm looking forward to our time together."

"Yes, well I'll be expecting a deposit in my bank account before we go any further, correct?" the woman said.

The Dutchman frowned. This was his project and he controlled things. Lucky for her, the serenity of the moment calmed him quickly. Though he needed her for the next few weeks, she would be dealt with afterwards. This was, after all, his last project.

"Check your account in an hour or so," he said. "When our charade is complete, you will be even richer. As long as all goes to plan."

"Blind and deaf too, correct?" she said.

As well as arrogant, the Dutchman thought. But then, that's why she was so good at this. A pity he wouldn't need her again. She would have made a lovely house pet. "You know the rules of the game, dear," he said and grinned.

"The game," she said and the Dutchman could sense disgust in the tone of her voice.

"Yes, my dear. Play the game well and you'll never need to work again. Make an incorrect move and you'll be shark bait before the month is through."

There was silence on the other end. The Dutchman could hear her breathing and knew he had shaken her, not just from his words but by the tone of his voice. He knew she was aware it had been no idle threat.

"It will all go as you planned," she resigned.

"Yes, it will," he said and pressed the end call button.

The Dutchman watched the scene from high above for a few moments longer, leaning over the edge once more to burn an image of the rocks below into his mind. He wanted to recall it at will over the next few days.

He then turned and headed toward the golf cart that would take him down the hillside to the lagoon where his Japanese-style villa lay.

The sea and I will yet again be satisfied, he thought quoting some obscure seventeenth century poet sailor whose name he had forgotten long ago.

Chapter One

Natalie Grainger was applying a last line of pale pink lipstick when she caught her lover's frown in the mirror.

"What's up Benny?" she said, her eyes dancing between his eyes and her own lips, pouted and already glistening from Benny's favorite rouge-colored gloss.

"That dress is pretty short isn't it?" he said.

Natalie laughed. "Your wife wears shorter."

Benny, or William Travis Benneton as the corporate world knew him, wasn't accustomed to being argued with. Especially from underlings. Natalie snickered. Yes, she was an underling alright, but she was no employee.

"You can't be late tonight Nat," he said, turning back to the living room. "You don't want to miss the boat, so to speak," he grinned.

"Cute" she said. He was referring to the annual company gathering aboard a tourist vessel, a thank you for all the underlings' hard work for the past year. She heard the front closet door open and a moment later Benny returned, raincoat casually thrown over his arm, a dark trilby hat in his other hand.

"I want you to meet someone tonight," he said, staring at her reflection in the mirror.

Now it was Natalie's turn to frown.

"I've told you Benny, I don't need an escort to functions, I'm perfectly fine by myself."

Benny bounced his hat off the edge of his elbow. He did things like that when Natalie questioned him. "You can't keep coming to events alone when you have no apparent purpose for being there."

"There are enough people there who know my, what did you call it… my purpose?" she said a little haughtily. "They talk to me, even if they're only doing it to please you."

"You need protection too," he said.

She turned from the mirror, one hand pointing the lipstick tube at him.

"You've been bringing that up a lot lately," she said. She moved closer to him, grabbed the hat and put it on her head at an odd angle. Benny smiled. "Is there something going on you're not telling me about?"

"Come on Nat," he said, straightening the hat on her head and pushing it forward to rest just above her eyebrows. "I'm the President and CEO of the second largest insurance conglomerate in the country; I'm always worried about security."

"You have bodyguards following Emma around don't you?" Emma was Benneton's wife. "I hear she's difficult enough to contain."

"Let's leave Emma out of this," he said. "I'm concerned about your safety and I want to hire someone to… well, to hang around."

"You should buy me a Great Dane, Benny," she said. "I don't need some brain-challenged muscle man 'hanging around'". She smiled, took the hat off and handed it to him. "Besides, you might get jealous." With that, she gently nudged him aside and strutted toward the front hall closet. She could sense Benny's eyes on her and she exaggerated her lower wiggle slightly.

"Just be nice tonight, okay?" he said, following her to the door, "and open to new friendships."

Natalie let him help her with her light coat then turned and looked him in the eyes for a few seconds. Benny didn't blink, or smile, or back away. He just stared back.

"You already have someone don't you?" she said, suddenly comprehending.

"Just be approachable tonight, that's all," Benny said. "I'll steal away some time after the cruise is in full swing. I'll need fresh air anyway."

"And Emma hates a strong, cold breeze, doesn't she?" Natalie said flatly.

Benny just sighed and opened the door. "I'll see you on the top deck around ten or so," he said, then added. "I've ordered a cab for you. It'll be downstairs in ten minutes."

"Gee thanks," she said, blowing him a kiss as he approached the elevator. She knew his limo would be at the front entrance waiting for him. "And Benny?" she called just as he stepped into the elevator.

"If I fall in love with your bodyguard, it'll be all your fault."

Benny held the doors back for a moment and stared at her, his eyes revealing a pained expression. Natalie instantly regretted her flippancy.

"I'm sorry," she said. "I'll be good, I promise."

She gave a short princess wave as the elevator doors closed taking Benny down to his awaiting car, his awaiting wife, and the dreaded three-hour cruise from Savannah.

Chapter Two

The air was chilly, despite it having been a scorching hot day. But as often happened in early fall in the Carolinas, once the sun dropped below the horizon, the advent of winter could be felt in the breeze.

On the three-level, open air tourist cruise boat, that breeze worked its way around the open dance floor where groups of three or four people, all dressed to the nines, schmoozed, hob-knobbed, caroused, and drank lightly; mostly because this was a work-related event and even though they were on a boat just off the coast of Hilton Head Island, it was still work. Spouses would have rather been anywhere else but the employees were ready to take advantage of Benneton Insurance's benevolence during this annual free excursion.

The boat wended its way along the Savannah River--the actual border between Georgia and South Carolina--around Cockspur Island, crossing the state border, heading out into the open waters of Colibogue Sound. They would slow to a crawl once it reached protected waters just beyond South Beach at the southern tip of Hilton Head Island.

Natalie was glad she'd let Benny talk her into the extra sweater. Despite this being one of the warmest falls on record, it would still be only sixty-five degrees, and out on the water it felt more like fifty. She was idly chit-chatting with one of the lower managers of Benny's company, a man who knew who and what she was but still treated her like another employee. She didn't really like the man but at least he made the situation as comfortable as it could be.

She eyed Benny, looking distinguished and commanding in his black tuxedo talking with one of his vice-presidents and his wife. Emma Benneton had her arm through Benny's and was laughing at whatever the men were saying. It seemed to Natalie that Emma was over-exaggerating her emotions but that's what trophy wives do.

Natalie must have been ignoring the guy she was talking to because he excused himself suddenly.

"Sure," Natalie said. "See you around." She swished her half empty glass of wine around a little and headed out to the aft deck. A few feet away, one guy, average looking at first glance but well put together, was alone, leaning over the railing, his highball glass in both hands as he stared out into the ocean.

Natalie waited until Benny briefly looked her way, then she casually walked over to the man and put her arm through his, leaning in close.

The man quickly turned his head to look at Natalie. His surprise was evident, though it didn't change to alarm, just curiosity.

"I'm Natalie," she whispered. I do hope your wife isn't just in the washroom."

"She may be, but the house is in Baltimore," he said. His voice was low and throaty, but friendly at the same time.

"Ahh," she said knowingly. She was used to talking with married men who didn't bring their wives to business social events. She liked them. And in the past she had seduced them, though she didn't like that aspect of her personality, and hadn't done it since meeting Benny, who had been the ultimate catch. *Take that Mom*. Married men are less demanding than single men her age. They know they can only offer part of themselves, so it was okay when she only gave them part of herself.

"I'm separated."

"Perfect," she said, pretending to smile. Damn! Separated men were usually still attached to their ex's, which meant part of her efforts could be listed as babysitting. But this one was cute after closer examination, tall with a full head of black bushy hair, the prerequisite five-o'clock shadow, and a nice smile. He'd be useful enough to piss off Benny. And he wasn't hard to look at. She briefly recalled her mother's standing comment that all the good-looking men were taken. Only the divorced or delinquent seemed to escape the wedding bells. Her mother was somewhat of an expert on the subject, having been through a few delinquent ones herself. This one was separated though, so he wasn't officially anything at this point. Maybe he could be persuaded to join the lonely single life, at least for tonight. Then neither of them would be lonely. Or single.

She pulled him away from the railing, and still arm-in-arm, strolled back into the parlor. She saw Benny's face break into a slight grin which agitated her immensely.

"It is getting crowded here," she said, turning her attention back to the man.

He nodded. She took one last look only to see Benny engaged in conversation again. His wife, Emma, was still perky, outgoing, and looking much too gorgeous for a fifty-something.

They reached the aft staircase and her new friend motioned for her to climb the stairs to the top level. She shrugged and led the way. It was open air up there and the wind rustled across the deck. Music from the band on the first deck was playing but not loud enough to hinder conversation.

She looked around. Conversation wasn't the main activity up here she mused. Couples were leaning against the railing, talking intimately or openly necking.

Natalie let go of the man's arm, suddenly realizing she didn't know his name. She was about to ask when a barely noticeable dull noise suddenly erupted into a roar. She wandered to the port railing to see a huge cigarette boat lurch into view from the bow of the boat, heading along the side in the opposite direction, creating waves that would likely jostle the party boat.

"Babes want a fast ride?" someone in the back of the boat yelled to no one in particular as they passed. Natalie figured they'd been drinking and the music coming from the speedboat's speakers was drowning out the music on the first level of the party boat.

Natalie reached out over the railing and gave the boaters the finger. The boat driver laughed as he roared past, zig-zagging dangerously close to the bigger boat.

"Are you working the party?" the man suddenly asked.

She spun abruptly, quickly forgetting the speedboat, ready to slap him. But just as suddenly she decided not to. His eyes weren't confrontational, not even inviting. They were just... well, grey. Maybe the ironic accuracy of the remark, or his apparent nonchalance in not knowing how close it was to the truth, caused her to sigh. Then she snickered, grabbed his hand and led him back down the stairs and to the edge of the parlor, partially hidden by the boat's superstructure.

"Thanks for the compliment. But no. I don't need to work it," she said. She pointed to the far center of the room where Benny still stood, working the crowd himself.

"That's my lover there," she said, moving aside so he could see who she was pointing to. "And his wife."

The man watched for a second then stepped back out of view.

"You expected her to be here?" he asked.

Her bluntness hadn't seemed to phase him. "She's always..." Natalie tried to think of the right word, then not coming up with anything witty said, "here." Then she turned away. "I need another drink," she said.

The man took her arm and steered her back toward the stairs and up to the open deck again. She followed. The bar up there wasn't as busy.

They got their drinks and strolled over to the railing again, watching the sun as it slowly lowered itself toward the far-off Atlantic horizon.

"What's your name?" he asked as they stared out into the darkening evening.

"Natalie," she said. "And you?"

"Drew," he said.

Not Andrew, Natalie thought, just Drew. Cute. Abbreviated name, likely matching an abbreviated lifestyle. She'd be willing to bet his ex had called him Andy.

"Why William Benneton?" Drew said. "He's awfully old for you."

She cocked her head and the corner of her lips twitched upward. "He's awfully rich."

"I see."

She watched his reaction, ready to tell him he didn't see at all and that it was none of his damn business anyway. Money was the great benchmark of success according to her mother, who, of course, had never managed to get past the array of rich wannabees that never seemed to amount to anything in the end. She was about to share that thought when the same engine roar as before came back on the opposite, starboard side.

They could hear the driver yelling back, the exchanges comical, childish and lewd. The speedboat wavered alongside, its inhabitants yelling at anyone who engaged them in banter.

Suddenly a loud boom came from nowhere and the whole boat shook violently. A woman on the other side of the deck lost her footing and fell. Her date helped her up. Drew grabbed Natalie's arm to steady her but she had already grabbed the railing.

"What the…" she exclaimed.

Surprisingly, the music was still going, the band obviously unable to hear any noise other than their own. But in the background a woman's scream came from below.

The first couple, now standing, the man's arm around his date, were leaning out over the railing, looking at something directly beneath them.

Natalie ran over to where they stood, Drew close behind. They leaned over the railing and peered out.

Directly below them, they saw that the cigarette boat had slammed into the side of the party boat, its fiberglass bow crushed almost flat. Flames were erupting from the side of the party boat where it had struck and there were pieces of fiberglass and wood floating all around the wreckage.

Four people were in the water, bobbing up and down.

"Get me outta here!" one of the men in the water screamed. His accomplices were too busy swallowing water to yell but they were obviously in the same state of distress.

A young man in a mariner uniform ran to the railing beside them and threw an orange life buoy to the guy in the water. Beside him on the deck, more people gathered to see what was going on. Natalie could see heads

17

popping out from the railing and windows of the two decks below them, the lower deck only a few feet above the smashed speedboat.

"Everything's fine folks," the sailor said, seeming only now to notice the hoard of people standing around him leaning over the railing.

He sounded calm, Natalie thought. But anguish was clearly etched on his face.

Drew suddenly turned and swiftly walked to the staircase, heading down.

"Hey, where are you going?" she yelled after him but he didn't stop or acknowledge her. She took one last look at the mayhem in the water below and followed.

At the entrance to the parlor on the second deck she found him staring into the crowd. He was looking for someone.

Most of the people had moved to the open railing and were all trying to get a glimpse of the spectacle. The atmosphere was surprisingly subdued, wonder and curiosity in the eyes of most people she could see.

The boat staff were attempting to organize a rescue attempt, seemingly in conjunction with others on the main floor below them. The flames weren't above that level yet but the smoke was and some were backing away, coughing.

Drew strode over to the railing by the door and Natalie went and stood beside him. She saw a greasy film of oil growing outward from the larger boat, surrounding the wreckage of the speedboat. She couldn't see any damage to the party boat but the hull swept inward below them so the actual impact point was obscured. The water wasn't putting out the fire though, she thought.

As the smoke intensified, some moved to the other side of the boat but most were still gawking at the railing. Several blue and white-clad sailors ran onto the deck and yelled for everyone to please move to the opposite side of the boat, apologizing as they went but insistent in their gesturing.

When no one responded immediately, they began grabbing people by the arms and when the passengers turned in annoyance, continued to apologize but dragged them away from the railing.

Drew took a step back and Natalie watched his face. There was anguish, yes, and annoyance. But with his jaw clenched and eyes riveted out to the horizon, determination seemed to be the dominant emotion.

"What's wrong?" she asked, grabbing his arm.

He shook his head but didn't look at her. His eyes began searching the room again. Natalie noticed his gaze land on Benny and his wife. They were being dragged away from the damaged side of the boat. Benny looked annoyed that someone was manhandling him and was trying to brush the guy off, but it was one of his bodyguards and he wasn't having any of it. Emma looked horrified, Natalie could see, but she continued to look over the railing until a uniformed sailor pulled her away.

Drew was staring at them. Natalie squinted. Oddly, she hadn't thought of Benny and what he might be doing during this escapade but now, with Drew's attention clearly focused on him, she turned him toward her.

"Hey, Benny can look after himself," she said. "He's got a whole security team." Surprised at her own nonchalance about her lover's safety, she grabbed Drew's other arm and shook him, forcing him to stare down at her. "Are we okay here?" she asked slowly. "Is this thing safe?"

Drew took one last look at the older couple, now being hauled off toward the staircase leading to the lower deck, and turned his attention to Natalie. As if suddenly realizing what was happening, he looked around the rest of the room and back to the aft of the boat. The angle had altered slightly, as if the boat was turning sharply and leaning toward one side.

"Come on," he said, grabbing her arm. "I doubt this thing can withstand a hit like that. If it can't we need to be near a lifeboat."

They ran upstairs and over to the opposite side of the deck where two large lifeboats were gently swinging on their davits. They bumped into people streaming up from the lower deck heading to both sides of upper deck. There were two boats on either side and it seemed they were accessed from this, the highest deck. It got crowded very quickly and Natalie moved to grab Drew's hand, gripping it tightly as the crowd grew thicker around her.

Each lifeboat's davits were controlled by a mini crane and white-clad sailors were squeezing their way toward the control boxes on both sides.

"Please… let me through," Natalie heard one of them say. "Ma'am, I need to get through." She watched as he continued to push and pry his way to the railing on the opposite side to the wreckage. The majority of the crowd had worked its way to that side of the boat as the floor was definitely angling more to the other side.

"Are we going to sink?" one older woman in a long, brown dress shrieked at a staffer as he pushed his way past her.

"How far are we from shore?" another asked.

"Are there enough lifeboats for everyone?" a man asked, grabbing a sailor as he pushed by.

Before he could answer, a tall, bearded man said, "What the fuck! This isn't the Titanic, lady."

There were a few anxious snickers, worried looks, and a lot of what Natalie thought was the visual expression of male bravado. But most people still slowly pushed toward the sections of the railing where the lifeboats hung.

Natalie watched as one sailor peered out toward where she thought the mainland was. She followed his gaze. It was nearly dusk and the shoreline wasn't clearly visible. There were one or two twinkling lights in the distance but she couldn't tell whether they represented small dock lamps or larger, far-off lights from houses and hotels.

"It's just a precaution folks," the sailor said. He was at the railing now, pulling open the lifeboat crane control box. "Please Ma'am, he said as he reached over a young woman who was blocking his way to the release mechanism. "Please, let me through," he said, more sternly this time. Clearly, he was losing his patience. Natalie listened carefully to his voice. The young sailor wasn't panicking but it was obvious he was trying to control his own fears. His skin was tight around his eyes and his lips were curled inward. This was no routine event and he was aware there was an element of danger. He was trying to be a pro but Natalie could see that the frenzied crowd was getting to him.

She'd lost track of her new friend but when he whispered into her ear, she turned her head and saw him staring at her intently.

"We're about a mile from shore," he repeated, briefly glancing toward the water and the twinkling lights beyond. "The water is going to be very cold." He turned her to face him.

"Can you swim?"

Chapter Three

"Are you friggin' kidding me?" Natalie said, hands on hips, her eyes blazing.

Drew looked back at the crowd jostling for position as close to the railing as they could get, pushing and shoving.

Suddenly the boat lurched again and settled into a noticeable starboard list.

Panic took over as several people screamed. Couples hugged, women buried their heads in their partners' chests. The men were mostly staring out across the darkening, wavy expanse of water between the boat and the shore, worry etched into their faces.

Some at the back of the crowd who clearly understood they wouldn't reach the railing and get close to the lifeboats, turned and headed down the staircase.

Drew grabbed Natalie's arm and propelled her along with the throng, down the staircase. At the second level, he pulled her away and swung her underneath, back to the port side of the boat. There wasn't much space between the stairs and the parlor wall, so there was only one other couple at the railing.

"It's a party boat, right?" the woman was saying to her date. "We're not so far from shore, are we?" The last words were raised in a panicked staccato pitch. The man looked at Drew and Natalie but no one said anything. Drew edged past the woman to lean over the railing.

He looked up. There were now two sailors trying to manipulate the crane mechanism which would send the lifeboat down the two levels to the water but they were struggling due to the angle. The lifeboat was now firmly wedged against the superstructure of the boat.

Drew stared back out to where the shore should be. There were a few twinkling lights in the distance but the darkening sky made it difficult to ascertain what they were, or how far away they were.

A small crowd gathered just below the stairs and one passenger held onto the staircase railing to steady himself. Drew figured he would have fallen over had his friends not gathered close to keep him upright. He was holding a beer bottle and its contents were sloshing out now and again, soaking his friends. One wiped his sleeve with disgust.

"Hey, we need a soundtrack. Where's Celine?" the drunk said, his words heavily slurred. One of his friends tried to grab the bottle out of his hands but failed and the drunk raised it higher, more beer sloshing out as he waved it around uncontrollably.

"Jesus, Frank, put your arm down," his friend said.

Frank resisted and his friend gave up, a look of anxiety on his face.

"Hey, are we going to sink?" Frank wailed, voicing the concern everyone was thinking but no one had yet vocalized. It had just occurred to him, it seemed.

No one answered. Drew told Natalie to stay by the railing then pushed himself through the gathering crowd across to the other side. He leaned over and looked down. Lots of debris but the list was greater than it had been a few minutes ago and the water was now lapping over the first floor deck. A sudden lurch and the list got even greater. Drew took one last look at the water that was now pouring into a couple of the windows closer to the bow.

A couple of shapes flew in front of him and a second later, bodies splashed into the water. He also saw people floating out of the lower level bow windows. People on the decks were yelling for them to stay calm till rescue came and some tried to swim back inside the windows. But more people were floating out and just bobbing around near the wreckage.

Drew ran back to Natalie and put his arm around her. She was shivering and he tried to block the wind that had picked up a bit. They looked up as they heard moans and loud voices.

People were trying to get into the lifeboat even though it hadn't been released yet. One of the sailors was trying to keep the exodus orderly but he wasn't having much luck.

A tuxedo-clad man popped his head over the edge of the boat and yelled at the others waiting to board.

"There aren't enough boats," he yelled and pointed toward the shore. "We'll have to swim."

There was muted conversation between several passengers and the staff and the older sailor suddenly put his hands up in surrender.

"Rescue boats are on the way," he said. "But they'll take twenty minutes or so. It's safer to stay onboard till they arrive."

"If the boat sinks much more, we won't be able to get off as easily." one older man said loudly. "I think we should all jump, then swim out that way--" he pointed toward shore, "--so we don't get sucked under if the boat goes down."

Natalie stared up and saw the incredulous looks on the faces of the men and women still crowded against the railing. This was a party boat, hired for a company function. How the hell did this happen?

As if to emphasize the need to take immediate action, the boat lurched again and the list became greater still. On que, one or two people climbed the rail and tentatively stepped out from the boat. Natalie stared as seconds later they bobbed up out of the water, sputtering, their faces scrunched with fear, eyes bulging.

Others followed until it became a steady stream of people jumping from the middle and upper decks. Natalie and Drew watched as women's dresses floated to the surface forming flower-like shapes on the water's surface.

The crowd in the water was surprisingly quiet, Natalie thought. As if reading her mind, Drew said, "It's got to be cold."

The couple beside them stared at Drew, then the woman turned to her date.

"We won't have to swim all the way, will we?" she asked, her voice catching in her throat.

"They don't count on these things sinking," her date said and turned to Drew as if for reassurance. "There are never enough lifeboats for anyone."

"Rescue boats will be on the way," Drew said, grabbing Natalie's hand.

"Can't we stay on board until they get here?" the woman asked, her tone frantic.

Her date looked at Drew who slowly shook his head.

"But the rescue boats have got to be here soon," she implored. Her date looked torn.

"If we're in the water, we'll be rescued first," he said, but didn't sound convinced.

The woman looked at Natalie and Drew, her eyes wide with fear. Her date's wide eyes made it clear he wasn't sure what to do.

Drew turned to Natalie, grabbed her hand and turned her to face him.

"Yeah, I can swim," she said, nodding her head. "Shit, it's gonna be cold."

Drew bent over and untied his shoes. Then he pushed his pants inside his socks. Natalie watched, then pushed her heels off with her toes. She wasn't wearing hose or nylons.

Drew looked at her. "That's good. You don't want anything dragging you down. We shouldn't be in the water long. The Captain will have radioed our distress. Boats from the harbors will already be on their way."

Natalie nodded her head, unable to speak at this point. This was crazy!

Drew grabbed her hand and, with his other hand, grabbed the edge of the stairwell above him and pulled himself, then Natalie up on to the railing.

Natalie glanced furtively at the other couple who were staring wide eyed, hugging closely. "You sure about this?" she asked.

Drew laughed then scrunched his face. "I'd rather take my chances out there than with this bunch. It's going down and the rescue boats will pick up stragglers first… They have to, they're all in the way."

Natalie looked out at all the bobbing people in the water. It was amazingly calmer out there than on the boat. Probably the numbing fucking cold!

Drew let go of the stairwell, and still holding onto Natalie's hand, balanced momentarily on the railing. He looked at Natalie and nodded.

She took a gulp and launched her body out into the unknown.

Chapter Four

Holy Shit!

    He hadn't expected it to be this cold. Upon impact with the water, Drew had tried to hold onto Natalie's hand but had lost his grip so he held out his arms horizontally to arrest his sinking. When his body slowed, he began pumping his arms and legs in a breast stroke upwards. In just a couple of seconds, his head broke the surface and he gasped for air.

    He was only ten feet or so away from the boat and he pulled himself around in a circle looking for Natalie. He heard a spurt behind him and turned to see her head pop up about five feet away. At first, he didn't recognize her; her hair had lost whatever styling she'd given it and was now long and straight, stuck to her face, cheek and neck. Her eyes bulged and she was breathing quickly, taking in huge lung fulls of air.

"Natalie! Calm down. We're okay," he yelled, swimming the short distance to her. With one hand he brushed her hair out of her fearful eyes. She grabbed his arm and he tilted her head backwards..

"It's okay, I've got you," Drew said, turning her around and leaning her back against his chest. He began to do a backstroke with his free hand, his other arm now around her chest. He pulled her along until they were a good twenty feet away from the boat. Eventually Drew felt Natalie's hand pull his arm away from her.

"I… I can do it," she stuttered, releasing herself, then turning and beginning to tread water. "How far do we have to swim?" Her voice had lost its panic but her eyes were still frantic.

"Not far," Drew said, looking around him. "Those shadows on the horizon, they're small boats."

She followed his gaze and began swimming toward them. Drew took one last look at the now heavily listing boat, people steadily leaping into the water, utter chaos having stricken the pleasure cruise.

He pushed both his legs and followed Natalie who, with a strong front stroke, was closing in on a mid-sized cuddy cabin racing toward them.

Chapter Five

Natalie watched as Drew closed the hotel door behind them. She shrugged off the blanket she'd been given on the boat.

"I have to get out of these wet clothes," she said, her voice stuttering a little. "I can't remember the last time I felt this cold." Her wet hair sloshed from side to side as she stepped into the bathroom and closed the door behind her.

The cruiser Captain had been a local resident of Hilton Head and he informed them that a search and rescue post had been set up at the Marriot, which was one of the island's luxury waterfront hotels and the closest dock to where the tour boat's SOS signal had originated. Apparently, it wasn't the first time the residents and local hoteliers had put together such a team, but this was the first time it had been due to a tour boat accident in the Sound. Regardless, the hotel was putting all the passengers up for the night, checking them off on a manifest list, and promising to give their names to the media so any inquiries as to their safety would be met with positive responses. They could, of course, call family and friends from their rooms, but the concierge urged everyone to look after themselves first with hot showers and warm drinks. They could make contact with the outside world after.

She heard Drew rummaging around in the room. He'd need to get dry too. She thought for a few seconds, then shrugged and stepped into the tub enclosure. He had been nothing but chivalrous throughout the ordeal, but that didn't mean she owed him anything more than her gratitude. He was a nice guy but not her type. Which, of course, reminded her that if her type was William Travis Benneton, maybe she needed to re-think her type-casting. After all, she had no idea where her rich, married lover and his wife were at this moment--maybe in a similar room just down the hall or maybe still bobbing up and down in the freezing sea. She shivered again at that thought and her immediate need to get warm took over. The water streaming from the shower head was hot and the steam was rising. Without another thought of Benny and his predicament, she stepped under the spurting stream.

She didn't hear Drew open the bathroom door slowly and enter. And, of course, she didn't notice him strip out of his soaked suit, underwear and socks either, throwing them on top of the pile Natalie had started with her own wet clothes.

She started as she saw the distorted shape through the frosted glass shower doors. Someone was walking toward her. She covered herself as best she could with her arms, in the back of her mind knowing he couldn't actually see anything other than a blurred body. "What are you doing in here?" she blurted. The distorted figure stopped just on the other side of the shower.

"I'm sorry," he said, "but I'm really, really cold."

"You couldn't wait?" she asked.

"I was hoping you wouldn't mind," he said, opening the glass doors and tentatively stepping inside.

Natalie stared at him, aware of their nakedness but also the absurdity of the situation. His eyes were pleading so she turned to face the back wall and began edging toward the rear of the shower enclosure.

Her initial thought was to scream but one look at his white face and quivering lips and she relented; some maternal instinct she didn't know she owned took over.

"Get under the water. You'll warm up quickly enough," she said. The shower enclosure was only a couple of feet wide and as he passed her from behind, she felt the edge of his penis brush against her buttocks. He had nothing to hold onto and she moved past faster.

Once past, she turned to see him leaning forward, head under the spray, arms braced against the front wall. She couldn't help herself from admiring his well-defined rear end as it jutted out toward her. She folded her arms as much to cover herself as to retain any heat.

"Sorry. You'll get cold again," he said, turning slightly. "I'm better. I'll wait now."

He held his hands out and she instinctively took them. He then steered her in front of him this time as they edged past each other again. Of course, this was more awkward because they were facing each other this time. Natalie had no way of covering herself as she passed within inches of his face. Her breasts brushed against his chest and she was horrified to feel her nipples harden upon the contact. His penis, now semi-erect, slid across her lower belly as it passed. She looked into his eyes but saw no malicious or even lustful expression. They stared at each other momentarily, Natalie unable to move. His eyes revealed nothing other than the fact he was studying her face carefully. She must look like a drowned rat, she thought, then tensed as his gaze briefly lowered to her erect nipples. His eyes were dark and mysterious but strangely expressionless. She wasn't sure what she was looking for; passion, lust, fear even. But his stare seemed to go right through her.

"This is embarrassing for you," he said once they had separated. "It's just that I was shaking so badly, I couldn't get relief from towels."

And with that, he quickly reached behind him and pulled the door open. As he stepped backwards out of the shower and gently pushed the door shut again, Natalie couldn't fathom why she felt sudden disappointment.

She finished showering and heard what she assumed was a hand warmer running. She turned off the water and stepped carefully out of the shower to see him still naked, bent slightly forward, rubbing his chest under the warm flow of air coming from the hand warmer.

She grabbed a towel off a nearby rack and wrapped it around herself. "What are you doing?" she asked.

He turned and she immediately noticed his fully erect member.

"You've never done this?" he asked, seemingly oblivious to both his nakedness and arousal. "It's the best way to dry off and warm up quickly," he continued. "I keep thinking I should put one in my apartment. I'd put it a little higher on the wall though."

Natalie laughed. "That's silly."

"Yeah?" He smiled. "Come try it. You'll be amazed." He stepped aside and gestured with one hand for her to bend down and try it.

She shrugged and placed her head under the nozzle.

"No, you've got to let it reach your whole body," he said. "Take your towel off."

She shook her head and the action loosened the towel enough to drop to the floor.

"That will work," he said, reaching for her hand and pulling her toward him.

Chapter Six

Natalie wasn't sure if it was the hot sun striking her face, or the incessant banging of doors that disturbed her but she awoke with eyes wide open and sat up abruptly. The bright morning sun was gleaming off the hardwood finishes on the table, the dresser and even the headboard, so much so that it was warm to the touch.

She wasn't the type to be groggy and forgetful when she woke up so she instantly thought of the events from the night before. It was hard to believe she had been on a sinking ship just a few hundred yards away from the island just hours ago. Equally hard was the realization that she'd jumped off the ship with a stranger and then spent the night with him in a hotel room. Then she thought of Benny. Did he get off the boat safely? Was he worried about her?

"Anyone here?" she called, and then quickly remembered his name. "Drew, are you in here?"

She got out of the bed and quickly realized she was naked. She never slept naked. Oh God, she thought. Where are my clothes? She'd thrown them in the corner of the bathroom before jumping in the shower.

The shower! Oh God!

As she passed the dresser, she saw a plastic bag with the Hilton Hotel's logo on it. She could see a pale yellow material folded inside. A small note was resting on top of the bag.

"All I could find on short notice. Back soon. We'll do breakfast. Drew."

She emptied the bag to find a flannel tourist track suit, similar to the ones she'd seen in every tourist gift shop she'd ever been in. This one had 'Hilton Head Marriot' emblazoned in green across the front. The top was a hoodie and she immediately pulled it over her head. The fleece was warm against her skin and though a little loose, it was probably the right size. She pulled on the fleece pants and checked herself out in the mirror.

"Ugh," she said. The saggy bottoms did nothing for her ass but it did look cute in a suburban housewife-going-to-the-gym kind of way. Of course, he has to be a nice guy, she thought. Not only chivalrous but thoughtful too.

"Damn," she said aloud. She had to sneak out of here, hail a cab, and get back to the safe haven of her condo where she could painfully and meticulously sort this mess out. She was pretty sure she and Drew hadn't done anything last night other than share a heated, lustful kiss in the bathroom, though the temptation for more had been palpable. More PTSD than actual longing, she thought. She remembered him bowing his head and apologizing, which surprised Natalie. He was tall, had a thick head of dark hair, the pre-requisite 5-o'clock shadow, and no beer belly. In fact, she'd gotten the hundred-dollar view outside of the shower and knew he was muscular and defined, not in a Venice-beach kind of way; more like a gymnast or maybe a boxer. He must have a girl somewhere. Hadn't he said he was separated? Maybe that had just been a line and all the chivalry and shyness was a con and he would come on stronger as the day wore on.

She flipped on the TV as she passed by, more out of habit than anything else. She found the noise made empty rooms a little less... well, lonely. She found a few complimentary wash-up items on the desk and carried them into the bathroom.

Last night had been many things: enlightening, frightening, and at times, oddly entertaining. But it had also been embarrassing. Though used to being placed in compromising positions by William Benneton when someone he knew approached them, she usually controlled them better because she always anticipated awkward moments when she was out in public with Benny, despite dreading them.

Last night, however, had been completely different. She hadn't been with Benny but on the outskirts of a 'Benny moment'. And she hadn't been in control of anything from the moment she'd set eyes on Drew. *God, I don't even know his last name!* Now, alone in the hotel room, she realized she'd made a complete fool of herself. That was annoying. She had promised herself that being William Benneton's mistress was bad enough, but one-night stands were something she'd given up years ago. God, that was the reason she'd become Benny's mistress. To jump into bed with every cute older man who professes to have a modicum of financial stability had been her nemesis for most of her early twenties. Hooking up with Benny had been justifiable to her at first. At least it was only one guy, and he definitely had money, and spent it lavishly on her.

So, why was she feeling guilty because she'd almost cheated on Benny? For God's sake he was married. Cheating was what their relationship was all about. Why should she feel guilty?

Then it dawned on her. It wasn't guilt, it was fear. Despite the absurdity of her relationship with Benny, she had stepped out of her comfort zone with Drew, despite nothing happening. Yet.

"We are here at the Hilton Head Marriot where several employees of Benneton Integrated Insurance Services have just spent the evening recuperating from a near-death experience out in the Sound. The only missing person reported thus far, after this terrible tragedy aboard the Savannah Princess last evening, is Mrs. Emma Benneton, wife of the company president, Mr. William Benneton."

The television announcer's voice cut through Natalie's thoughts like a dagger. She dropped the soap and ran into the main room.

Benny was in view beside the reporter, staring out into the ocean. He looked different; stressed but not in the same manner as usual. Work stress made his forehead crease into little lines. This was a different stress. She listened as the commentator continued.

"Several boats of all shapes and sizes from various local marinas came to the rescue of some--" he referred to his notes,"--some eighty-six passengers on the ill-fated tour boat. Mrs. Benneton, along with three other women and two children, were helped aboard the Creole III by her husband and two other men who we have since learned were employees of Mr. Benneton's. The boat made it to shore and everyone was taken into the Hilton Beach and Tennis Resort. According to Mrs. Jay Featherstone, that was the last they saw of Emma Benneton. They assumed she had found her husband in the hotel or had gotten a ride home or somewhere else."

The camera shifted to a view of a middle-aged woman who stared into the lens. She had obviously attempted to straighten her hair but must have been missing the right tools because it looked as if she'd just gotten out of bed.

"It was very confusing here last night," she said. "We weren't sure if we were supposed to stay in the lobby and wait for our husbands, get a taxi home, or wait for the police. We just didn't know." She shook her head vigorously as if to underline her confusion. "Everyone was running in different directions and nobody really knew what to do. Eventually we were given rooms and told to have showers and get warm until someone came to fetch us. We hadn't noticed Mrs. Benneton had gone until later when the policemen came asking about her."

Natalie grabbed her clothes and stuffed them into the gift shop bag. She then raced out the door and headed to the elevators.

Emerging from the elevator on the lobby level, she was surprised to see a lot of people milling about, most of them in track suits similar to hers. Some looked tired, others forlorn, lost. A lot of the women, especially the older ones looked hideous. Devoid of any kind of make-up, many of the socialites had been reduced to their haggard selves and yet others were hiding in corners of the lobby, trying not to make eye contact with anyone. Men were in small groups everywhere, talking and sipping coffee from small Styrofoam cups.

She couldn't see Drew anywhere but since all the men were wearing the same track suits, she had to look carefully. He wasn't in the lobby. She looked through the patio doors where she could see others standing in clusters around the pool area. Beyond the pool, the Atlantic lapped against a small strip of sand. Between the pool and the ocean, there was a small treed area.

She almost missed him.

Under one of the trees, far off to the left, Drew was talking to another man, the latter hidden from view from low branches. Drew had on a track suit too, his blue, but with the same hotel logo on the back. The two men were well secluded from the other groups of people, almost on the beach itself.

Natalie started to turn. She had to get out of here. She couldn't face Drew at the moment. Suddenly a stiff breeze moved one of the tree branches enough for her to get a quick glimpse of the man Drew was talking to. She stopped walking. She recognized that face. The man was wearing casual dress pants and a button-down white shirt but it was undoubtedly the same man she and Benny had met in a trendy restaurant in Washington just last week. Benny had told her he was some big shot in the government. Natalie remembered the man had been cordial, even conversational. But she had felt he had hidden secrets. And was good at keeping them.

What the hell?

She watched them talking. They weren't angry at each other so this wasn't a confrontation. In fact, the other man put his hand on Drew's shoulders at one point as if comforting him.

At that moment, the man turned for some reason and saw Natalie staring at them from a hundred yards or so. Drew turned too and saw her. The two men exchanged a quick word and then Drew began walking toward her, a determined look on his face, his pace quick and steady. The other man simply turned and walked along the beach away from the hotel.

Natalie didn't like the look on Drew's face. Besides, what was he doing talking to someone Benny did business with? Who was this Drew guy anyway?

There was something not quite right here. Natalie quickly strode down the patio steps toward the sand. She didn't want to make a scene in front of everyone.

"Hey, good morning princess," Drew said, grabbing her arm and steering her away from the doors and off to a line of chaise lounges behind the pool.

"You're hurting me," Natalie said.

Drew released his grip and moved his arm to her waist, pulling her close. Natalie pushed the side of his stomach trying to get him out of her space. Drew held on and smiled.

"You were out like a light when I left the room," he said to her, his smile wide. It didn't reach his eyes.

"Emma Benneton is missing," she said, squirming within his embrace. Drew let go but stood his ground, his face so close she could smell his breath; a little minty, like toothpaste.

"I know," he said.

"And why are you talking to one of Benny's business associates?" she said, turning to face him, hands on hips. Now that he had let her go physically, she felt she didn't need any more distance and stood eye-to-eye. She had to bend her neck slightly upwards since he was about four inches taller than her but she gave it her best tough bitch pose.

Drew didn't say anything right away but just stared at her. He appeared to be making a decision. He reached for her arm again but Natalie stepped back quickly.

"What aren't you telling me, Mr..ah, what is your last name anyway?"

He stared at her for a moment and then his cold expression broke and he grinned. He stepped back leaving a more acceptable space between them.

"Look, he's just concerned about some rich people's whereabouts, and I was telling him who I'd seen at the hotel. That's all."

Natalie frowned. "What were you smiling about?"

"My name is Scanlon, Drew Scanlon," he said. "Pleased to make your acquaintance."

"Are you kidding me?" she said, hands firmly on hips.

"I can explain," he said. "But not here. You need to come with me. I promise, I won't hurt you or do anything you won't like."

Natalie tilted her head sideways. This was weird.

"Where?" she asked.

He stared at her for a moment, then sighed and said: "William Benneton's." Then, without worrying about whether Natalie was following or not, he turned toward the patio doors. He pulled a cell phone from his pocket and began dialing. Apparently, he felt his name dropping had been sufficient enough to entice Natalie to follow him.

It was.

Chapter Seven

Drew hadn't counted on Natalie knowing who Frank Daro was. The fact that William Benneton had taken her to a meeting with the Assistant Director of the CIA was unnerving, but for Natalie to remember Frank and mention it to a total stranger—him--was not good. Drew had agreed to meet Frank at the beach as soon as he'd found a scribbled note slipped under the hotel room door early that morning.

"I wouldn't have thought sinking the boat would have been part of the plan, Frank," Drew had said, staring out to where the tour boat had made its last gasp and slipped beneath the relatively shallow waters on the edge of the Continental Divide.

"These things happen," Frank said, tossing his head indifferently. "A little overkill on their part, I agree, but no one else is missing and no one really got hurt, right?"

Drew knew Frank's concern for others, especially regular citizens, was virtually non-existent so he was simply placating him.

"Besides," he continued, "the end result was acceptable, wasn't it?"

"You mean me half drowning in the coldest water I've been in since last year's Polar Bear dip?" Drew said. "Or the fact I ended up rescuing your contact's mistress because no one else seemed to give a shit."

Frank cocked his head. "Oh?" A mischievous grin replaced his usual stark purposeful expression.

Drew sighed. "No Frank, nothing happened," he said, a twinge in his gut telling him that he had questioned that decision a couple of times since waking up and staring at Natalie's innocent, naked form, laying on the bed. It was a strange feeling; one he hadn't felt for longer than he wanted to admit. "She is oblivious. Safe, but oblivious." He glanced briefly at the hotel and the swarm of grey and green-clad patrons filling the breakfast room and overflowing onto the patio. "And Benneton is safe," he said.

Frank took a small, noticeable step back, as if ensuring he wasn't directly in Drew's personal space.

"Yes, and Emma is gone," he said, slowly.

Drew stared at him for a moment, then with a puzzled expression said, "It was part of the grand plan, right? We just didn't know when."

Frank shrugged. Drew turned to stare back out to the sea. Frank watched him carefully. "We had a meeting early this morning," he continued. "We think we may have misread the signs leading up to this."

Drew turned, his eyes intense, the puzzled expression morphing into one of anxiousness. "You had someone on the inside and you missed the fact that today was Emma Benneton's breakout day?"

"You should have known too," Frank said, stabbing Drew in the chest with his finger.

"I'm not privy to the Dutchman's schedule Frank. You knew that going in."

Frank lifted his chin in exasperation. "You need to speak with Benneton, see what he knows, if anything," he said.

"I don't work for you, remember?" Drew said. "My job is to keep an eye on the girl, and wait for the Dutchman's next instructions. You guys need to clean up your own mess."

Frank stared at Drew, not saying a word. His eyes were slightly warmer than usual, Drew thought. But neither man said anything for several moments. Finally, Frank put a hand on Drew's shoulder.

"You know you have to find her, Drew," he said slowly, calmly and, to Drew's thinking, somewhat comforting tone.

"I'm aware of that."

Frank put his other hand on Drew's other shoulder and turned the slightly taller man to face him. His cold eyes were back but the hands-on Drew's shoulders were somehow reassuring and convincing simultaneously.

"Everyone's focus was on Benneton," Frank said, his tone firm. "Now we wipe our hands clean and let the local authorities handle Emma's disappearance. Maybe even the FBI."

Drew stared into the man's eyes. What little compassion Frank Daro had for any other human being seemed to be welled up in his eyes. It surprised Drew a little.

"The Dutchman will reach out to Benneton eventually. Meanwhile, the locals won't stand a chance," Frank said. "She's long gone. I can't convince the Company to take that as a threat against Benneton until it actually becomes one."

"It was a threat to Benneton the day we all agreed to this."

Frank nodded. It was a very touchy subject and Drew knew Frank wasn't going to muddle things by talking too much. Drew would come to the right conclusion sooner or later and Frank knew it. Drew knew it too. But he was trying to fight it, whether that was rational or not, fair or even self-destructive. He didn't work for Frank Daro. But Frank and he had a mutual connection in this case. And Frank was playing Drew to make him do what he wanted, regardless of where Drew's allegiance actually lay.

"There's something else too," Frank said, finally letting go of Drew's shoulders. He put his hands in his pants pockets. "If Benneton doesn't do what he's supposed to, then the girl will be next."

Drew's head shot up.

"You know what she is to him," Frank deadpanned.

Drew frowned. *The primary reason I didn't take that next step in the bathroom.* Frank's gaze wandered past Drew then bounced back again.

"Once they realize Benneton doesn't care for his wife as much as they think he does…" Frank paused as Drew winced. "They'll go after Natalie Grainger quickly."

"Then put a team on her," Drew said.

"She may be a clean way to get to him," Frank said. "Besides, we can't operate on US soil, remember?"

Drew rolled his eyes and shook his head.

"It is fortuitous you were assigned to Ms. Grainger. Take her to see Benneton. That added pressure will ensure he works with us. He'll get it. He's a smart man." Frank shuffled his feet, his brows furrowing. "This could be the break we've been waiting for," he continued. He then reached out and touched Drew's arm. "Watch her for now till I can figure out if that really is their next play."

Drew's cheeks raised as his eyes scrunched. "Are you serious?"

"Emma is the priority right now," Frank said, his cold, business-like, CIA-like expression returning in full force. "I promised Benneton we'd do this without endangering anyone." He took a step back. "So, I need you to find her quickly for both our sakes."

Drew swung his head around vigorously as if trying to shake the thoughts out of his brain. He turned to the sea, then to Frank, then glanced back to the hotel behind them. That's when he had seen Natalie standing just on the main deck of the lounge. She was staring at them, hands on her hips. She looked ridiculous in the spa-getup they'd all been provided. In any other situation Drew would have snickered. But she looked annoyed, confused, angry.

"Shit!" Drew exclaimed. "She's seen us," he nodded toward the girl.

Frank turned and stared back at her.

"Take her to Benneton," he said. "She doesn't know who I am. He'll tell her a story, calm her down. Get her out of here, at least until they make their next play. I'll call him so he's prepared for you."

Drew gave Frank one last exasperated look, was about to tell him to stop giving him orders, then realized the futility of that idea. They both turned and walked in separate directions; Frank along the water's edge toward the next resort, Drew toward Natalie.

He watched as she stepped off the patio and started heading toward him on the sandy path. She had a determined look on her face that matched her sharp pace. He straightened his shoulders. As he got closer to the girl and saw the multitude of expressions flowing across her face, he realized this was going to be one hell of a long day.

As she met him a few feet from the steps where the sand met the patio, he reached out and grabbed her arm and squeezed, warding off any outburst.

"Good morning Princess," he said, mustering as much warmth as he could into his voice as he spun her back toward the patio.

Chapter Eight

"So, are you going to answer my question?"

Natalie's arms were folded and she stared at Drew. She had followed him out through the hotel lobby to a waiting black limousine, complete with uniformed driver. Reluctantly, she had gotten in, hoping that he was, indeed, taking her to see Benny, wherever he was.

Drew's demeanor had changed dramatically over the past few moments. He seemed less expressive, slumped in the back of the limo, staring out the window, his eyes not seeming to focus on anything in particular. It was as though he had detached himself from the situation and didn't feel the need to communicate. He was a completely different guy to the one she had come close to entangling herself with the night before.

"What question?" he said in a monotone voice, still staring out the side window. They were driving away from the ocean, along Pope Avenue towards William Hilton Parkway, the main thoroughfare on the island and the fastest way to return to the mainland.

"Who are you?" Natalie asked. She caught the driver staring in the rearview mirror but he was looking at Drew not her.

"I told you already," he said, turning to look at her. His tone was plain, almost businesslike. Gone was the affable dude from the night before. "My name is Drew Scanlon and I'm just trying to be a friend."

Natalie laughed, though her heart wasn't in it. "If you were my friend you would tell me why you were talking to one of Benny's business associates."

Drew stared at her but she couldn't tell if he was thinking, studying her, or even aware that she was waiting for an answer. He seemed so indifferent, almost somewhere else at the moment.

"It's complicated," he said and turned back to the window. They turned onto the Parkway and started going a little faster. Natalie knew that if they were going back to Savannah, they would have stayed on Palmetto Bay Road. She had visited friends on the island last summer. Though still on the main island highway, they were actually heading north toward the small airport that the 35,000 island residents used for quick trips back to the mainland.

"Where are we going?" she asked. She was getting a little nervous. She didn't care if he'd said they were going to see Benny, she wasn't flying anywhere with this guy. She'd thought Benny was at the hotel, or maybe another one nearby. She didn't really know Drew and regardless of how chivalrous he had been last night, he was definitely acting weird now.

"It's not far, just relax and enjoy the view," he said. "It will all make a lot more sense once we arrive, don't worry." He'd sighed after which made Natalie think that perhaps he was trying to convince himself.

"Are we flying back to Savannah?"

Drew's head spun around. "Who said anything about flying?" His eyebrows creased and he lifted his hands, palm upwards. "Look, I know none of this seems logical at the moment but I assure you Mr. Benneton will explain everything."

"Benny's still here, on the island?" Of course he was, she thought. They were still looking for Emma probably. Much as she disliked the woman because of, well because of who she was, she had never wished her any real harm. She hoped the woman had been rescued.

Just before the road turned inland toward the airport, they turned off heading toward the gated communities of Port Royal and Port Royal Sound.

After a few minutes of meandering tree-lined roads, they turned into a driveway adorned on either side by large brick walls. The large wrought iron gate was open and a policeman stood at the entrance. The driver rolled down his window and spoke with the officer briefly who waved them on.

The home looked like it could have been part of The Great Gatsby set; the version with Robert Redford. Beautiful brick buildings formed an L-shape, all English Tudor style with paned windows, green slate roofing, and beige wooden trim. As they pulled around the circled driveway in front of what was obviously the main structure, Natalie saw police cars parked haphazardly near the main entrance which was a covered portico leading to two massive wooden doors. On her left was a long, one-storey building, surrounded by lush shrubs and small trees. Paned windows circled the building just a few inches below the roof line and ended in a ground to ceiling window facing the driveway. Sunlight shone in from all the windows illuminating an oblong indoor swimming pool.

She turned to Drew when they stopped in front of the large front doors, but he just got out and waited.

"Who the hell lives here?" she said, admiring the gorgeous setting, once the driver had ceremoniously opened her door to let her out. It must be almost a hundred years old, she thought. "And what's going on?"

Drew stared at her. Then he raised his eyebrows. Natalie suddenly got it.

"You're kidding," she said. "He never told me about it."

Drew shrugged.

"Thank God you're okay Natalie."

The voice was deeply resonating and very familiar. Natalie turned to see William Benneton standing just outside the huge doors, both wide open revealing a wood enhanced foyer beyond.

"What's going on, Benny?" she said, walking toward him and accepting a quick kiss to her forehead. Whether he was going to embrace her or not, she didn't know because she brushed past him quickly and stood in the center of the foyer. It was magnificent: dark, exotic wood everywhere, tiling that glistened intently from sunlight that crept in from several small circular windows just above eye level. And there were people everywhere. Most were uniformed policemen who seemed to be guarding the entrance to what looked like a large office.

"I'm glad you're okay," he said, trying to grasp her arm. She avoided it and began walking down the hallway that led to what she assumed was the rear of the house. All the activity seemed to be centered around the office where other men in suits were setting up small machines on a huge desk and running wiring to other machines set up on the floor. Natalie moved down the hallway toward a large den. No one was in this room but there was a large curved leather couch set in front of a huge fireplace. There were windows along the one side on two levels, one set above the other. Sunlight filled the room, offering a cozy, old world charm atmosphere. Natalie dropped onto the couch and poured a glass of red wine from a decanter that was sitting on the square glass coffee table. Benneton followed and stood next to the fireplace, making no further attempts to get close to Natalie. Drew ambled in along with another man in a drab suit.

"We'll be ready in about forty minutes Mr. Benneton," drab suit said. "If it's alright with you, I'd like to settle into my room." He looked at Natalie briefly and then his gaze moved to Drew who had settled into a high-backed leather chair on the opposite side of the room. "And you are?" he said, looking at Natalie.

"They're just family friends, Detective Carmen," Benneton said. "Here to console me while we wait for something, anything to happen."

Detective Carmen clearly didn't think that was a good enough explanation, but since Benneton's tone was a little shaky, he returned his attention to him.

"That's fine sir," he said. "Once everything is in place, the team will leave and there will just be my three associates, yourself and," he gestured to Drew, "anyone you feel you need with you during the ordeal. Perhaps we could go over some protocols a little later? I can have the office order some food in if you wish."

"That won't be necessary Detective," Benneton said, shaking the man's hand and steering him to the double French doors. "My cook will serve dinner as usual. I'll inform her that you'll be joining us." He turned to look at Natalie. "My friends won't be joining us for dinner so we can go over your plans at that time, I'm sure."

Carmen nodded and left. Benneton pulled the doors shut and resumed his spot in front of the fireplace. Natalie had leaned forward, glass of wine in one hand, her one foot tapping the carpeting. She looked up at Benneton.

"Where's Emma?" she asked quietly

Benneton gazed at his feet while he shifted them. "I don't know," he said. "I haven't seen her since putting her on the boat with those other women. I went to the hotel where the boat dropped them off but there's no sign of her. And, of course, she didn't come home."

Natalie winced at the word *home*. She knew Benny had secrets. Hell, *she* was one of his biggest ones. But he had never mentioned a home, nor a mansion for God's sake, on Hilton Head. Is this where he was when she couldn't reach him on weekends sometimes? Did Emma come with him?

"The police think she may have been abducted," Benneton said. "That's why they're setting up the recorders and such. They think we'll get a ransom call sometime soon."

"Why would they think that?" Natalie asked. "Maybe she got a cab last night and went back into town."

"She would have come here," Benneton said. "It's one of her favorite places."

Natalie winced again. That answered one of her questions anyway. "Benny, why would someone want to kidnap Emma?"

"To get to Mr. Benneton, obviously."

Natalie had forgotten about Drew. He had said it casually but noticed that Benneton nodded in agreement. Drew crossed his legs, looking very comfortable in the overstuffed leather high back. He looked at Benneton as he continued. "There had been threats for the past few weeks which is why she had security guys with her at all times."

"Is that what you are, security?" Natalie asked, staring at Drew.

"Mr. Scanlon is a special kind of security guard Natalie," Benneton said. "His job is to make sure that those things most precious to me aren't harmed."

"He's not very good then is he?" Natalie said, turning back to Benneton.

"Why do you say that?" Benneton asked.

"Because Emma's missing," Natalie said. "Obviously he wasn't paying close enough attention to your most precious things," she said, hissing out the last three words.

"Actually, he did Natalie," Benneton said. "His job is to look after you."

Chapter Nine

"So, this is the guy you were talking about last night at my apartment?" Natalie asked incredulously.

"I was going to find time to introduce you during the voyage but--"

"But you beat him to it," Drew interjected, smirking.

"I didn't realize you had met," said Benneton, looking at Drew. "but I'm glad you did. I can only assume you looked after her during the ordeal?"

"Looked after me? Jesus, Benny, I told you I don't need a babysitter, I can look after myself."

"Under normal circumstances, yes, but this was unusual," said Benneton.

She stared at him for a moment. "No Benny, you've been planning to have me watched all along," she said, her voice rising slightly. "And you weren't planning to wait until I agreed either. Not if you were going to introduce me to him--" she threw a thumb toward Drew, "--last night. And how exactly were you going to introduce him Benny?" She shifted in her seat. "'Hey honey, this is a friend of mine who's going to pretend to be your date for tonight. Act like a normal couple while Emma and I act like the perfect couple too.'"

"That wasn't the idea at all," Benneton said. "I had intended to--"

"And how could you possibly know last night was going to be an unusual circumstance?" Natalie interrupted.

Benneton and Drew glanced at each other.

"What?" Natalie asked, switching from one to the other. "What aren't you telling me?"

"We didn't know anything would happen last night for sure," Drew said. "But we knew something was going to happen sooner or later."

"What is he talking about?" she said, looking at Benneton, her eyes pleading.

"There have been threats," he said quietly. "Against Emma."

Natalie was stunned. She put the wine glass down quickly and brushed her hands through her hair.

Drew came and stood beside Benneton. It was a subtle show of mutual camaraderie. "Mr. Benneton has been receiving threats stating that if he didn't agree to change certain corporate policies then they would kidnap his wife and that if he didn't agree to their demands at that point, then he would never see her again," he said.

"I didn't take it seriously at first until I began getting follow-up messages stating that I was running out of time," Benneton said. "I couldn't go to the police because I didn't have anything concrete to tell them. My only option was to… well, to go elsewhere."

Natalie noticed Drew cock his head and give Benny an odd stare. "Those two big guys who were with you last night?" Natalie asked.

Benneton nodded. "When that speedboat hit the tour boat, we all just reacted as anyone would in an accident situation," he said, walking toward the window and looking out. "Looking back at it now though, it seems the whole thing could have been an elaborate plot just to get Emma away from the guards, and me."

Natalie swung on Drew.

"So, what did that guy at the beach want, the one you saw before we came here? Did he have something to do with it?"

Benneton turned quickly and looked first at Natalie, then Drew. 'What guy?"

Drew was calm, his legs crossed at the ankles.

"She's talking about Frank," he said slowly.

Benneton stared at Drew for a moment. "Frank is a business associate. Benneton said, turning to Natalie, his voice stoic, his gaze hard and unyielding.

"He came to the hotel to catch up on things," Drew said.

"What things?" Natalie asked, not sure which person to address, her eyes darting from one to the other.

"Frank is a kind of a—um, a specialist in this kind of thing," Benneton stammered.

Natalie wasn't sure what to think, let alone say, so she just continued to stare at both of them.

"They had your schedule well ahead of time," Drew said, clearly trying to steer the conversation away from the man on the beach. "And they planned the accident. Maybe they didn't anticipate it being quite so catastrophic, or maybe they didn't care if there were other casualties."

"The accident made the whole thing easier for them," Benneton agreed.

"They could have had someone on the inside," Drew said. "Someone on your staff."

Benneton said nothing but nodded his agreement. He was deep in thought, his body turned toward Drew. He'd forgotten about Natalie, she thought.

"So that's why the police are here?" Natalie asked. "You're waiting for the kidnappers to call with their ransom demands?"

"We already know what their demands will be," Drew said, turning toward her.

"And that's why you have to get out of here, now," Benneton said, walking over and grasping Natalie's hand. "Mr. Scanlon is going to take you somewhere safe. I won't know where it is, so there's no way I can be forced to tell anyone."

"Wait a minute," Natalie said, grasping Benny's other hand and gripping it tightly. "Why do I have to go somewhere, and why don't you want to know where I'll be?"

Drew and Benneton exchanged glances. Drew walked over to the big bay window and stared out into the darkness, giving them a little privacy.

"Because we think they'll come after you next," Benneton said quietly, looking into her eyes. "And I can't let that happen. Frank assures me that Mr. Scanlon here is capable of making people disappear. And that's what I've asked him to do with you."

"Benny?" Natalie gripped his hands harder. She turned to look at Drew. He was still staring out the window. "Why would anyone want to hurt me? I'm not important to anything you do. Once you get Emma back, things will go back to normal." She grinned despite herself. "Well, as normal as can be expected."

"No, Natalie, they won't," he said, his face tightening a little. "They will know they can use you to get to me. So you need to go with Mr. Scanlon now. I need to know that you are very safe. I want to make sure this time. I was too slow with Emma and I didn't take them seriously. I can't make that mistake with you." Natalie noticed his eyes moistening.

"I don't want to go anywhere Benny," she said. "You need me here. Maybe I can help, or at least keep you company till they find Emma."

"I don't think they'll find Emma," Benneton said, letting go of Natalie's hands and standing up. She looked at him questioningly.

"Why not?" she asked.

"Because there won't be a ransom."

Chapter Ten

"So where are we going?"

Drew grimaced.

They had left Bennington's house quickly once Detective Carmen had interrupted to say they were ready to test the phone recording equipment. Benneton's parting embrace was firm and at the same time tender. Confusing, Natalie thought. Benny was never overtly affectionate, which made the whole scene surreal.

She had been whisked out of the busy house and escorted to the limo once again, where for the first few minutes, no one had said anything. The driver simply stared ahead and drove.

"Are you going to tell me?" she asked again. "I don't even know what to pack."

"Your bags are in the trunk," Drew said.

Natalie stared at him, then as the limo turned right onto Dillon Rd and the Hilton Head Island Airport entrance, she looked out the side window in the direction of Port Royal.

"This was all planned?" she asked, incredulous.

"Actually no," Drew said. "It's mostly reaction. Had I been given more time, I would have thought of a change of clothing."

Oddly enough, Natalie hadn't thought about clothing. She'd been too bent on figuring out what was going on. She should have asked Benny if she could borrow some of Emma's clothes. They were similar in size, though Emma was a good twenty-five years older. Something about that bothered Natalie but she chalked it up to mild jealously that a woman old enough to be her mother could wear the same dress size she did.

"When Mr. Benneton realized his wife was actually missing," Drew continued, "he called one of his Savannah employees who went to your apartment and packed a few things." He smiled. "We didn't want you to do anything you would normally do in case they were waiting for you somewhere. So we took the liberty." He finished the sentence by opening his arms, palm upwards in a 'you know the rest' gesture.

"Besides, you won't need much clothing where we're going. And if they forgot something we'll just buy a new one."

She looked at him quizzically.

"So you have known about this for a while?" she asked.

"I have had a plan ready to implement as soon as it became necessary," he said. "It became necessary this morning after Mr. Benneton told me his wife was missing."

Natalie thought about that for a few seconds. "Can I use your cell?"

"No."

Natalie angled her head and glared at him.

"It's important that no one know where we're going," he said. "Otherwise, it's a pointless move."

"You want me to fall off the face of the earth?" she said. "My friends, my sister, they'll be wondering where I am."

Drew leaned forward to speak to the driver. "Have you got them with you?" he asked him. The driver nodded, reached into the glove compartment and came out with two small 4 x 5" postcards. He handed them over the seat to Drew, who handed them directly to Natalie. On the front was a picture of a large hotel located on a white sandy beach. She flipped it over and saw that it was from The British Colonial Hotel in Nassau, Bahamas.

She looked at Drew.

"No, that's not where we're going but before we take off, if you would be kind enough to write one to your sister and another to one friend who can be counted on to blabber it to all your other friends, we'll put them in the mail. They've already been postmarked from the Bahamas."

"My friends don't blabber," she said defiantly, not knowing what else to say.

"Tell them you're away for a couple of weeks with a business associate and that you'll send more postcards," he said. "Mr. Benneton assures me they'll think nothing of it. You've done it before."

"That's because I usually go somewhere with him," she said, staring at him defiantly.

"Well that's not going to be possible this time," Drew said. "I'm afraid you're stuck with me for the duration."

"So back to my first question," she said. "Where are we going?"

Drew looked at his watch as the limo slowed to a stop in front of the small terminal.

"You'll find out in about an hour or so," he said, opening the door and climbing out. He turned and leaned back in. "You might want to buy a magazine and maybe a t-shirt; there's no movie on this plane, it's too short a trip."

Natalie sat staring out the front window of the limo. There weren't many people about and most were arriving not departing. Should she make a run for it? Go home and figure out what to do?

Unfortunately, Benny was all she had. And he had wanted her to go with this guy and disappear for a while. She looked out the side window. Drew was staring back, a medium sized travel bag in each hand.

Maybe it was the picture of the hotel by the beach. Maybe it was the sight of Drew who, despite having a good three or four years on her, really wasn't that hard to look at. Or maybe it was the fact that she couldn't think of another choice since this seemed to be Benny's idea. She opened the door, smiled thinly, and followed Drew into the terminal. She hated the fact that she was used to taking orders from men.

Chapter Eleven

Located just 300 kilometers below Puerto Rico, the island of Sint Maarten is the smallest land mass in the world that is owned by two countries. The northern side is governed by the French and is called St. Martin, whereas the southern portion forms part of the Dutch Antilles governed by the Kingdom of the Netherlands.

Sint Maarten is also very civilized, which comes as no surprise to anyone who has dealt with the fastidious Dutch or conversely the sophisticated French. However, English is the predominant language as this is also the focal point for various surrounding islands catering to the nouveau riche.

Natalie knew none of this. What she did realize very quickly is that this particular Caribbean trade wind breeze was like nothing she had ever felt before. After passing through the small customs desk, her first glimpse of the island was through the clear glass windows that displayed an assortment of cacti and gently bending palm trees. Though the terminal allowed the tropical sun to illuminate every nook and cranny, it wasn't until she passed through the sliding entrance doors that the full impact of the tropics attacked her senses.

"My God this is beautiful," she exclaimed.

Drew was crossing the two-lane road that separated the terminal from the main parking lot. He seemed to be searching for someone or something.

"In my opinion, it is the most magnificent island in the Caribbean," he said. "But I'm no travel agent."

Suddenly noticing a single white van out of a line of several, he waved his arm. A black man waved back. Dressed in a white concierge outfit, he reminded Natalie of Isaac Washington from *The Love Boat*. They headed toward him.

The black man opened the rear door and took the bags from them.

"Mr. Scanlon, I assume," he said, his voice drawling in a manner that seemed to compliment the gently bending palm trees surrounding the parking lot. "My name is Oliver and I am at your service, sir, madam." On the word madam, he bowed slightly in Natalie's direction. Natalie smiled.

"The villa is ready for us, I trust?" Drew said. He didn't introduce Natalie to Oliver. The man nodded enthusiastically and opened the sliding side door, offering his hand to assist Natalie.

"Thank you, kind sir," she said.

As Oliver exited the parking lot, they passed a long line of parked jets.

"Do you see that grey one at the end miss?" Oliver gestured to the plane. "That belongs to Mr. John Travolta. He comes here often with friends."

Natalie smiled. She liked the man instantly, his ever-present smile comforting and reassuring.

"He owns a home here, does he?" Natalie asked.

"No, I think he just, how do you say it, freeloads off his friends," Oliver said, grinning. "Actually, he usually takes his yacht to St. Barths where several actors have homes but the landing strip there is too small for his large jet, so he lands here. If he is on the island, you might see him at Tantra's. We will pass it shortly."

As they circled around the airport and headed north, Natalie watched as other jets were coming in to land.

"Aren't they flying a little low?" she asked.

"If you stand on the beach directly in front of the fencing that ends the runway, the propulsion will knock you over, even throw you into the sea," Drew said.

Oliver nodded his head enthusiastically. "You must experience it before you leave, miss," he said. Natalie smiled and nodded, already distracted by the constantly changing scenery.

Sint Maarten only has one main road that allows drivers to circle the entire island in just over two hours. All other roads lead to the interior where it becomes more mountainous, though the word mountain is a misnomer. The highest point on the island is Pic du Paradis at 424 meters. Many homes and villas are nestled on the interior slopes, all with astonishing views of the surrounding waters. The coastline is dedicated to resorts, hotels, small villages, and some of the most remarkable French restaurants outside of Paris.

At each turn of the winding road, Natalie would see either astounding resort facilities or rundown, thatched roof homes. They seemed to share the limited space with ease and certain nonchalance. Obviously, this was a place of incredibly rich or devastatingly poor. Natalie saw no evidence of middle class. No suburbs, no low-income housing.

"Everyone is smiling," she said to no one in particular.

"This is Sint Maarten," Oliver said proudly. "And this is the best place to work in the Caribbean."

Natalie noticed he hadn't said the best place to live.

"Were you born here Oliver?" she asked.

"Oh no, miss," he said. "I am Jamaican. I came here as a teenager. Soon, I will bring my little sister here to work." His voice rose slightly as he puffed up his chest. "This is where it's at, man!" he exclaimed.

Natalie laughed and even Drew grinned. He hadn't said anything but had let Natalie and Oliver exchange banalities while he perused some papers he had pulled from a file he had been carrying.

"Oliver, how far is our villa from Marigot?" he asked.

"It is at the end of the peninsula sir, just at the mainland," Oliver replied. "You will like it there. Some of the best restaurants on the island." He leaned backwards and winked at Natalie. "And some of the best shopping too! Though I would also suggest Philipsburg on the Dutch side."

"I don't think we'll have time to go to the other side Oliver, but thank you," Drew said, his voice taught.

Oliver appeared to pout but said nothing.

"So, we are staying on the French side of the island?" she asked, addressing the question to Drew.

He looked up from the papers.

"We will see about renting a scooter so you can discover the pleasures of the French capital, Marigot," he said. "But you will have to stay close to the plantation, so to speak. The French are better at keeping to themselves. The Dutch side is a little more in touch with the world, if you catch my meaning."

"Hmmm," Natalie said quietly. Oliver eyed her in the mirror and winked again. She smiled. She would have to find out how to get in touch with Oliver. Should Drew become boring, she had an idea Oliver would be a fun date in a brotherly kind of way. And, of course, he had a vehicle which may come in handy.

After twenty minutes or so, Oliver turned off the main road which seemed to be heading inland. The scenery became more natural with white sanded beaches and smaller but more expensive looking homes dotting the coastline every few hundred yards or so. Once in a while plush and colorful foliage would hide the sea from view but it would return at the next bend in the road.

"How long will we be here Drew?" she whispered.

"As long as it takes," he said, still reading the papers. Was he immune to the beauty of the surroundings?

"And how long should it take?" she asked.

He put the papers back in the file and placed it beside him.

"Until they find Emma," he said.

"I thought they weren't supposed to," Natalie questioned.

Drew sighed. "One thing at a time Natalie. I suggest you just enjoy the diversion for the time being. We'll know more in a couple of days, I'm sure."

He smiled what seemed like a genuine smile but Natalie didn't know him that well yet. He'd already deceived her once and it had seemed to come easily for him. She wanted to hate him for that but she reasoned that he really hadn't betrayed her in any way, just not told her the whole truth when they'd first met on the boat.

God, she thought. That seems like so long ago but it was only yesterday. Perhaps Benny was right. A change of scenery was a great way to forget what's going on elsewhere. She looked out the window as Oliver turned inland and they began a slow ascent up one of the ever-present hills.

It was hard to think of Emma, even Benny, when all she could see in front of her was lush, tropical flora and fauna. Maybe she could do this, she thought. She looked over at Drew. He sensed her gaze and turned to look at her.

"Welcome to paradise," he said and pointed through the windshield.

Directly in front of them, nestled between two huge trees was a small stucco'd bungalow with a huge wooden door directly in its center.

Oliver turned in to the semi-circular driveway, stopped the van at the door, and jumped out. He quickly slid the side door open and held his hand out to Natalie.

"This is one of my favorites," he whispered as she stepped out. Then louder, so Drew could hear also. "We are at the geographical center of the island and that is why this villa is called No Limits."

"I don't understand," Natalie said to Oliver.

"You will," Drew said. "Come on." He led her to the front door, opened it and stepped back allowing Natalie to enter first.

As she walked through the front door, Natalie noticed several things. She noticed the stark but tasteful furnishing, she noticed there were very few walls and that somehow every room flowed into the next, and she noticed the stunning 180 degree view of what must have been the Caribbean Sea well in the distance below them. She also noticed an aqua green-colored infinity pool fill the frame of the huge, open patio doors. But most of all, she noticed that breeze; warm and comforting. It encircled her physically and emotionally.

"Now I get it," she said. "No Limits."

Chapter Twelve

Oliver dropped the bags in the foyer and Drew grabbed his and took it into the first bedroom down the hallway. The bed was a canopy style with green drapes to match the green sheets. He went to the next bedroom that was more light pine and white sheets. He threw his bag on the bed and returned to the foyer.

"Yours is the first bedroom to the right," he said to Natalie. "Oliver, it's been a pleasure." He handed the driver a fifty-dollar bill. "We'll be sure to call when we need transportation and a guided tour.

"There is a jeep tour that you could join from one of the resorts in Marigot," Oliver said. "Highlights of the island, lunch at Oyster Bay, all in about four hours."

"Actually, there's a scooter around here somewhere, I'm told." Drew said. "I'm sure I can navigate the island; after all, it's only about twenty or so miles long."

Oliver looked briefly disappointed but quickly recovered, elegantly kissed the back of Natalie's hand and said goodbye. "Enjoy your stay on our magical island!" he exclaimed as he left., then just before pulling the front door behind him, "And remember: no limits!"

"Are all the people on this island that friendly? Natalie asked, once Oliver had left.

"Tourism is virtually the only industry here, so I would guess they are," Drew said.

"Have you been here before?"

"Yes," Drew said. "It is a very sophisticated island."

"You seem to know quite a bit about it," she said.

"It's called reconnaissance," Drew said and smiled. "Get to know enemy territory before you attack."

"We have enemies here?" she asked, frowning.

"Figure of speech, sorry." Drew said, pointing to a set of patio couches facing each other on a covered portion of the deck. "I'll map out a route. You go and cool off."

Natalie walked through the open living area straight to the huge floor to ceiling patio doors that stretched the full length of the room. She opened one side and was immediately embraced by that warm, comforting breeze. The entire coastline was spread before her and she was surprised at how low and flowing it was. The so-called mountains were little more than hills and she could see straight to the water's edge despite it being more than a mile away.

"It's magnificent," she said, staring out toward the Caribbean. "Somehow I thought there would have been more trees in the tropics."

"I suppose it depends where you go," Drew said, walking up behind her. He didn't touch her but Natalie sensed his presence. She recalled her carnal thoughts in the shower last night.

"I was thinking since we haven't done any shopping, that perhaps tonight we could have dinner in town," Drew said quietly. "it will give us a chance to see where all the stores are."

Natalie just nodded, not trusting herself to speak. He was so close, she could feel his breath on the back of her neck.

"This side of the island is French," he said. "The other side is Dutch. I think we'll enjoy the French food better, don't you think?"

She nodded again, then reached for the patio door handle and pulled it open.

"Why don't you go for a swim first?" he said. "I'll see about finding that scooter."

She was still staring out the window, not daring herself to look at him in this close a proximity. In a few moments, he moved away, heading to the front door.

"I'm sure they packed a bathing suit," he said over his shoulder. "But if not, you could always put on a party dress. You swam well in that kind of outfit last time." The door closed behind him before she could respond.

Chapter Thirteen

Natalie sat on the edge of the elliptical pool, her legs dangling in the water as she pulled her hair back into a pony tail. Suddenly an engine sputtered to life then, after a few moments, settled into a steady tinny sound similar to a lawnmower. A few seconds later Drew stepped through the patio doors and motioned to her.

"Come on, we've still got a few hours of daylight. Let's go discover the island." He was wearing a pair of cream linen pants rolled up above his ankles and a loose-fitting, pink linen island shirt.

Natalie laughed. "Well, you're certainly not questioning your masculinity, are you?" She got up, grabbed her towel from one of the lounge chairs and walked toward him. "Pink shirt and capri's!"

Drew tilted his head as the corner of his mouth raised. "Cute. Don't bother changing; I'm sure we'll find somewhere else to swim. Might want a hat though, and maybe some shorts. The seat gets hot in the sun."

When Natalie saw the scooter she stopped short.

"We're both going to fit on that thing?" It was obviously old, though admittedly she didn't see any rust. But the yellow paint was fading and the seat was very, very tiny.

"We won't be going that far," he said, then laughed. "And we won't be going very fast. Come on."

He pulled it off its parking stand and manhandled it toward the villa's drive while Natalie raced inside for a hat. He straddled it and moved as far forward as he could. He then patted the remaining portion of the seat behind him.

"Your taxi awaits, Madame," he said.

After a few minutes, Natalie forgot about the uncomfortably tight quarters and relaxed her legs. She didn't want to get cramps from squeezing the machine too tightly. And she thought she might be hanging a little too tightly onto Drew's waist. The tiny machine didn't seem to go much past twenty miles-an-hour anyway so she felt pretty safe.

What really was grabbing her attention however was the scenery. The main road winded around the edge of the island, following the shoreline closely for the most part. Occasionally, the road would duck inland to swish by a small village, or more commonly, the grand entrance to a resort, hidden behind palms and other thick-leaved trees. The numerous hills were on the inland side whereas every now and again, the other side would reveal yet another breathtaking view of the Caribbean Sea.

They stopped at a couple of bars along the way, one in a village and right up against the street. They met some of the locals there and Natalie was amazed that despite their obvious poverty, they were all happy and genuinely friendly, the children especially. She'd heard horror stories of children in the islands chasing tourists for change or to sell them beads and things. But the children chasing around the bar were content to play with balls and dogs, occasionally brushing up against her as they raced past laughing and shouting. Drew asked what the popular beer was and they were handed two Carib. Drew frowned when he saw the alcohol content was only 3.5%.

"It'll take a few of these to cool me down," he said smiling and brushing sweat from his brow with bottle in his hand.

They finished, waved goodbye to the bartender and followed the signs to Grand Case. It was the first time they had been off the main road, and they stopped at a second bar--tiny shack actually--overlooking the bay and had another couple of beers along with a plate of what they were told was sautéed shrimp that had been dusted with herbs and spices. When dipped in an accompanying thick green dip, the taste was very creole and Natalie figured that was the influence. She figured they were still on the French side of the island.

She worried a little that Drew was drinking so much but she sensed he hadn't lost his balance yet as they putt-putted along the rutting roads at little more than a snail's pace.

When Drew turned left on yet another side road--this one not even paved and full of deep holes--she became concerned that if they accidentally drove into one, he may not be responsive enough to pull them out quickly. She began to think of how she could gracefully jump off the back of the scooter without skinning her knees, or worse, getting trapped underneath it, should Drew drop the machine.

"Do you have any idea where we're going?" she said loudly into Drew's ear.

He turned his head and said just as loudly: "Actually, the bartender back there told me about a beach up here. I've heard of it and he says this is the back way."

No kidding, Natalie thought. "What's so special about this beach?" she asked.

"You'll see," Drew said. She decided to leave it at that since he appeared to be concentrating on dodging the larger pot holes.

The road ended at a parking lot that was nothing more than a leveled beach area behind several shacks. In between the shacks, Natalie saw the familiar azure blue water. It looked a little rougher here though.

"We're on the Atlantic side of the island now," Drew said, lifting the scooter onto its parking stand and watching it sink a few inches into the light sand. He pushed it a couple of times to be sure it wouldn't fall over, then grabbed her hand and headed between the shacks.

It could have been the amazingly large and non-stop waves that made this place so memorable. Or it could have been the numerous boats pulling wave-jumpers and parasails. It could even have been the beautiful, warm sand that allowed her feet to settle into gently, encasing her toes like bath salts.

But there really was no doubt that the most memorable feature was the fact that most of the tourists were naked.

And for a lot of them, it wasn't an attractive sight.

Drew laughed at her expression and she punched him. He led them into the shade of one of the shack's large umbrellas. Four stools were placed up against a hole in the side of the shack that served as the bar and Drew ordered yet two more beers.

"Actually, I'll have something with an umbrella in it, if you don't mind," Natalie said, trying to take her eyes off one particularly large man lying prostate on a lounge chair, his parts exposed fully to the sun.

"What happens when his… thing gets sunburned?" she asked no one in particular.

"His wife will have to rub aloe vera all over it, I should think," Drew said.

The bartender nodded his agreement, grinning from ear to ear. "Many make such sacrifices every day just for the pleasure of knowing what the remedy will be," he said and laughed heartily.

"Rum punch for the lady," Drew said as the bartender handed over a tall glass full of what looked like Coca-Cola. A blue parasol attached to a straw adorned the edge of the glass. "Welcome to Orient Beach," he added. "Apparently, the only *official* nude beach on the island."

The bartender winked at Natalie. "Official, yes," he said, pronouncing yes as "yays". "But not the only one." When he smiled, he exposed a row of teeth that gleamed in the sunlight. He had no shirt on and Natalie was tempted to lean forward to see if he had pants on but shook off the urge.

A younger woman walked by closer to the edge of the water. Her breasts, though large and round, sagged just a little but grudgingly, Natalie had to admit the rest of her was well proportioned. She had a wrap tied at the waist, hanging down one side, but it was see-through so the intent was lost on Natalie. As she looked around at the twenty or so people in various states of nudity, she felt a little more secure about her own body though; always a good thing for a woman. She smiled.

"You like the view here?" Drew asked, grinning, as he emptied his beer by putting his head back and guzzling the bottle's contents. The bartender placed another one on the bar without being asked.

"The service is attentive," she said and gestured to the waiter's glistening torso. "I wonder what else is on the menu."

Drew laughed.

After a few moments, he grabbed her hand again and led her to the water's edge. A couple of large rocks were protruding about six feet out of the water just a couple of feet in and Drew helped her atop one where they sat and watched the various water activities being performed before them.

All-of-a-sudden Drew pulled off his shirt and slipped into the water. He began swimming, then stopped and stood facing Natalie. He had his baseball cap and sunglasses on and the water was up to his shoulder level.

"It's gorgeous," he said, loudly enough for Natalie to hear above the crashing waves. Other rocks in the area prevented the full intensity of the waves to get close to the shore and Natalie figured maybe they had been put there for that purpose. "Different to swimming in the pool," he said and floated on his back to prove the point. Natalie had heard somewhere that the ocean's salt water density around the Caribbean islands was higher than most other places and that you could float without much effort.

She pulled off the shorts she had put on over her bikini bottoms and carefully edged in. The water was surprisingly warm and she was swimming immediately, heading to where Drew stood.

As she came closer, Drew ducked under the water as if reaching for something. He came up with something in his hand. His bathing suit. Natalie stopped swimming and planted her feet on the sandy bottom.

"You're in your underwear?"

"I don't wear underwear," he said grinning.

He thinks we're just going to jump into a cozy relationship because I was stupid enough to fall for his charm and chivalry once. He brings me to a nude beach, takes off his clothes and figures, what, that I'm going to glide over there and we're going to make out in the water? She stared at him for a moment, his grin growing wider.

She turned and began swimming back to the rock to retrieve her shorts. Suddenly the sight of the naked tourists nauseated her.

"Hey, where are you going," she heard Drew say. "What's wrong? It's a nude beach. I thought we could, you know, do as the Romans do," he pleaded.

What did that mean? Cavort in the water like ala-Caligula? Not likely.

Suddenly the intensity of her situation engulfed her. The near drowning and swim to shore in Hilton Head; the flight to an unknown tropical island;

Drew being an asshole. She grabbed her shorts and strode out of the water, heading back to the bar.

"Can a lady get a cab around here?" she asked the bartender who was grinning. He'd probably seen Drew's stunt and thought she was some prissy ice queen or something.

"There's usually a couple waiting behind," he said, the smirk dimming at the sight of her determined expression. "Look for a white minivan," he said in a more subdued manner.

"I'm sure he'll settle our bill," she said, pointing to Drew who, thankfully, was still standing up to his neck in the water, probably still naked. She stormed around to the rear of the shacks and saw what had to be a cab parked by the edge of the clearing. It didn't say taxi anywhere but there was a taxi-thingy mounted on the roof so what else would it be? The driver saw her coming and doused his cigarette--at least it looked like a cigarette--and opened the rear door for her. Natalie took one look back at the beautiful water, shook her head, and got in.

How did Benny expect this to work, she thought? Send her off to an island with some stud, just to keep her safe. Was he that dense? Or did he expect her to get entangled with someone else and forget about him? Maybe that was the game. Maybe he was remorseful about what was happening to Emma and his plan was to re-sort his marriage, for what, the fifth time?

"Where to miss?" the driver said, staring at her in the rearview mirror. *I must look angry.* She forced a slight smile.

"Do you know where the No Limits villa is?" she asked hopefully, realizing it was the only landmark she knew.

"In the Terres Basses peninsula, yes," he said, returning the smile. "Very nice places there," he added. "I have cousin who cleans some of them every weekend. No Limits very nice. Top of world, no?"

"Yes it's beautiful, thank you," she said. And they drove off. Natalie didn't turn to see if Drew had noticed she'd left. She'd worry about what to say later, once she'd had a chance to sort this out and decide her plan of action. First thing was to call Benny from the villa and find out what the plan really was.

She stared at the enormous cacti edging each side of the road as they passed some small but well-appointed condo resorts. Obviously this was the front entrance to the famous nude beach.

No limits, she thought. No limits my ass.

Chapter Fourteen

Drew was angry. Natalie had left the beach without him. But he wasn't overly surprised to find her standing by the kitchen counter, arms folded, a sour expression on her face.

"There are no phones," she said adamantly, her arms unfolding quickly sweeping in a large circle to encompass the entire home.

"None of the villas have phones," he said. "Everyone relies on cells, especially visitors."

"Do you have a cell phone? she asked.

"In my backpack, yes."

Her eyebrows furrowed. She obviously hadn't thought of searching his bags. "Can I use it?" she asked, moving toward the bedrooms.

"No," Drew said, grabbing a beer from the well-stocked fridge. While taking his first sip, he could see Natalie staring at him from the corridor. "Nobody can know where we are Natalie, you know that."

"I want to speak to Benny," she said.

"Him especially," Drew said. "He was afraid that if they came after you, they could use him to find out where you are."

"That's stupid."

Drew laughed. Natalie's eyes narrowed.

"What are they going to do, torture him," she said. "For God's sake Scanlon, they're kidnappers, not terrorists."

Drew watched her for a few moments. "So it's Scanlon now?"

"Damn it Drew, I'm not your plaything!" she said and began to sob.

Should I comfort her? Drew thought. No, that would make it worse. She belonged to William Benneton and although that relationship was just as screwed up as anything he could hope for, he had no right to take advantage of this.

Natalie dropped her hands and let out a deep sigh. It appeared she couldn't pretend to be angry anymore. Drew figured she was still annoyed with him but all she wanted was answers. Trying to get her to frolic with him in the ocean had been a dumb, impulsive idea. He wouldn't let it happen again. But damn it, she was so alive, so unpredictable, so damn alluring.

But of course, he knew where this was all going and getting involved with the security was not only dumb but deadly. Benneton would have wanted a replacement if he knew what had almost happened last night in the hotel. And the Dutchman? Well, he didn't want to think about what that guy's reaction.

"Look, I'm sorry about this afternoon," he said, moving closer to her.

Natalie moved away quickly and went to the couch facing the outside view.

"You were just taking advantage of the situation, I can't blame you," she said. "Benny set this up."

"Benneton had no idea we would end up in a hotel together last night," Drew said. "That wasn't part of the plan."

"Oh, and swimming naked in the Caribbean is?" she said.

Drew looked down at the floor. "No, that's not part of the plan either. I'm sorry. I just got caught up in the moment. It won't happen again, I promise."

Natalie looked at him and must have found something sincere because to Drew's relief, she leaned back into the couch cushions and visibly relaxed.

God, she is beautiful, he thought. In a girl next door kind of way. Maybe that was why he lost his edge while around her. Ever since first seeing her on the boat, he'd felt a tingle in his stomach that he hadn't felt before.

He shook his head and finished his beer in one gulp.

"Let's go into town like we'd planned and have supper. Later we'll get groceries for a couple of days. I don't want you to be too visible, even here," he said.

"Is this to be my jail cell?" she said.

"You could do worse," Drew said. "Look, I won't do anything I shouldn't okay; no getting naked in public."

"Or jumping into the sea fully clothed?" Natalie interrupted, grinning.

"Or sneaking into your shower," he said and watched Natalie's face redden. *Shit, shouldn't have said that.* "Well, I can't complain about getting cold here, so there's no excuse," he added quickly.

"You won't need an excuse," Natalie said defiantly. "I can lock the door to the bathroom here, I checked."

Was she playing with him or just making a statement without trying to look angry? Either way, she was off limits now. He had a job to do and when it was over, he'd never see her again. And she'd be happy. So long as he didn't confuse things.

"We'll call Oliver to come get us," he said. "We have nowhere to put groceries on the scooter."

She nodded.

She doesn't want to be back in close quarters on the scooter any more than I do, he thought.

"So when can I call Benny," she asked.

"When Mrs. Benneton is back home," he said.

Natalie was staring out the windows. Drew noticed a faint moon rising slowly above the horizon despite it still being light out.

"Or dead," she said.

Chapter Fifteen

Oliver had seemed surprised to hear from them so soon but he had happily agreed to drive them into Marigot, which was only a couple of miles away as the crow flies, but a ten-minute taxi ride along the winding roads that led from the hilltop to the French capital of the island.

As they rode past what Oliver described as the village square, Natalie noticed the size of some of the late model yachts docked all along what appeared to be a public marina.

"A lot of the boats you see here are owned by people in villas near you," Oliver said happily.

Natalie thought the town looked very European which seemed natural considering it was, after all, a part of the French West Indies. The streets were narrow and seemed to be staged in an ever-enlarging circle, much like she recalled cities like Paris and Rome were. Tourist shops, high end real estate offices, and expensive looking retail stores lined the streets. Oliver was forced to drive slowly due to the number of people walking. She cringed a few times as small scooters squeezed by them, missing both the van and pedestrians by mere inches. Oliver didn't seem fazed, however, and soon drew up in front of a colorful, brightly lit restaurant with large windows exposing diners at white clothed tables. It seemed to be very full and waiters in white shirts and tiny black bowties were bustling between tables quickly.

"Le Chanteclair," Oliver announced. "I recommend the Parisian Tartare highly and be sure to have a shot of Guavaberry to end your meal."

"Is that like a cognac or something?" Natalie asked him while Drew fished around in his wallet for a tip.

"It is the local liqueur made only here," he said proudly. "Kind of a peppery taste." He leaned in closer and whispered, "My wife uses it a lot when she cooks. Adds flavor and keeps me mellow." He laughed and Natalie squeezed his arm as she laughed along with him.

"Thank you, sir," Oliver said as Drew handed him a couple of Euro notes this time. "You have my number. Just call whenever you're ready. I'm never more than a few minutes away."

The restaurant could have easily been in any metropolitan city, except that the open windows welcomed the unmistakable Caribbean trade winds inside. That blended with the delightful smells from the kitchen to create a fragrance of extravagant tranquility.

Drew and Natalie were settled into a table for four near the front of the restaurant, it being one of the only ones available, and Natalie enjoyed people watching for a while, commenting on the diversity of shapes, sizes, ages and nationalities. Drew for the most part was quieter, letting Natalie do most of the talking in between courses of fine French cuisine.

During one of the pregnant pauses, Natalie quietly said, "In a different time and place, I would enjoy exploring everything the islands have to offer," she said, emphasized the word everything. "But I am who I am and as absurd as it sounds, I am loyal to Benny. Do you understand?"

Drew smiled, not quite a genuine smile, Natalie thought, but at least he's wasn't arguing.

"I understand Natalie," Drew said, "and once again, don't worry. It won't happen again. My job is to protect you and then send you back."

He'd said it with an expressionless face and Natalie was surprised at how much his sudden lack of interest disappointed her. Was she hoping he would have fought for her? *What an insane predicament this is.*

The waiter talked them into ordering Brioche Vendéenne, for dessert and as he returned with the magnificent chocolate delight presented on a stark white plate, Natalie noticed that a four-piece band was setting up at the back of the restaurant. Several waiters began to clear some of the tables nearby, creating a dance floor of sorts. The people who had been at those tables wandered over to those at the front of the restaurant and joined them at whatever empty seats they could find.

One attractive, older blonde headed directly for their table and addressed Natalie.

"Do you mind if I join you?" she asked.

Natalie wasn't sure what Drew felt about that but as he stood up, took her hand and lead her to the chair opposite Natalie, his opinion seemed apparent.

"Please," Natalie said, motioning for the woman to sit. She was perhaps twenty years older than Natalie, in her mid-fifties and well-tanned but she had a younger countenance enhanced by the chic wrap she wore around her waist, the crisply cut white blouse, and stylish, avant-garde four-inch heels right out of the latest Vogue. Natalie felt suddenly outclassed being in the presence of such a well-preserved island sun-goddess, and of course, Drew's attentions weren't helping to boost her confidence.

"You're here alone Ma'am," he said, leaning in and touching her arm lightly.

"Please, ma'am was my mother. I'm Diane. Diane Losier," she said extending her hand first to Natalie and then Drew, who held it just a second or so longer than Natalie thought necessary. Her grip was firm, a hidden strength that surprised Natalie a little as she looked so, well, model-esque.

Drew introduced themselves and Natalie wondered briefly why he hadn't used fake names. She smiled to herself, realizing she'd probably been reading too many psychological thrillers lately.

"My companion is usually here for the Blatten Brothers." she pointed toward the band that was just completing setting up and was now testing the microphones. "But he's out getting last minute supplies for an outing tomorrow. I'm afraid he'll likely miss out tonight."

"We weren't aware there was music tonight," Natalie said, looking at Drew for reassurance. He just shrugged.

"Oh, you must stay," Diane said and patted Natalie's hand. "You'll love them. They play every Wednesday and Thursday night and are the island's best kept secret." She winked and Natalie couldn't help but smile in return. The woman was cosmopolitan and damn near perfect but she seemed genuine enough, and probably a lot of fun. *Just what's needed right now.*

"We only just arrived. Our taxi driver picked this place for us," she said. "I think he knows all the best places to go."

"You're lucky you didn't get one of the resort drivers," Diane said. "Bar owners pay them to take tourists to the typical traps. Too many big men in flowered shirts for me." Her laugh was short and high pitched. She threw her head back and her curls bounced around her face before settling in nearly perfect order again.

The band began with a bluesy rendition of a *North80East* jazz hit and Natalie relaxed. Drew ordered more drinks for everyone and they settled into light conversation about some of the places Diane thought the couple absolutely had to see while visiting the island. After a while, several people had jumped onto the dance floor and when Diane grabbed Natalie's hand, she laughed and let herself get dragged out. She appreciated that the woman hadn't asked Drew to dance. Maybe he didn't know how anyway. She caught a glimpse of him watching them and smiling. No, someone like Drew just had to know how to dance. Diane was definitely a good dancer though and seemed to like being the leader which suited Natalie fine. She was used to being led around a dance floor by Benny, albeit stiffly. She felt a brief pang of guilt at enjoying herself when Benny was likely pacing back at home, anxious for Emma's safety. She shook her head and laughed. God, a shrink would have a lot of fun with that one.

When Diane was pulled away by a handsome forty-something she seemed to know, Natalie headed back toward the table, only to be headed off by Drew coming onto the dance floor.

"Come on, now's no time to take a break," he said and whisked her back to the center of the floor.

Okay, so he was good, twirling and swaying and always holding onto one or the other of Natalie's hands at all times. He directed her around the floor like a competitive ballroom dancer. Natalie laughed and Drew smirked confidently.

When the band slowed it down to a romantic ballad, Drew pulled Natalie closer, placed his arm firmly at the small of her back and blended into what Natalie could only describe as dirty dancing. She hadn't danced with anyone this fluid for a long time and she let herself go with it, though somewhere deep inside she knew it was probably a mistake. His aftershave was stronger at such close proximity and she marveled at how it instantly sparked memories of the night in the hotel. It seemed like a dream but the musky scent, mixed with the effects of about four glasses of red wine now, reminded her of his urgency and she found herself grinding into him a little harder.

When the song ended, they held onto each other for a moment, then Drew gruffly pushed away.

"I have to make a phone call," he said, looking at her briefly but avoiding eye contact. "Stay with Diane. I'll be right back." And with that, he turned and headed toward the front entrance.

Damn it! She knew there was an animal attraction between them. *Am I teasing him? Yeah, of course I am. Benny, you idiot, you should have hired an ugly bodyguard cause I'm not sure how long I can keep up this chastity thing.*

She laughed as she returned to the table where Diane sat, a glass of wine in each hand. She handed one to Natalie.

"You two just get married or something?" she asked.

"Oh God no," Natalie exclaimed. "He's a business associate. Kind of." Diane raised her eyebrow and Natalie laughed.

"Business must be good," Diane said and they clinked glasses.

Chapter Sixteen

Drew had never been this frustrated before. Natalie was driving him crazy. Her innocent girl-next-door beauty mixed in with the knowledge that she was somebody's mistress made him think lude thoughts of her constantly. Coming to an island had not been the smartest idea since everyone here wore as little clothing as possible, including Natalie.

They should have gone to Alaska.

Once outside the restaurant, he pulled out his cell, scrolled down to the number and pressed enter. It was answered on the second ring.

"We are on schedule?" The voice on the other end was gruff and resonant of a European accent.

"Everyone is in place," Drew said, idly watching the passers-by who thought nothing of a guy standing on the sidewalk talking into a cell. Probably trying to find his girlfriend who had disappeared into a shop somewhere along Boulevard de France. "Has the other guest arrived yet?"

"She is arranging transfers in the Caymans as we speak and should arrive tomorrow night," the man answered. "But that is my concern not yours. Your worry is to keep your charge in place for another seventy-two hours or so. Then she can do as she pleases."

Drew wiped his brow. She'll run back to Benneton.

"I think I'd like to meet this one," the voice said, his tone lightening slightly.

"We've never done that before," Drew said, suddenly alarmed but not really sure why.

The man either hadn't heard him or didn't care. "I'll arrange something."

"She has to return, you know that," Drew stated.

"I decide who returns and who doesn't," the man exploded. There were a few moments of silence. Drew knew better than to aggravate him. He could hear heavy breathing on the other end. After a while, the breathing lightened and a calmer voice said, "Just bring her along Mr. Scanlon. All will be fine." The phone went dead.

Drew watched the tourists and locals wander by the restaurant. The street was well lit up with stores and eateries open despite the later hour. The music from inside the restaurant wafted out onto the street and occasionally passers-by would dance a short jig to the beat, laughing and hugging their partners. The real world gets put on hold for five or seven days as cold northerners bask in the Caribbean heat and forget about their lives back home. In another time, Drew could have done that, perhaps with Natalie. But right now, he needed to focus. This new twist had him worried. And he needed to think it through so that Natalie would, indeed, return to her lover. Drew shuddered and was a little surprised at the twinge he felt in his lower stomach.

What a waste.

The evening wound down after that. Drew's scowl convinced Natalie that his phone call had put him in a bad mood. She didn't want to ask him about it in front of Diane but she wondered if something had happened back at Hilton Head.

Diane had dragged her up to the dance floor a couple of more times but the energy had worn off and by eleven, the women had had enough.

"Let's go shopping tomorrow," Diane had asked Natalie after thanking Drew for picking up the tab. Natalie had expected Drew to offer some excuse as to why she couldn't go and was surprised when he nodded and said that was probably a good idea. He had calls to make in the morning and Natalie wouldn't get another chance to explore the island's many shops. He had even suggested they go to Philipsburg, the capitol of the Dutch side, famous for its discount jewelry stores and Fifth Avenue style boutiques.

"Let's meet at nine in the square," she said.

"We'll get Oliver to drive you down," Drew had said. With a quick wave, Diane left and Drew stood to go.

"Have they heard from the kidnappers?" Natalie asked.

Drew frowned. "I wasn't speaking with Benneton," he said.

Natalie arched her eyebrows.

"That's one of the calls I'll be making in the morning," he said, walking to the door, obviously hoping she would follow. Natalie quickly caught up with him just outside where there were still a lot of tourists wandering around.

"You're upset about something," she said.

Drew looked in both directions, apparently looking for Oliver's white cab. Since most were white, they couldn't tell until the vehicles were virtually in front of them.

"I'm just tired," he said, brushing his hair back over his forehead. His bangs swung right back in a straggly manner, curling just above his eyebrows. "It's been a hectic last couple of days, don't you think?"

"Nothing a little shopping won't cure," she said brightly. "Good thing you're not coming, you'd spoil it."

"I thought you were homesick?" he said.

Natalie turned her head away from him for a moment, then once she had control of her expression again, turned back.

"I am used to being disappointed Mr. Scanlon," she said calmly. "I have learned to make the best of the moment at all times."

Drew grinned. "Yes, I still remember one moment in particular."

At that moment, Oliver honked his horn as he edged to the curb. Natalie opened the front passenger door and jumped inside, forcing Drew to open the sliding side door and get in the back.

Get me out of here Benny. Or we'll all be sorry.

Chapter Seventeen

Natalie hadn't expected Drew to be up the next morning, so she was surprised to see him talking to Oliver out by the van taxi. Oliver was urgently nodding his head as if taking important instructions. As she came closer, Drew stopped talking and glanced over at her.

"I'm going into town later," he said. "Perhaps I can meet up with you somewhere for lunch."

"I have no idea where we'll be," Natalie said. "Diane is the tour guide."

"Tell her to bring you to the Ocean Lounge. I'll make reservations."

Natalie stared at him, and then saluted. "Yes sir."

Drew grinned. "Thank you, Oliver," he said, shaking the man's hand which seemed an odd thing to do to a taxi driver but Natalie went around the van and jumped into the front seat.

The old Jamaican seemed on edge as they drove away, looking in the rearview mirror regularly until the villa was no longer visible. His fingers tapped the steering wheel nervously and his usually gleeful expression was dour.

"What did Mr. Scanlon want, Oliver?" Natalie asked. Oliver stiffened slightly then slowly turned his head toward her.

"He said to make sure we went directly to the Town Centre, Miss Natalie," he said quietly. "And to not stop anywhere on the way."

"I see. Did he tell you why he doesn't want us to stop along the way?"

Oliver fidgeted in his seat. "He only say I make sure you don't use a phone anywhere. He even tell me to keep my cell in my pocket." The poor man was distraught.

Natalie conjured up a laugh, unconvincing to her ears, but Oliver's fingers stopped tapping and he looked at her questioningly.

"There are some problems at work back home," she said. "We are here to get away from it. Mr. Scanlon thinks that if I talk to anyone back at the office, I'll get upset. He wants them to solve the problem themselves and when we go back, everything will be back to normal. That's all. Nothing sinister, Oliver." She patted his leg and smiled. She hated that lying came so easy to her but being with Benny had taught her to ramble off mistruths without a second thought. She had to put poor Oliver at ease. Then maybe later, he would let her use his cell phone.

Oliver's shoulders dropped significantly and his arms bent a little at the elbow. The familiar carefree expression was reforming slowly.

"It not right for a man to control the woman," he said, his eyebrows curving down. "Woman is here to make man's life easier."

Natalie laughed, genuinely this time. "That's a woman's role in life is it? To make man happy?"

Oliver squinted, his quizzical frown making Natalie giggle.

"Women shouldn't work outside home. Woman learns to cook, to clean, to wash clothes. They need someone to do that for. Then they happy. And if wife happy, then I have no problems," he said and grinned.

"Happy wife, happy life. Is that it?" Natalie said, smiling despite the incongruity of Oliver's essentially sexist attitude. She knew that it was simply island native life as it had been for centuries.

Oliver laughed too. "Yes, when my wife happy making me happy, what I have to complain about?" He waited, then began singing the refrain "Don't worry, be happy!" from the Bobby McFerrin hit of the late 1980s.

They drove in silence for a while and as the outskirts of Marigot came into view, Natalie said, "If I ever want to borrow your cell phone though Oliver, you'll let me, won't you?"

Oliver smiled. His hands were steadily drumming the wheel again but this time to the beat of the song he was still humming. His chin bounced in and out to the beat as he replied. "I'll think about it, Miss Natalie. When woman happy, Oliver happy."

She patted his shoulder and a moment later pointed Diane out to him. She was standing by a small blue car, the make of which Natalie didn't know.

"Be sure to call if you need a ride home," Oliver said, waving his cell phone around and laughing as he drove away.

"New friend?" Diane asked, getting into the car.

Natalie giggled. "He likes women to be barefoot and pregnant, I think."

"Yuk!" Diane said as they drove toward the main street. "Don't get too close to the natives dear. Next thing you know you'll be dancing in a grass skirt on the beach by a fire and chanting voodoo lyrics."

Natalie looked at her companion to be sure she wasn't serious but Diane's straight face eventually formed a small grin.

"He's a nice man. He worries about me, I think."

"Isn't that Drew's job?" Diane said.

"Drew is looking out for me, and in his own strange way, I think he likes me. But I don't think he worries about me," she said.

"Sounds like a little trouble in paradise," Diane said staring at the pedestrians crossing in front of her. When the way was clear, she turned right onto Rue de Hollande and headed south out of town.

Define paradise, Natalie thought. At home, seeing Benny once a week at the apartment condo he pays for. Rarely going out in case they are seen by the wrong people in public, and always, always making sure he's happy. She laughed. Maybe Oliver was more of a philosopher than he imagined.

"What's so funny?" Diane asked.

"Sorry, just thinking you're right. We are in paradise. And what does one do in paradise other than swim and drink rum punches?" She looked over at Diane.

"Shop!" they said simultaneously.

* * *

Diane headed along the main road with Simpson Bay Lagoon on the right. After a mile or so, they passed signs stating they were now entering the Dutch side of the island. The road wound around mountains and small villages. After Pelican Key, they began climbing and the extended views of the Atlantic were breathtaking.

"That has to be the most beautiful beach I've ever seen," Natalie said as they crested the mount after Little Bay and slowly came down the other side.

"This is Great Bay," Diane said. "Phillipsburg is at the far end; see where the two cruise ships are."

To Natalie, the giant floating cities seemed out of place and over-scaled for the size of the bay but the water was the kind of greenish blue you only see on calendars.

"My partner docks his catamaran here," Diane added. Natalie realized that Diane always called him her partner, not husband, boyfriend, whatever; an interesting relationship, no doubt. The boat was obviously his toy. "He's likely there now," she added.

"Will he be joining us for lunch?" Natalie asked.

Diane seemed pre-occupied with steering the car around the tight curves. "Oh no, Manfred doesn't eat on the island much, he's too used to his private chef. He does a little shopping but likes to stay on the boat all day, even when docked." Diane continued driving and eventually they entered Phillipsburg which seemed older and less sophisticated than Marigot but much, much busier.

"You live on the boat?" Natalie asked.

Diane was slowing to turn into what appeared to be a municipal parking lot. She pulled into a spot, turned off the ignition and turned to face Natalie, her expression serious, an internal debate occurring.

"Manfred doesn't come here much," she said pointedly. "Only when I want other human companionship. Or to shop," she said, smiling a little. "He owns an island just out there," she pointed in the general direction of the Atlantic. "You see, he's very, very rich." She sat looking at Natalie as if waiting for a response.

Natalie stared back. Rich men were no mystery to her. Maybe if Natalie explained her situation with Benny, the woman would understand they were kindred spirits of sorts. But not yet.

"Then that means you're buying lunch," she deadpanned. They stared at each other momentarily and then both broke out laughing as they stepped out into the eighty-two-degree tropical heat.

* * *

Philipsburg is known for its wide array of jewelry stores, high-end clothing and accessory boutiques, and a plethora of tourist souvenir shops. The streets are narrow and the Walter A. Nisbeth Road runs along the back of the shopping district, along the shore of the Great Salt Lake, which turns the town into a peninsula of sorts. All the shopping is closer to the Caribbean side of the strip of land, restaurants on the Boardwalk being the final layer before running into Great Bay, about four streets later. Visitors by the hundreds converge on the less than one-mile-long shopping district and haggle for the best bargains they can get. Often, due to the time restraints of the cruise ships, the haggling is rushed and merchants, though experienced in dealing with various nationalities, recognize they are all under time pressure to get the deal done.

Diane explained that during the day, the population of the shopping town nearly doubled due to the number of people invading the stores from the ships. By late afternoon, a lot of the shops close since the cruise ships leave around five o'clock. They see no reason to stay open for visitors who are here on week-long vacations. They have much more time to shop and don't need to be catered to in the same rush fashion.

"I used to tell them I was a tourist from the boat," Diane laughed. "But they all know me now so it doesn't work as well."

Natalie bought a new Dolce-Gabbana purse, an authentic Panama hat made in Ecuador, and an extra, extra-large Bamboo Cay island shirt in subdued pink for Benny. The hat was a bit manly but Diane said it gave her a spunky look and complimented her rounded face, so she went for it.

Natalie told Diane about meeting Drew at the Ocean Lounge and Diane thought that was a great idea.

"It's at the end of the boardwalk at the cruise ship pier," she said.

"Here in Phillipsburg?" Natalie asked, surprised that Drew had guessed they would be coming here.

"No surprise," Diane said in response to her quizzical expression. "It's a small island and the daytime fare is much better on the Dutch side. French cuisine is reserved for romantic evenings."

They continued walking the three or four streets that made up the shopping district, sipping Carib beer they bought for $2 American each at wooden stands erected on virtually every corner. When they discovered the market place, Natalie even picked up a couple of handmade stone turtles that she thought would look great on her coffee table. Diane said they were mass produced and sold all over the Caribbean but Natalie smiled and said she didn't care. They would remind her of her whirlwind visit to Sint Maarten.

By one o'clock, laden with shopping bags, they headed toward the boardwalk which meandered along the beach. Tiny bars and eateries with colorful sun umbrellas and comfy lounge seating dotted the pathway. At one point, Natalie stooped to get a handful of sand and saw that it wasn't sand at all but tiny shells, ground down by the water into a semi-sharp covering that Diane said was difficult to walk barefoot on for any great length. She said it was this material that made Sint Maarten beaches so clean looking, especially when set against the turquoise hue of the Bay's shallower water.

The Ocean Lounge was busy since it was lunchtime and this was the closest restaurant to the ships. Diane explained that since all dinners were served aboard ship as it sailed from one destination to the next, lunch was the only meal tourists could enjoy on any of the islands. Some of the less adventurous would not wander far and that's why the Lounge boasted a full house virtually every day from eleven-thirty to three o'clock or so.

"Drew said he would call ahead to reserve a table but I don't know if he was able to," Natalie said looking at the bustling establishment, white clad waiters and waitresses hustling from table to table. She noted that most of the patrons were likely American, obvious from the size of bellies and type of food, all greasy, arrayed on the bamboo tables.

"Don't worry, we'll have the best view in the house," Diane said, stepping under the thatched awning and grabbing Natalie's hand.

The maître'd was a short, black man in a white linen shirt with a bright yellow tie.

"Ms. Losier, so good to see you again," he said. "Your other party is already seated. This way, please." As he led them into the restaurant, Diane leaned into Natalie's ear.

"Manfred owns it," she said and smiled.

Chapter Eighteen

Diane was smiling but Natalie wore a frown as both women approached Drew who was seated at a table by the open air window, facing the beach. Directly behind him, visible through other windows was the bow of a huge cruise ship poised as if to bear down and crush the restaurant any second.

"How did you get this table?" Natalie asked as they sat down. The maître'd took drink orders from the ladies and left.

"When I called for reservations this morning, they were booked so I thought I'd better come and meet you. Then we could go somewhere else," Drew said, leaning back and directing his conversation to Diane now.

"Then when I got here and mentioned I was meeting a Diane Losier, he brought me here."

"That was very good of him," Diane said matter-of-factly.

Drew nodded. "Apparently you pull some weight here," he said nonchalantly, sipping his own dark cultured drink.

"Diane owns the restaurant," Natalie said.

"Actually, Manfred does," Diane corrected, her smile vanishing. "Along with a lot of things on the island."

"Sorry," Natalie said. "Diane's hus...ah, partner owns the restaurant."

"Good thing," Drew said, gesturing with his thumb over his shoulder. "Half a city just unloaded from that ship and all the males hit the bar while the women headed into town."

"I think we ran into a few of them," Natalie said, "literally." Both women laughed. Natalie reached down and pulled out a couple of the things she'd bought and showed them to Drew.

They ordered food, Drew searching the menu diligently to find anything that wasn't deep fried. He settled on mussels in a coconut cream and rum sauce. The women both ordered the daily fish special with salads.

Part way through the meal, Natalie excused herself to go to the bathroom. She seemed to be waiting to see if Diane would join her, but the other woman continued to eat and didn't acknowledge the subtle invitation so Natalie went alone.

"Of all the incredible places to eat on this island, I wish you hadn't chosen here," Diane said, putting her knife and fork down despite her fish being only half eaten.

"It's a landmark and is easy to find," Drew said. He didn't like his decisions being questioned, especially not by Diane. Besides, there were other reasons for being in this location.

Diane didn't make eye contact with Drew but her eyes roamed the beach as if looking for someone.

"She's a nice girl," she said, her eyes still roaming.

"Yes, she is," Drew said, taking a big gulp of his drink.

They both stared in different directions, saying nothing, deep in their own thoughts, until Natalie returned. Drew hoped she didn't sense any change in the chemistry amongst them and immediately initiated conversations about the various stores in the town and other aspects of island living in which Diane contributed actively.

Eventually the conversation turned to activities they were going to do while visiting the island.

Natalie looked at Drew. "I hadn't thought of anything particularly," she said. "I don't know how long we're going to be here."

"Then you have to come sailing this afternoon," Diane said.

Drew was staring out toward the beach.

"On your partner's boat?" Natalie asked.

"If you call it a boat, he'll throw you overboard," said Diane laughing. "It's a sixty-five-foot catamaran and it's his pride and joy. That's why you have to come. He insists I go with him once or twice a week and, quite frankly, I find it boring. I would absolutely love the company and I'm sure you two would thoroughly enjoy it."

Drew's gaze came around to Diane but he said nothing until he realized Natalie was waiting for him to reply.

"It is a beautiful day," he said quietly, "and we had nothing else planned."

"I don't have a bathing suit with me," Natalie said.

Diane pointed to the town.

"Another excuse to shop," she said, grabbing Natalie's hand.

"It's called the Elyssa," she said to Drew. "On dock C, just over there." She pointed in the general direction of the marina just the other side of the cruise ship dock. "Manfred will be aboard. Just introduce yourself. Come on girl, I need a new suit too!"

Drew watched as the two women nearly ran out of the restaurant. Diane stopped briefly to speak with the maitre'd, pointing back to the table, and then dragged a laughing Natalie out onto the boardwalk,

The maitre'd came over and began clearing the table.

"I need to store my scooter here for a few hours," he said to the man. "Is that a problem?"

"Of course not," he said without looking up from his task. "Put it near the back kitchen entrance. It will be safe."

Drew stood, dropping a few dollars onto the table.

"Thank you, Mr. Scanlon," the man said. "Always a pleasure. "Please give my regards to Mr. DeVries. I hope he finds time to visit us this time around."

Drew looked at the small Jamaican momentarily. The small man sensed the gaze and looked up to see Drew's expressionless face.

"Did I say something wrong Mr. Scanlon?" he asked, his voice quivering slightly.

Drew was going to reprimand the man but instead decided it wasn't worth the effort. He sighed, shook his head and headed out of the restaurant.

The maitre'd stood watching, sweat beading on his forehead. He watched as Drew headed to the parking lot, then used the table rag to wipe his brow. He didn't think he'd done anything wrong but since Mr. DeVries had bought the restaurant a year ago, he wasn't really sure what he should say and do half the time.

He watched as Drew walked back along the boardwalk, heading straight toward the marina. These people made him nervous though he didn't know why. Even the woman had a cold stare sometimes that reminded him of his wife's mother when she was annoyed with him for something he didn't know he'd done. But she usually only came to the restaurant a couple of times while on the island. Next time she would likely bring her companion, the owner.

And that he never looked forward to.

Chapter Nineteen

Natalie had never been on a catamaran before. They looked so much bigger than a regular sailboat. Benny had a forty-foot C&C that he sailed around Hilton Head and the inner harbor, and she'd been on it a couple of times but it seemed narrow compared to the Elyssa.

As she and Diane approached, Diane yelled, "Permission to come aboard Captain," winking at Natalie.

A grey head popped up on the opposite side of the bulkhead.

"Ah, you're here," he said. He had a European accent; Dutch Natalie assumed. He was thin but healthy looking for a man whose face said he had to be in his sixties. No paunch, thick arms, and very agile. He practically hopped to the edge and extended his hand out for the women to grasp and jump aboard.

"This must be the mysterious Natalie," he said, pulling her up and over onto the deck. "I have already heard so much about you but Drew never explained how lovely you are."

Natalie wasn't sure why she would be considered mysterious and wondered exactly what Drew had explained, but smiled as the man helped Diane aboard. She watched Diane take off her sandals and put them in a basket on one of the seats. Natalie noticed the man was barefoot too so she bent to take her sandals off.

"It's safer in bare feet," Diane said.

"And shoes scuff up the deck," the man added. "I'm sure you don't want to be swabbing all afternoon, eh?" Manfred said.

"Natalie, this is my companion, Manfred," Diane said as the older man grabbed Natalie's hand again, turned it over and kissed it quickly. "Businessman, sailor, and swashbuckling wannabee," Diane added.

Natalie laughed but stopped quickly when she noticed Manfred scowl momentarily. Diane had been calling him her partner all day but suddenly he was her 'companion'. And the swashbuckling wannabee quip had clearly annoyed him.

"You have sailed before?" Manfred queried, his accent evident on the 's' in sailed. He gestured for the women to sit on the pre-formed seating area at the stern of the boat. Natalie knew that catamarans were designed with two hulls connected by a deck, thus the extra width. She'd heard they were a more stable boat than a single hull.

"Only a few times," Natalie said. "I have a friend who sails along the Carolina coastline. I've never crewed or anything but I do love the scent of the ocean, and the wind, of course."

Manfred smiled widely. Natalie sensed she'd said something appropriate.

"You haven't sailed until you've been on a vessel like this," he said, his arms taking in the entirety of the boat.

"Feel free to wander around. Diane can show you the nets at the bow. If you don't mind getting a little wet, it's thrilling to lie on them as we sail. If you concentrate, you can imagine being a fish. "

He then excused himself and climbed over steel ropes and supports, heading toward the bow.

Just then, Drew came from below with drinks in his hand. He didn't say anything immediately and she noticed him eyeing her from head to toe. She flushed at the raw attention.

"Nice suits," he said eventually, leaning forward and handing a plastic glass to each of them. "Manfred has a supply of rums that would rival a Manhattan nightclub. This one's Cuban."

The women had only been gone less than an hour and already Drew was chummy enough with their host to be rummaging through the bar.

"I never drink this stuff at home," Diane said. "But it seems so appropriate in the tropics don't you think?"

Natalie realized she'd never asked Diane where they were from or if they stayed on the islands, or the boat, for extended periods.

"Just make sure you have a glass of water for every rum or you may fall overboard," Drew said.

The women relaxed. Diane seemed content to sip her drink and sunbathe. Natalie watched the people in nearby boats and marveled at their opulence. The Elyssa looked very new and was larger than those nearby but across the marina, she noticed two very large yachts tied up to the concrete pier.

"Movie stars, rich businessmen and a lot of European royalty dock here all the time," Diane said, following Natalie's gaze.

"That one there," she said pointing to the larger of the two yachts, "belongs to a Sheik from Dubai. He's here for a month with his--" she thought for a moment "--sixth or seventh wife, I think. Manfred has been aboard for drinks, a past acquaintance I gather."

"You didn't go?" Natalie asked.

"Sheiks treat women like chattel," Diane said, waving her hand dismissively. "And one thing I don't do well is sit quietly in a corner, look pretty and wait for the big man to feel the need to use his chattel."

Natalie laughed as Diane smiled and sighed. "Manfred knows better."

Manfred had prepared the boat and asked Drew to cast off the bow rope. Diane got up and did the same at the stern without being asked. The motor was quiet and the boat drifted slowly into the harbor, around the wooden docks and out into Great Bay.

"It'll be calm until we get into the Atlantic," Diane said, returning to sit beside Natalie. "He'll want to put her through her paces to show off, so if you get a little seasick later, the head's down there." She pointed to the open cockpit.

Drew was up forward manhandling the smaller jib sail and Manfred was uncoiling rope. It was strange how the two men seemed to work so well in tandem despite not knowing each other or even talking about the various tasks being performed. She hadn't known Drew was a sailor. Of course, she didn't know anything about Drew really but obviously Manfred trusted his skills.

Diane suggested they sit atop the cockpit and laid out towels for them. The breeze was steady and warm and Natalie closed her eyes for a moment as her long hair blew straight backwards. She'd heard others talk about the trade winds, how it cleared up sinuses and enveloped you like a huge hair dryer. She wished she had come here a lot earlier in her life and experienced what so many returning Caribbean tourists took for granted. She'd spent many a summer up north in the Finger Lakes as a child, and in Florida as a guest of various love interests, but she'd never felt this combination of clean, fresh, warm air. It was all-enveloping and intoxicating.

When she opened her eyes, she noticed Drew staring at her. He quickly turned away and popped into the cockpit where Manfred was manning the huge, stainless steel wheel.

Diane was lying back, eyes closed, enjoying the sun. She was in great shape for an older woman, Natalie thought. Though well proportioned, now that she was wearing only a bikini, Natalie could see her well defined arm muscles and tight stomach. She probably works out daily, Natalie thought. Isn't that what rich women do every day? Despite her comments about not being just a plaything for her man, Natalie figured she likely kept herself in such good condition to maintain her companionship with Manfred. She briefly wondered why the boat had been named Elyssa and not Diane. Maybe he'd been married before. Maybe his wife was Elyssa and Diane was his partner for the Caribbean. Kindred souls for sure, she thought and frowned.

As the Elyssa left the protection of the bay mountains and headed out into the Atlantic, the waves got a little bigger and the boat began a steady rocking back and forth, almost bouncing over waves as they headed due Southeast.

The two women sat talking while the now brisker but still warm wind whipped around them. Manfred and Drew scurried about the boat pulling lines and tightening ropes so that the bright white sails remained taut. The boat was lightly bouncing on the starboard side as the winds lifted the port side out of the water now and again then gently let it drop back into the swell. Eventually Manfred announced that they were set for a while. He and Drew retreated to the stern steering wheel where they picked up their drinks and stood talking while Manfred kept the big boat on a steady path into the wind.

"Would you like to try the nets?" Diane asked as they swiftly passed a couple of small islands that appeared to be uninhabited except for scores of colorful birds.

One side of Natalie's mouth crept up as her eyes widened slightly. "It's safe, I suppose?"

Diane laughed, grabbed her hand and pulled her down the sloping deck toward the bow of the boat and the net that was strung between the two hulls of the catamaran. About ten feet of net was exposed to the elements and Diane slowly edged out into the middle, pulling Natalie with her. Natalie could see the ocean whipping past just inches below her as the boat crashed through the waves and bounced gently.

Sitting with legs straight out in front of her, Diane explained how she would grip the net with her hands so that she didn't bounce around too much when the waves got a little bigger. Natalie's eyes bulged and Diane laughed.

"Once past these last few outer islands, we'll be exposed to the full force of the Atlantic for a while," she said. Don't worry it's fun and as long as you hang onto the rope, you won't bounce off.

As if on cue, the boat rose a little higher on the starboard side and the main sail fluttered as if being bombarded by a large stick over and over. The bouncing became more insistent and Natalie felt her hands tire from gripping the net so hard.

After a few minutes, the repetitiveness of the wave's actions and the boat's responses became almost relaxing. Natalie caught a glimpse of Drew and Manfred, still at the wheel, in what seemed to be heated discussion. Though maybe it just looked that way because they were yelling to be heard above the noise of the wind in the sails.

Without warning, a large wave hit the bow and engulfed the entire front of the boat, including Natalie and Diane. Sputtering after it passed, she swung her head vigorously to get the hair out of her eyes. Diane was doing the same but laughing heartily also.

"I forgot to tell you about that part," she said. "You can see them coming." She pointed in front out toward the waves that were coming at the boat on a forty-five-degree angle. "Look for the white caps."

Natalie was soaked through but since she was in a bathing suit, there didn't seem to be anything to be concerned about, other than her hair. She stared ahead, looking for white-capped waves.

"Relax, that's as bad as it gets," Diane said. "In fact, when the next one comes in, let go of the net and let the wave surround you."

Natalie looked aghast but Diane assured her that the water could only push her backwards. The net was shaped in such a way that as long as they were low in its cradle, the waves weren't strong enough to physically move them far.

Another crest crashed over the bow and Natalie reluctantly released her one hand. She bounced sideways and losing her balance, fell sideways into the net. She heard Diane laughing. A few seconds later, another wave swept across the bow. This time Natalie tentatively let go and felt herself get lifted an inch or so, carried backwards, then dropped and pressed back against the net a few inches farther back. What a feeling! She noticed Diane, legs up in the air, bouncing on the net beside her as wave after wave swept the bow of the boat each time it sank into the trough that preceded a large white-capped wave.

After a while, she felt bruised and the salt was getting into her mouth. She felt thoroughly soaked. Diane, as if reading her mind, nodded her head backward and they both edged toward the deck. They crawled back to their towels and stretched out under the sun. Diane said she was going below to get more towels and crawled to the port side where Drew helped her down into the cockpit.

Natalie pulled her hair back and formed a loose bun, then sat up, arms folded around her legs and stared forward. Though still wet, the sun's intense rays and the warm breeze surrounded her in a comforting embrace.

The Security

She turned at the sound of muffled voices and saw her three companions talking intently in the cockpit. She couldn't make out any words but both Drew and Diane looked agitated. Manfred, on the other hand, appeared calm, though when he spoke, Natalie could see his Adam's apple extend as he spoke, connoting an effort in being heard. Must be really windy back there.

After a few moments, Diane returned and handed Natalie a soft hair broach which Natalie used to make a more comfortable pony tail out of her hair. Diane quietly did the same.

"Are we turning back soon?" Natalie asked.

Diane looked straight ahead and pursed her lips.

"Manfred wants to stop in at St. Barths," she said. "You've heard of the island?"

Natalie knew it to be the haunt of the rich and famous. Movie stars, rich businessmen and their families either owned villa's or rented them on the tiny island that was said to be so expensive, tourists only visited; few could afford to stay there for more than a night or so. She'd read that was why the powerful and famous had been going there for decades; they had the place to themselves pretty much.

"He has to meet someone," she said still staring straight ahead. "We'll have a late afternoon snack. I know a great place near the pier."

Natalie could see that Diane was upset but decided not to ask her about it. They didn't know each other that well yet and she sensed Manfred got his way most if not all of the time. Actually, Natalie was glad. She could use a break from the bouncing and the salt in her mouth was getting very annoying. A cool umbrella drink would clear that up in no time. Diane had probably been to St. Barths many times. For Natalie though, it would be a pleasant surprise. She could tell Benny all about it when she returned home. Of course, he'd probably been there. With his wife.

Chapter Twenty

Natalie's first impression of St. Barths wasn't the pristine beaches, the lush plant life, or even the rolling mountainside. It was the boats. Hundreds of them, lined up along the entire length of the harbor. And not just ordinary boats. Even from a distance, she could tell these were vessels you didn't see every day. Excessively long and two or even three stories high, these were floating luxury cottages.

As they maneuvered around even more opulent yachts were anchored to various white-painted buoys dotting the harbor. They sailed gently into the protected main harbor of the capital city of Gustavia and Diane pointed toward a particularly large yacht docked dead center forcing all shipping to go around it.

"That's Paul Allen's," she said and when Natalie looked at her quizzically, "Co-founder of Microsoft."

"Too big to dock?" Natalie asked

"Just over four hundred feet, I think. I'm told that on New Year's Eve, he sends shuttle boats ashore and lets anyone get on. It's so big, he doesn't care who comes aboard so long as it's full of happy, drunken people."

Drew expertly dropped the sails, stuffing them into the forward cabin through an open hatch. Manfred steered the Elyssa toward a long concrete docking area that was, for some reason, empty.

"Have your passport ready," Diane said, pointing to a small wooden building just off to the right of the dock. "We just entered France."

Natalie blew air out of her mouth quickly. No one had mentioned passports and she was thankful she carried hers in her purse at all times when travelling. She wondered if Drew had remembered his and was relieved to see he was holding it between his teeth as he jumped ashore to tie off the bow line.

Manfred did the same with the stern line and then held out his hand to help the women.

"We can only dock here for a couple of hours," he said. "But that should be long enough. I must meet someone but I'm sure you will enjoy exploring the downtown for a while; perhaps get a drink or two?" He handed Diane a wad of bills--Euros Natalie assumed--turned and walked off into the crowd.

"Come on," Diane said. "I know a lovely place where we can get a drink and watch the local action." With her head she nodded at a group of shirtless young men cavorting in front of a jewelry store across the street.

Natalie laughed and followed Diane down the narrow street. Cars were bumper to bumper and she briefly wondered why they even had cars here. She remembered reading in a Vanity Fair article last year that the whole island was only a few square miles in size.

"I'm going to go and find another t-shirt," Drew said. "I only brought the one and it's a little sweaty."

"Playing tourist are we?" Natalie said.

Diane was frowning. "We'll be at Le Deurne," she said.

"Fine, I'll meet you there in a bit," Drew said and loped off in the same direction Manfred had gone.

"Come on. It's siesta time. All the locals will be heading back to their villas for a nap before supper," Diane said. "It's the best time to star gaze."

Natalie recalled the article saying that many of the island's luxurious villas were either rented or owned by New York ultra-rich, European royalty, and of course, Hollywood stars. But she hadn't really thought she would see anybody just wandering around the tiny port town.

La Deurne was little more than a few wooden tables perched on the edge of the pavement where the two main streets merged. The roof was nothing more than an extremely large umbrella which prevented sunlight from directly hitting the patrons but did little to stop the warm breeze from penetrating its depths.

Most of the tables right at the front were occupied so they settled at one on the edge of the pavement where they had a perfect few of the tiny cars and scooters all vying to enter the sharp right turn that took them from the downtown core to the pier. It reminded Natalie of any port city but in miniature. Car after car edged by them and tires squealed as they took the tight turn at one or two miles per hour. Where do people drive to in a place so small?

After two Margarita's, both women had settled into a comfortable silence, just people watching and enjoying the breeze. Diane nudged her a couple of times to point out notables. The first time, when she explained that the couple holding hands across the street, gazing into one of the many store windows was Roman Abramovich, a Russian businessman who owned an $89 million-dollar estate overlooking Gouverneuer Beach.

"His daughter?" Natalie asked.

"His wife. Dasha something or other," Diane said. "She's twenty-six I think."

"If he's that rich, doesn't he have bodyguards?" Natalie asked, looking around for guys in black suits with little wires attached to their ears.

Diane laughed. "Nobody cares here," she said. "That's why the rich love it. I heard a story that Steve Martin used to disguise himself when he first started vacationing here. Then he realized that no one bothered him when they found out who he was anyway. So he bought a villa just up there," she pointed up above the stores toward the mountainside that encircled the port town.

A few moments later, she nudged Natalie again and this time Natalie needed no explanation. Jimmy Buffett's straggly hair was easily recognizable. He was meandering down the road in animated conversation with a dark-skinned man. No one was paying attention as they strode by, occasionally sipping the beers they were holding.

"This is one of the only Southern islands where he hasn't put up one of his insipid Margaritaville's," Diane said, shaking her head. "So this is where he likes to vacation. None of this bunch would eat that crap anyway."

Natalie laughed.

They ordered another drink and Natalie sat back, her sunglasses perched on the edge of her nose. She was now looking at every person walking by to see if she recognized any more celebrities. She figured she had met quite a few of the East Coast's elite at parties Benny had taken her to over the past couple of years and wondered if she would recognize any of them here. It would be interesting to see how old their partners were.

She briefly wondered if Benny had ever been here but then shrugged the idea off. He would definitely have brought her if he had.

Then Emma Benneton walked by.

At least it looked like Benny's wife, across the street, surrounded by three men who seemed huddled close to her. Natalie jumped up to get a better view. The woman was just turning the corner on the other side, heading away toward the other side of the harbor.

Perhaps it was because she'd been thinking of Benny and she was subconsciously looking for someone who looked like Benny's wife. But it couldn't be. She'd been kidnapped. They were waiting for the ransom to be paid so she could return home. There's no way she was here on St. Barths.

But damn, it looked so much like her.

Natalie grabbed her purse and half ran past the other tables in a race to get out of the bar and chase down the woman. Bewildered patrons frowned as she brushed past them.

"Natalie!" Diane yelled. "What's the matter? Where are you going?"

Natalie kept her eyes on the corner as the woman in question turned to talk to one of the men she was with. That profile, that way her mouth curled when she spoke in anger. It was Emma!

"Natalie. Wait!"

Natalie heard Diane yelling after her and she turned her head quickly to see that she was racing after her.

"It's Emma!" she screamed back. "Benny's wife. She's here!"

Diane stopped in her tracks. "Natalie!" she yelled. "Don't, please! Come back!"

As Natalie turned back she noticed Diane pulling out her cell phone but she couldn't wait to explain. If it was Emma Benneton, she had to reach her, find out if she was okay.

As Natalie turned the corner, pushing people aside as gently as she could, she saw even more people coming at her. The road was jammed with tourists and locals, walking on the sidewalks, the street, everywhere. She frantically searched the area but couldn't see Emma's blonde head.

She quickly walked ahead a few paces, looking in the store windows, then across the street, ahead again. Nothing. The woman had disappeared.

Was it Emma? Or was she just looking for someone she knew in the crowds of people and someone like Emma had sparked her subconscious?

"What's the matter?"

Natalie looked up to see Drew walking toward her. He had a new t-shirt on with *St. Barths, Home of the Rich and Infamous* emblazoned across the front. His eyes were boring into her and when he reached her, he grabbed her arm, spun her around, and began walking back to the corner.

Natalie pulled her arm away.

"No, I saw her. I saw Emma Benneton."

Drew's forehead creased as he squinted.

"What? That's crazy," he said. "She's not here. She's hidden away somewhere waiting for...", his voice trailed off and he gently steered her forward again. "Natalie, it couldn't possibly be Mrs. Benneton," he said calmly. "That's absurd, you know it."

Natalie looked at him. His jaw was twitching slightly and his eyes were a little wider than usual. She took one last look over her shoulder and then let him lead her back toward the bar.

Diane was still in the middle of the street and was putting her cell back into her purse. She looked relieved when she saw them coming toward her.

"My God, I was worried," she said. "What happened?"

"Natalie thinks she saw someone she knew," he said, his head tilted slightly. Diane stared at him, then her gaze softened as she took Natalie's hand.

"Goodness, I thought you'd seen a ghost, you took off so fast," she said.

Diane's smile seemed forced to Natalie but perhaps she wasn't accustomed to having people race off, knocking people and tables askew. As they walked past the entrance of the bar, she noticed the patrons glaring at her. Perhaps Diane had been embarrassed.

"I'm sorry Diane," she said. "I really thought I'd seen Emma."

"And who is this Emma you keep mentioning?" Diane said.

Natalie hesitated.

"She's an old rival," Drew said," who couldn't possibly be here because we know she's somewhere else."

Natalie looked at him, the corner of her mouth curling upwards, her eyes darting from side to side. She sighed and turned back to Diane.

"He's right. It couldn't be her. But it sure did look like her," she said, only half convinced. She had only gotten a glimpse of the woman but when she'd turned to talk harshly to the guy with her, that expression was unmistakable.

If it wasn't Emma Benneton, it had been her universal twin.

"Come on, Manfred is waiting at the boat," Diane said.

"You called him?" Natalie asked

Diane's head snapped backward and her eyes widened.

"I just thought that if he was finished he could have helped me find you," she said quickly. "But he said he'd wait at the Elyssa for us and that we need to get going. We're going to lose the sun on the way back. He was sure you wouldn't get lost since Drew was looking out for you."

She was looking at Drew as Diane said the last part and he stared back and shrugged.

"And I did find her, didn't I?" he said.

Natalie sensed a tension between the two that she didn't immediately understand. "Come on then. I could use another drink though obviously I've had too many already," she said.

Drew grabbed her hand and they all walked back along the Rue du Bord de Mer toward the main dock where the Elyssa bobbed in the gentle harbor waves.

Chapter Twenty-One

As they motored out of Gustavia's harbor and both Drew and Manfred began preparing the sails, Natalie stared at the plethora of boats dotting the scene. She realized this was a picture right out of Hollywood and that she would likely never see anything like it again. Even Sint Maarten didn't offer such a flagrant display of wealth and opulence.

Diane had gone into the hold to get sweaters as the sun was descending and the warm Caribbean trade winds were slowly turning into your standard Atlantic Ocean stiff breeze.

She watched as Drew carefully folded the jib so that, when raised, it wouldn't tangle. He snaked the lines around the outside of the halyards, feeding it to the winch where he loosely coiled it around a couple of times.

"I saw her you know," Natalie said as he released the rope.

"What?"

"Emma. I saw her."

"It wasn't Emma," he said, walking toward the bow.

"How do you know? It could have been. Shouldn't you be at least a little concerned?" she said, slowly following, hanging onto halyards as she edged forward.

"She was kidnapped, remember?"

"Since when are you an expert on kidnapping?" she said.

Drew's head tilted slightly and the edge of his mouth rose to form a grin.

"Okay, but you don't kidnap people. You just protect people," she said.

He tilted his head further and accentuated the grin.

"Oh shit," she said.

"Look, let's just say I know how kidnappers think," he said, "and they don't bring their victims to exotic Caribbean islands, trust me."

"How can you be so sure?" Natalie said, one hand on her hip, the other gripping the final halyard tightly as the boat began to bounce a little as it left the harbor and headed into open water.

"I just know, okay" he said.

Something about his stare told her she should drop it but she didn't like her ideas being dismissed so flippantly.

"I think we should check," she said. "When we get back, we should phone Benny and find out if he's communicated with the kidnappers yet. Maybe he's got some ideas about it."

"You're not phoning Benny. Not yet." Drew hissed.

"You keep saying that but you don't say why."

"You know why. He can't be distracted right now. He needs to concentrate on getting his wife back safe and sound. He doesn't need your hysterics getting in the way."

"I am not hysterical," Natalie said, releasing the halyard and placing her left hand on her hip to match the right one. She swayed a little but her anger was grounding her at the moment.

Drew turned away and looked out into the ocean.

"Don't ignore me Drew Scanlon," she said loudly. "If it was Emma I saw, then something weird is going on here."

"You okay?" Diane said. Natalie hadn't seen her climb up and come forward. She handed over a sweater and gave Natalie a quizzical look.

"I'm fine," Natalie said, staring at the back of Drew's head. After a few seconds, she turned and started heading back to the safety of the center portion of the boat. "I have to go back there to put this on," she said, holding out the sweater. "I can't keep my balance here."

"Sure, okay," Diane said. Drew didn't seem to hear their exchange or was ignoring them, so Diane looked at the back of his form momentarily, then held out her hand to help Natalie reverse her steps more easily.

"Let's sit here and watch the sun go down," she said. "It'll get cold once it sets and we may want to get behind the transom for cover then."

Natalie nodded, braced her feet a little wider and quickly pulled the sweater over her head. She sat beside Diane and both women quietly watched the waves quickly pass by as the Elyssa cut through them.

Once clear of the islands, Manfred set the main sail and shortly after Drew came to the middle of the boat to pull the jib up and tie it off. Manfred then cut the engine and the wind found the sails and filled them with a *thwack* which made them go taut again. It was suddenly eerily quiet, the only noise being the gentle crash of the bow as it bounced from wave to wave.

Drew stood just inside the curve of the jib, having a clear view of the ocean in front of him. He appeared to be deep in thought and since Natalie was pissed at him anyway, she reluctantly agreed when Diane suggested they move back behind the transom.

When the boat suddenly lurched to port, Natalie thought Manfred was just making a course change, though an abrupt one. But then the weight of the boat shifted as the main sail whipped across the deck in search of wind that was now coming from the port side.

"Aargh" came a wail that was suddenly cut off.

"Man overboard," Diane yelled as she jumped up.

Manfred was staring at the main sail as it quickly filled with wind and the boat speed picked up again.

"Drew's gone," she yelled again, climbing over the seat to tap Manfred on the shoulder. In response, he simply looked over the side of the boat, his hands still on the wheel. He turned to Diane.

"I don't see him," he said calmly.

Natalie scrambled to the rear net and looked behind the boat. She searched the water's surface frantically for a few seconds, then saw a black thing bobbing above the waves about fifty feet behind them.

"There!" she yelled and pointed. Diane followed her gaze but Manfred continued to watch the sail. Diane was standing beside Manfred now and Natalie could see she was yelling even though she was just inches from his face.

As if reluctantly, Manfred turned the wheel so that the wind escaped from its grasp on the sails. The boat still had momentum and as the bow slowly turned, Natalie could see they were getting farther away. Drew's head disappeared every time a wave rolled by and she had to concentrate to maintain visual contact.

"Hurry!" she said. "He's being tossed all over the place."

Diane was untying a circular life buoy that had been attached to the side of the boat and was making sure the rope was securely attached.

"Go to the bow," Diane yelled at Natalie, "and direct him to Drew. He won't be having a clear view directly in front once we turn completely."

Natalie nodded and, on hands and knees, scurried forward to where the pontoons jutted out into the sea. She chose the starboard side pontoon and edged right to the end where, once she grasped the railing, she stood and willed her eyes to find Drew again. The boat was slowly turning and she'd lost her bearings completely.

"There, there!" Diane was yelling and pointing to a spot just to the right. Natalie followed her arm and felt a knot in her stomach as she didn't immediately see Drew. Then, a black speck caught her attention in the corner of her eye and she quickly turned to see Drew's head bouncing as another wave crashed over him and buried him momentarily. She assumed Drew was a good swimmer though she wasn't sure if he was good enough to stay afloat in this melee. Even so, being tossed around like this would wear anyone out very quickly.

Manfred seemed to be moving in slow motion but Natalie could see that Diane was speaking to him rapidly. She looked angry. Was the old man not such a good sailor? Was that what Diane being angry about, that he had made a silly mistake that had put a guest's life in danger?

A few moments later, the boat was heading straight for Drew's bobbing head and Natalie leaned out over the railing making sure she never lost sight of him. As they came closer, Manfred climbed to the deck and began lowering the main sail. The jib was flopping in the wind, blocking her sight of both him and Diane now and again. Then she heard the tiny blurt of the engine starting. She saw Diane at the wheel now. She looked up to Natalie and pointed to the life buoy and mouthed "you throw it from the bow".

Natalie carefully walked back to the cockpit, grabbed the buoy and dragged it and the attached rope back to her perch at the edge of the pontoon. The boat had slowed and was flat, making the trip back and forth less dangerous, but they were still moving quickly. As she looked down

125

into the water, she realized she'd have to anticipate their movement when throwing the buoy or she could miss Drew by quite a few feet.

By about thirty feet they could see that Drew had tired considerably. He was flapping his arms rapidly just under the surface to keep his head afloat but she could see that he gasped for air now and again. Salt water in your lungs didn't help breathing she knew. She'd experienced that when simply swimming near the Atlantic shore back home.

She pointed to Drew with one hand, arm fully extended so Diane could trace the direction, and held onto the buoy with the other hand. Diane's eyes were riveted to Natalie's arm, her gaze breaking every few seconds to peer over the side herself. Natalie didn't know if Diane could see Drew but the boat was steadily approaching him. Their direct angled approach to Drew was forcing the boat to cut through waves like a power boat and it began to bounce up and down erratically. Diane steered into the troughs of the waves in an attempt to soften the impact but Natalie would frantically wave showing that they were moving away from Drew.

What seemed like half-an-hour later, Drew's facial expression was clear from about fifteen feet away. His face was white, his black hair matted against his face haphazardly. His arms weren't moving as rapidly as before and Natalie was afraid that if she didn't get the buoy to him with her first attempt, he may drop under the waves before they could turn and pass by again.

She kept her one arm pointed to Drew and as they closed, it came closer and closer to the boat. She hoped Diane knew not to drive the boat right over his head but had no time to look at her, let alone yell anything. Drew was getting close. His eyes were gripped onto hers and as she lifted the buoy and gripped it with both hands, he nodded his understanding.

As the bow of the pontoon drew almost perpendicular to Drew's bouncing form, Natalie tossed the buoy out to the starboard side of the boat about ten feet or so. As the boat continued its motion, the buoy floated calmly in position, the rope depleting slowly as the bow moved past Drew.

He kicked a couple of times and just as the rope became taut and began to follow the boat, he grabbed the circle with one hand, then the other. Almost immediately he was dragged along with the boat toward the stern.

Grabbing the handrail for support, Natalie stooped and raced back over the deck, then over the cockpit, and almost fell into the stern netting. Drew was being towed behind the boat about five feet but he now had blood flowing from a gash in his forehead.

"He must have hit the side of the boat," Diane said as she edged up beside Natalie on her hands and knees. She grabbed the rope and began to pull. Natalie turned her head quickly to see that Manfred was back at the wheel, staring straight ahead, appearing not to be interested in the rescue. She focused her attention back to Drew and grabbed the rope ahead of where Diane was pulling and began pulling too.

Drew slowly came closer but he wasn't kicking or attempting to swim at all. His eyes looked glazed and Natalie wondered if he'd given himself a concussion.

Eventually, Natalie was able to grab his hands, then his arms. Then together, she and Diane manhandled Drew onto the net. Once safely aboard, they both fell back against the net, exhausted from the effort.

"I'll get the first aid kit," Diane said and slithered back to the cockpit.

Natalie leaned over Drew and stroked back his hair to reveal a long gash just above his right eye. It wasn't deep and head wounds always bled profusely, she knew. But his eyes still looked a little distant. Was it a concussion, or just a sign of exhaustion?

His lips moved and he tried to say something but it just came out as a groan. Diane returned with a little red medical kit. She found some gauze and alcohol and began cleaning the wound. Drew winced a little but didn't cry out. She then applied some polysporin and placed a piece of white gauze over the gash using adhesive tape to secure it to his head.

The motor stopped and the boat settled into a gentle sway. Manfred suddenly appeared leaning over them.

"He'll be fine," he said matter-of-factly. "Just don't let him doze off." And with that, he turned and headed back to the cockpit. Within a few minutes, he had the main sail raised, the jib set, and as the boat once again caught the winds, they began to sail.

Diane was staring at Manfred, her gaze impossible to decipher.

"How did that happen?" Natalie asked quietly, looking at Diane for an answer.

"Manfred was impatient," she said still staring at him, "He didn't yell a warning before the jibe." Her cheeks were tight and she spoke through barred teeth.

Drew reached out and touched Natalie's arm. When she looked down, he was trying to smile though it was clear his facial muscles were telling him that kind of movement would be painful. He opened his mouth and when only another groan escaped from his lips, he sighed and tried to nod his head as if telling Natalie not to ask questions.

She gripped his hand. "Just rest," she said. "But don't sleep. I think you've got a concussion."

"It's a good thing he works out regularly," Diane said. "Most people would have tired very quickly in these waters."

"How do you know he works out," Natalie asked.

Flustered, Diane quickly replied, "Oh, he mentioned it once.at the restaurant I think." She said and unfolded her legs to get up. "I'm sure he's going to be fine." She patted Natalie's arm and walked toward the cockpit where she just stood beside Manfred as he concentrated on manning the boat alone.

Natalie looked down at Drew. He wasn't sleeping but he wasn't all there either, she could tell. His eyes seemed to be staring into the sky. As she watched, his head turned to her and his gaze reached her eyes. He nodded slightly, squeezed her hand, and went back to staring straight up. She laid a towel over his him and shifted herself so she could lay his head in her lap.

What had that been about? she thought. Had Manfred deliberately turned the boat so that Drew would be knocked in to the water? But why? Especially if he was willing to rescue him?

It was as if Manfred had been teaching Drew a lesson. But about what? They hadn't known each other before today.

She looked down at Drew. He would be out of commission for the rest of the day. She would make sure he rested back at the villa.

And then she would sneak into town and call Benny. She needed to get out of here.

Chapter Twenty-Two

Natalie watched as Drew slowly performed laps in the pool. He had risen early and she had heard the splash moments later as he dove in. She had waited a while until her nostrils were aroused by the aroma of fresh coffee and padded into the kitchen to pour a cup. He must have started the machine before swimming.

She sat on one of the chaise longue's beside the pool, sipping and taking in the majestic view. There was a small island in the distance and she made a mental note to ask someone what it was. She hadn't been able to sneak out and find a phone the night before. Drew had stayed out on the veranda till very late, half dozing. She had felt obligated to shaking him once in a while to ensure he wasn't succumbing to a concussion. He seemed to appreciate it and while she sipped white wine and stared out at the sea and stars, he just stared into space. Both were lost in their own thoughts.

During one of his Olympic-style turns, Drew stopped suddenly, swam to the pool's edge and pulled himself out.

"I see your experience yesterday hasn't put you off playing in the water," Natalie said.

Drew dropped onto another chaise beside her. He didn't towel off but simply brushed back his hair, lay back and began soaking up the sun.

"I can only sink six feet in there," he said, nodding toward the pool. "And I'm sure you'd save me again if I got into trouble."

"If it hadn't been for Diane, I'm not sure we would have saved you."

"Hmmm," he said, closing his eyes.

"Speaking of whom, I'm supposed to meet her for lunch, remember?"

"I'll drive you," he said, without opening his eyes.

"You don't have to. I can call Oliver."

"It's not a problem. I have to go into town anyway."

Natalie studied him. He seemed relaxed, almost lackadaisical. But she sensed he wasn't going to let her go too far on her own.

"Are you picking me up then?" she asked.

"No, I figured Diane might bring you back. Maybe you can invite her for a dip and some margaritas."

"What if she wants to invite Manfred?"

"No!"

She grinned. From what Diane had eluded to yesterday, she'd likely prefer to enjoy an early evening social without her partner anyway. Strange that Drew was intent on driving her into town but wasn't worried about how or when she returned though.

"I'll be ready in ten minutes," she announced. "You'll dry quicker with a towel."

As she walked through sliding patio door entrance, she turned to see that he hadn't moved. She noticed his body was almost dry, though one or two glistening drops of water were still sliding down the center of his chest, disappearing into the top of his bathing suit. She quickly averted her eyes and began thinking of what to wear for lunch.

Chapter Twenty-Three

Diane had chosen a small bar on Maho Beach, one of the most famous locations on the island. Situated at the edge of the main runway into Princess Julianna International Airport, incoming jets soar overhead less than twenty-five feet above the heads of sunbathing tourists. The Sunset Beach Restaurant was on one side of the beach with an unobstructed view of incoming landings.

Conversation was light and Natalie chose not to discuss the mishap with Drew the day before. Diane had appeared to be angry with her partner at the time and Natalie saw no need to bring up the subject and risk putting her new friend into a foul mood.

The occasional airplane landing forced conversation to an abrupt halt throughout the restaurant as the engine noise was deafening. But the sight of a huge 747 gliding in less than an hundred feet away and only several feet above the ground took Natalie's breath away every time. She laughed along with everyone else when one idiot bather stood upright, arms extended at the water's edge. When an Air France 707 descended over the beach toward the start of the landing strip just thirty or so feet from the sand, the jet thrust lifted him off his feet and flew him backwards several feet into the sea. There was a universal gasp until the guy popped his head up a few moments later and waved to everyone assuring them that, though stupid, he was still alive.

Natalie fidgeted and glanced at her watch as Diane casually discussed food and places to go on the island. Relaxation came naturally to a woman who seemed to do little other than shop and dine out, Natalie thought.

"You know, you're supposed to be on holiday," Diane said, putting her hand over Natalie's wrist, hiding her watch from view.

Natalie smiled.

"Any other time, I would enjoy it," she said. "But I have a lot on my mind. And I miss my, ah, friends back home."

"Goodness, you must have pretty amazing friends if they have the power to take your mind off all this," Diane said, sweeping her hand around the dingy, crowded bar.

They both laughed and sipped their Carib beer.

"It's just that this was a last-minute excursion," Natalie continued, deciding to confide in her new friend. "I had to get away from home quickly."

"That sounds ominous," Diane said. "Are you safe? Are you in some kind of danger?"

"No. At least I don't think so," Natalie said, brushing a hand through her hair roughly. "It's very complicated and I'm not sure I can explain it but I'm pretty sure I'm safe. Drew is looking out for me."

"Well he doesn't seem too worried about anything," Diane said. "In fact, he seems to be enjoying himself, like he'd planned this trip."

Natalie looked out at the gently wavy Caribbean and nodded. "Yes, it's what he does, so I guess being calm is just part of the job."

"I really thought you two were a couple," Diane said quietly.

Natalie looked at her for a moment then sighed. "No, he's kind of a bodyguard, I guess."

"Oh my!" Diane exclaimed. "You really were in trouble. But I don't understand, why come here?"

"I don't really know why he chose here, but like you say, he seems to have it all planned out," she said. "But I think I've had enough."

"What do you mean?"

"I need to know what's going on back home," Natalie said, looking at her watch again.

"Are you hiding from something, someone?"

Natalie pushed back her chair and crossed her legs.

"That's just it," she said. "I'm not sure anymore why I can't be there. I'm not the one in trouble." She crossed her arms momentarily and looked up to the ceiling. "It doesn't really make sense that I'm here enjoying myself when Benny is back there worrying about things."

"Who's Benny?" Diane asked, leaning forward, her voice lower.

Natalie uncrossed her arms and stared at Diane for a moment. She took a deep breath.

"He's my lover," she said finally and watched as Diane arched her eyebrows and leaned back in her chair. Natalie kept going. She'd started now and she needed to get it all out.

"He's a very rich, very powerful southern gentleman," she said, grinning. "And I'm having an affair with him."

Diane clapped her hands together and leaned in again.

"Oh, tell me more," she said.

"It seems he was getting threats against his wife—that's the woman I thought I saw yesterday on St. Barths--and he was worried that they might come after me too."

"Who is they?" Diane asked.

"That's just it, I have no idea. Drew whisked me away so quickly that I never had a chance to ask Benny anything."

"So, your Benny must have hired Drew," Diane said.

Natalie thought for a moment. "Well, that's what he said. He's been bugging me to hook up with someone for ages. You know, someone I could be seen with, who could take me out to places where Benny can meet me, you know." She laughed at Diane's expression.

"It sounds very complicated," Diane said.

"That's what I thought too. Besides, I didn't want to hang out with some escort or something just waiting for a chance to get Benny alone," Natalie said. "He was the one who wanted to do so many public things. I was quite happy to just enjoy his company in the apartment."

"Wouldn't that get a little boring after a while?" Diane asked, her skepticism causing Natalie to laugh.

"Yes, I suppose it would," she admitted. "But we've never gone long just being alone. Benny has so many engagements to attend, and he loves having me around when his wife doesn't go with him. I guess I've never had the chance to find out if I'd be bored or not."

"Drew isn't a bad, ah, escort," Diane said, grinning, "if you have to be seen hanging around with somebody."

Natalie's head dropped and she stared at Diane from under hooded brows.

"No, and under other circumstances, maybe," Natalie admitted. "But I love Benny." She suddenly pushed her chair back and stood up.

"I've got to use the loo," she announced. "I think I saw one on the outside of this joint. I'll be right back."

Diane watched as Natalie spoke briefly to the bartender as she passed the bar. She then walked outside to where Diane knew the washrooms were as they were public washrooms used by bar patrons and beach goers alike.

After a few moments, Diane sat forward quickly. She looked around and then went up to the bar.

"My friend was looking for the bathroom," she said. "Long, straight black hair. American?"

"Oh her," the bartender said, continuing to dry beer glasses as he spoke. "No, she wanted to know if there were public phones nearby. I told her there was a box across the street in the souvenir shop." His puzzled look followed Diane as she nearly ran toward the exit.

*   *   *

"Hello!"

Natalie smiled at the sound of William Benneton's gruff voice.

"Benny, it's me. I'm sorry, I just had to talk to you."

"Natalie!" Benneton's voice rose and words gushed over the phone line. "Where are you? I hadn't heard a thing. I've been so worried about you."

"I'm in Sint Maarten," she said tentatively. "Drew brought me here, like you wanted him to."

"He told me he was taking you to a busy tourist hotel in the Bahamas," Benny said. "I've been calling every couple of days but no one has heard of you, or him. Are you using different names?"

"Benny, we're in the Dutch Caribbean. Sint Maarten. I thought you knew. I've been waiting to hear that everything's okay and I can come home."

There was silence briefly. Then, a little more gruffly, "I see. But you're okay, right?"

"Of course," Natalie said. "But I've had enough. I want to come home."

"And I want you to come home too, right now," he said. "I've been looking for you all over. I even hired a detective to try and track down Drew's trail."

"You mean, you didn't know where I was? Drew didn't plan it with you?" She was sweating a little and wiped her brow with her free hand.

"I have to tell you what's going on Natalie," Benneton said. "But not over the phone. Take the first flight you can to., say Miami. They'll have flights going there every day. I'll meet you at that hotel we love in South Beach, the--"

"The Beachhead Marriot, yes, I remember," Natalie interupted, turning from the phone in time to see Diane on the other side of the street, watching her. Natalie waved and Diane, an annoyed expression on her face, walked quickly toward her.

"I have a friend here," Natalie said. "She'll help me get back."

"But Drew will--" Benneton began.

"Forget him," Natalie cut him off. "He's the cause of all this. I'll meet you at the hotel by ten tomorrow night, I promise. Love you!" She quickly hung up the phone and grasped Diane's hands as the other woman approached.

"Diane, you have to help me get out of here," she exclaimed, turning her from the booth and striding back to the bar. "I'm leaving as soon as I can but I need you to help me get a flight. Do you know any travel agencies nearby?"

Diane seemed to be in deep thought as they strode back into the bar, back to their table and picked up their drinks to finish them. Suddenly Diane smiled, slammed the beer bottle down on the table and grabbed Natalie with both arms.

"I can do better than that," she said and steered Natalie to the bar where she laid a few bills on the counter, winked at the bartender, and pulled her outside.

"When Manfred's doing his thing on the boat, I often get homesick and take the jet to the States to see my kids," she said.

"I didn't know you had children?" Natalie said.

"Hey, you're not the only one with little secrets," Diane said. She patted Natalie's arm as she waved over one of the taxis from the ever-present long line of cabs that circled the beach.

"I fly over every three weeks or so, stay for a couple of days, and come back," she explained. "You go pack and I'll go to the boat, let Manfred know and he'll have the jet ready for us later this afternoon. We'll be in the States by tomorrow morning."

"Diane, that's too much to ask, honest," Natalie exclaimed, though her eyes were glistening.

"Don't be silly. It's an adventure," she smiled. "Besides, I haven't seen the kids for a few weeks. I'm due. Manfred will understand completely. He'll be happy I'm bringing someone along. He likes you, anyway."

Natalie turned her head and frowned. Then she grinned.

"Oh-my-God, that would be awesome," she finally exclaimed.

Diane opened the rear cab door and was about to get in when Natalie grabbed her arm.

"Look," she breathed. "Drew's watching us. I told him to meet us for lunch in Philipsburg."

Natalie waved but Drew just stared and didn't make any motion toward them.

"He won't let me go," Natalie said under her breath.

"He won't know," Diane said. "Smile and wave, then get in. He'll think we're heading into town to shop before lunch or something."

Natalie waved again, pointed to her watch and raised two fingers demonstrating two-o'clock. She hoped Drew would understand that meant she was going shopping for an hour and would meet them at the restaurant. Instead, she would head back to the villa, pack, and meet Diane at the airport. She assumed that's where Manfred's plane would be.

Drew continued to stare as Natalie got into the cab and hotched over to the other side to allow Diane to follow behind her. The car interior obscured her view of Diane just before she bent to get in, so she didn't see the other woman motion to Drew with a quick slash of her hand across her throat. Drew's lips tightened and he responded with a nod. Then he turned and walked back toward the scooter.

Chapter Twenty-Four

Despite hanging around with rich men with lots of toys, this was the first time Natalie had traveled on a private jet. As she stepped into the cabin the smell of leather and mahogany overwhelmed her senses.

Then she saw Drew, sitting comfortably in an enormous high-backed easy chair half way back, and she focused in on one sense: Fear.

"What are you doing here?" she asked.

Drew's expression was stony.

"He's coming with us," Diane said from behind. Natalie spun around and faced Diane who was holding both their carry bags.

"What is this?" she sputtered. "I thought you were my friend. He's not going to let me go back to Benny!"

Diane opened her hands and the bags dropped unceremoniously to the floor. She then tightened her right fist and drove it into Natalie's stomach.

"Ahh!" Natalie saw stars at first and then felt as if someone had snatched all the air from around her. Her knees wobbled and she felt herself folding downward. She moved a hand to protect her face then quickly put it back to her stomach when she hit the floor. The throbbing was like nothing she'd ever felt before and just catching her breath was taking all her concentration.

Drew jumped up.

"Leave her, she's fine," Diane said. "I'll tell the pilot we're ready to go."

Natalie opened her eyes to see Drew looking down at her, his eyes wide and his lips tight.

"No, I will," he said, stepping over her and heading to the cockpit. "You look after her. She's not going to let me touch her."

Diane looked puzzled momentarily, then grinned. "She's not going to like me much anymore either," she said.

Natalie heard the cockpit door open but she couldn't move yet and so she just clutched her stomach and stared at the plush carpeting.

"You're lucky," Diane said. Natalie tried to look up but her hair had fallen over her eyes and Diane was a blur. God her stomach hurt.

"The second Manfred asked to see you, I knew it would come to this," Diane continued. "Be thankful he knocked Drew overboard and not you." She settled back into her chair, picked a magazine from the rear of the seat in front, and began shuffling through pages. Natalie managed to sit up, her legs under her, one arm still holding her stomach. The pain was subsiding and her breathing was returning to semi-normal.

A moment later the cockpit door opened again and Drew stepped out. His expression had become even stonier. He leaned down to help Natalie get up into her seat. Natalie tried to shrug him off but his grip on her arm was too tight.

"Let go of me asshole," she managed. Diane smiled but didn't look up from her reading.

Drew released his grip on Natalie when she was seated, more or less upright. "I'll get you some water," he said and walked toward the back of the cabin.

Natalie spun around, as quickly as she could considering her insides felt like someone had stapled her navel to her spine.

"Don't bother." she began but gasped as she watched Drew turn quickly as he passed Diane, lean down and snake his arm around her neck squeezing her throat. Her eyes bugged in surprise and she began thrashing but Drew now had his other hand under her one arm, his fingers clasping his other arm in some kind of choke hold.

Diane's face went a deep red, then just as quickly relaxed. Her eyes fluttered a couple of times and her grip on Drew's arm loosened and eventually her hands fell away revealing several bleeding welts on his arms from where Diane had dug her nails in.

Natalie watched as he gently lay her sideways, her head leaning against the side of the cabin's interior wall.

"Come on, we don't have much time," he said, staring at Natalie.

"What's going on?" Natalie stammered, her voice hoarse, her brain grasping to catch up with the action of the past few minutes.

"We have to get off, now!" he said, grabbing her arm with one hand, and her bag with the other.

"That's not mine," she said, flustered.

Drew dropped the bag and picked up the other one. She stumbled to keep up as he practically dragged her forward. Her breath was back but her stomach still ached.

"The pilots?" she said. "Aren't we taking off?"

"Not on this plane."

"They'll stop us," she said, looking at the closed cockpit door, willing it not to open.

"No, they won't." he said, opening the outside cabin door. "Shit!"

Natalie looked over his shoulder and saw the steps had been taken away. It was a seven- or eight-foot drop to the tarmac. She looked back at the cockpit door.

"You didn't, did you?"

"What?" he said, throwing the bag to the tarmac. He turned to look at her. "I am many things Natalie, but I'm not a killer. They're unconscious, but only for about ten to fifteen minutes so we have to get off, now!" He pushed her in front of him and she hesitated, knowing what he wanted her to do but unsure of how to land.

He pushed in front of her.

"Look, I'll go first," he said. "You jump right into my arms, okay?"

She looked at him, bewildered and watched as he leaned out of the cabin doorway, and then dropped out of sight. She leaned forward and watched as he landed on his feet and immediately rolled forward into a somersault coming up a few feet away. He shook himself off quickly and stepped back directly under the doorway.

"I'll break your fall," he said. "Go!"

Natalie looked at him, his arms outstretched, face anxious. A few minutes ago he'd watched Diane punch her and done nothing. Now he expected her to trust him to jump into his open arms?

"Argh!" she yelled as she leaned out and aimed directly for Drew's chest.

She hit him hard and they both went down but it seemed to be slow motion. They hit the ground with a jolt and Drew swore loudly, but Natalie felt only a painful jolt in her shoulders. Oddly, it replaced the pain in her stomach. She lay on the tarmac, sprawled over Drew, staring into his eyes, not four inches away.

"You know, any other time, this might be funny," she said, his eyes only inches from hers.

"Tell that to my back," he said gruffly.

Natalie disengaged herself from him and got up. Drew followed, a little slowly, she thought.

He retrieved her travel bag, grabbed her hand and pulled her away from the plane.

"This way," he said. "We haven't got much time."

He headed across the tarmac, not in the direction of the main entrance where they had originally come from but to the side of the building, past a sign stating *Employees Only*.

"Where are we going?" Natalie asked

"Not where we *were* going," Drew said.

"You had this planned?"

Drew looked over at her, his lips curling up on one side. His eyes widened slightly as he stretched his arms.

"Do you think I'd plan to have you jump out of an airplane on top of me?"

Natalie cocked her head, puzzled.

"Forget it," he said. "I called a friend to come get us. Let's go."

Drew dragged Natalie out through a door and they entered a corridor. Natalie heard voices and music. The corridor led to the airport's public departure area, though right at the end by the main doors.

Drew glanced in both directions and Natalie unconsciously did the same, not knowing who or what she might be looking for. A white minivan stopped at the curb just outside and Drew, seeing it, pulled Natalie through the main doors. Oliver smiled as he took the bag from Drew and grasped Natalie's hand.

"I'm glad you decided to stay a little longer, miss," he said, his whitened teeth glistening in the tropical sun.

Chapter Twenty-Five

Oliver had dropped them off at an obscure, behind-an-alley bar that he assured them was used almost exclusively by locals, having no appeal to tourists. But its dingy, corrugated interior was a welcome sight to Drew. He wanted to be sure no one would find them for a couple of hours at least.

Oliver took Natalie aside while Drew pulled out their bags and asked if she was being forced to do anything against her will. "This no place for tourists," he said, his face scrunched. Natalie made eye contact with Drew who kept his distance and merely held her gaze. She kissed Oliver on the cheek, thanked him for his concern, and told him they were fine. They just needed to leave the island quickly, without anyone knowing. Oliver assured them he would have his phone with him at all times and would be ready to whisk them anywhere they chose, anytime. Drew shook his hand and said that indeed, they would be calling him as soon as he could arrange a flight.

Drew then went to a corner in the bar, pulled out his cell phone, and began keying in numbers. Not sure what else do to in the situation, other than panic, Natalie asked the bartender for a rum punch.

A few minutes later, Drew joined her at the bar.

"We're flying out in twenty minutes," he said.

"Wow, how did you get a flight that quickly?" Natalie asked.

Drew stared at a faded picture of one of St. Maarten's beaches that hung behind the bar. "I have a few friends nearby," he said.

"I don't understand what's going on Drew," Natalie said. "And once we slow down, you're going to tell me, aren't you?" She placed the palm of her hand over top the back of his and gently squeezed it. Drew turned to her and his eyes searched her face momentarily.

"We have to get out of here first," he said. "Then I'll tell you everything I can."

"What can't you tell me?" she asked, nervous.

"There are parts of this that are out of my control," he said, staring at the picture again. "And I'm not sure it's all over just because we got away from them."

"Them? You mean Diane? Who is she, really?"

Drew took a big gulp of his beer and stood.

"We have to go. Oliver will be here any minute," he said. When Natalie didn't make a move to get up from her stool, he leaned on the counter.

"If we stay here, they will eventually find us," he said. "And if they do, we won't be going anywhere for a while, I guarantee you."

"Benny will find me," she said.

"William Benneton has no idea where you are," Drew said, grabbing her hand and pulling her up. "And even if he did, he wouldn't come. He can't."

Natalie pulled her arm out of his grasp. She'd told Benny they were on Sint Maarten, but if they left, he'd never find her.

"Why wouldn't he come? He just told me on the phone he was worried sick because you hadn't told him where we were." She stood glued to the floor, her hands on her hips, her glare boring a hole into Drew's brain. He could have grabbed her, she knew. He could take her wherever he wanted, regardless of even Oliver's protests, she thought.

But he didn't. He simply picked up the bags and said, "It's complicated Natalie. Very complicated. It will all make more sense soon. But you have to come with me. You're not safe here." He then turned and walked out of the bar.

Natalie stared after him. The bartender had been watching them and when he grinned, his yellowed pointy teeth suddenly reminded her that predators come in all shapes and sizes, often when you least expect them. She jumped up and followed Drew.

"This thing won't make it to the States," Natalie exclaimed. Oliver had dropped them back at the airport but not at the terminal. He had gone through a mesh gate at the other end of the runway, closer to the town, and driven right up to a tiny, red and white Cessna, complete with propellers and, from what Natalie could tell, just four seats.

"We have to stop somewhere first," Drew said. "Then we'll head back home tomorrow morning."

"There are international flights leaving here all day long," she said. You couldn't get us on anything?"

"They'll be watching the airport. It's the only one on the island, remember?" He opened the door of the small propeller plane. Inside, a man in a flowered shirt and blue baseball cap was adjusting dials. He didn't say anything to them.

"This is a private plane, owned by someone I know," Drew said. "They'll be looking at international flights, not short island hops."

"You keep saying *they*. Who are *they*?" she asked as she settled into the tiny back seat and watched as Drew shoved their bags unceremoniously under the seats, pushing them as far back as he could.

"We're going to see the one who started all this," he said. Then he grabbed her hand and looked into her eyes. "And you'll get some answers."

Natalie had thought he had all the answers. It was unnerving to realize that he may be a little mystified by recent events too.

"Where is this person we're going to see?" she asked.

"We'll be landing in St. Barths in less than an hour, ma'am," the pilot said.

The increased volume of propeller noise prevented Natalie from saying anything but her thoughts were racing as they taxied out to the runway. Sunset was about twenty-minutes away and the calm Caribbean beckoned as the tiny plane cruised down the lone runway, only just clearing the Sunset Beach bar. Natalie could see the patrons on the patio watching idly as the little plane rose ever so slowly higher and higher above the open water.

She didn't think they were going to see Jimmy Buffet.

The Security

Chapter Twenty-Six

Natalie's first exposure to St. Barths had been one of a magical, fairytale island worthy of a Disney film full of wealthy, eccentric characters.

This time was different. Maybe her trepidation with all the mystery surrounding this visit aided in creating a sense of foreboding. Or maybe it was because the island didn't appear as ostentatious from this angle and in twilight; nothing but trees as if they were flying into unchartered territory in the Amazon valley or something.

As they crested a tiny mountain and began descending, she did see a couple of colorful buildings perched on the mountainside, jutting out from the land, seemingly pushing trees and shrubbery out of the way demanding exposure to the warm tropical sun. Natalie counted three or four only as they flew lower and lower. She assumed they were some of the expensive villas she'd heard about; private hideaways costing $20-30,000 a week just to rent., *The views must be out of this world.*

The plane seemed to float onto the runway and they stopped just a few short feet from the end. A plane any larger than the Cessna would never make it, she thought.

The terminal, if you could call it that, reminded Natalie of a fancy sales trailer you might see on the empty land designated for high-end condos: tiny, expensively decorated, and sparsely populated. Only one customs officer greeted them and quickly whisked them through once he'd stamped their passports. They jumped into an awaiting jeep and drove off along a surprisingly modern road, toward what seemed to be nothing more than forest.

"Where are we going?" Natalie asked.

"To see someone," Drew answered dryly.

Natalie frowned. "You said that already, but who?"

Drew didn't turn to face her but stared ahead as if watching where the driver was going.

"I have questions too," he said, still staring ahead, intent on the direction they were going. "We'll get answers together."

"But I--" Natalie began but Drew held up his hand to stop her.

"Please Natalie," he said. "Enjoy the view. And trust me, okay?"

Trust him. Is he kidding? But she could tell he was concentrating on watching the road. She assumed he'd never been to this part of the island before and for some reason, wanted to remember how to get there from the airport. Or maybe how to get back to the airport should they have to leave in a hurry. She laughed. She was getting paranoid, she knew. But who wouldn't at this point?

When the taxi crested a hill and began its steep and slow descent into the capital of Gustavia, Natalie's fairytale thoughts returned. In the distance, the ocean glistened, the lowering sun sparkling off the gentle white caps flowing briskly into the main harbor. Adorning virtually every inch along the perfectly square inner harbor were opulent, gleaming yachts, tied stern first, each one reaching out into the bay like fingers of varying lengths, widths and bold colors.

Unlike her first visit to the star-struck island by boat just two days prior, Natalie marveled at how quainter the town seemed from this lofty angle. By boat, the visitor is quickly immersed into the bustling town where hundreds walk around aimlessly, seemingly coming from and going to nowhere in particular.

Between the dock and the road they were slowly traversing, perfectly linear rooftops were covered in either light gray or vibrant red shingles. It was as if someone had decided that roofs could only be one color to ensure uniformity and sophistication. She recalled Bavarian villages she'd seen on a trip to Germany a few years ago, having come upon it in a similar fashion. She smiled. The harbor though, dotted with scores of fiberglass monuments to affluence, added an element of playfulness, as did the lush greenery of the low-lying hills surrounding the harbor, branches gently swaying to the tactile beat of the tropical breeze.

This was a place where chic, affluent people came to do nothing. Far away from the fans and minions, Gustavia allowed freedom to be normal: well, as normal as you could be with facilities and amenities handy and ready to cater to your every whim and fancy. Tourists simply didn't belong here and Natalie felt very much a tourist as the taxi meandered around turns and switchbacks, slowly descending toward the main road at harbor's edge.

About one block up from the harbor the taxi stopped in front of a quaint hotel that looked to be one of the original buildings from the early 1960s; days when the island was less a rich playground and more of hidden gem, albeit one only the rich could afford to reach.

Drew paid the driver and grabbed their bags from the trunk. As they entered through thick, frosted glass doors, they were met with décor straight out of Casablanca: dark wood trim offsetting cream stucco walls, a few bistro tables on one side and a large oak reception desk on the other. Even a large tropical fan in the center of the entranceway turned languidly, a slight breeze emanating downward from its efforts.

Directly in front of them, a narrow elevator door opened and a woman stepped out. Her coiffed hair jostled slightly as she walked but the rest of her body was controlled and poised like a movie star intent on ignoring the fans. Then she smiled and headed straight toward them, arms outstretched.

Drew embraced her and kissed her gently on one cheek. He then stepped back leaving the two women facing each other.

"I'd like you to meet my mother," Drew said.

"Hello Natalie," said Emma Benneton. "I've been dying to meet you."

Chapter Twenty-Seven

"Emma Benneton is your mother?" Natalie said, glaring at Drew.

"You look like you could use a drink my dear," Emma said, grasping Natalie's elbow and pulling her toward a set of double French doors that led to an outdoor patio.

Natalie waited for Drew to respond but when he didn't, she let the other woman lead her out onto a quaint patio on the edge of a street that ran behind the hotel. The hotel was situated on the incline of the hill so the view above the rooftops of the buildings between the street and the harbor was unobstructed. Natalie glimpsed the glistening azure blue harbor before Emma pushed her below a sun umbrella and into one of four wrought iron chairs surrounding a matching round table.

"I don't understand," Natalie said, alternating her stare from Emma to Drew. "If this is your mother, that means you've known where she was all the time. You could have told Benny." She stopped suddenly and brought her hand to her mouth. "Benny is your father?" she exclaimed.

Emma laughed. "Benny? That's cute."

"Mother," Drew said, his head tilting to an angle, his eyes warning her not to go any further. "This is a shock to her, as you well anticipated." He looked at Natalie. "Benneton is not my father."

Emma stopped laughing but her lips still formed a smile as she looked Natalie up and down.

"Well, he certainly didn't do you justice," she said. "I had no idea you were so, ah so perky, yes that's the word for you, perky."

"You knew about Benny and me?" Natalie asked. "I mean, he actually talked to you about me?"

"Oh, I know quite a bit about you Natalie," Emma said, spreading Natalie's name into three syllables, 'Nat-a-lie'. "And what I don't know, I'm assuming my son Andrew does. So, you see, this is a long overdue meeting."

At least she had a different name for him. Andrew was motherly, whereas Drew had reminded her of a Harlequin character. She wasn't sure anymore. Emma continued.

"I couldn't be sure that William would go through with paying the ransom. There was always the possibility that once I had staged my kidnapping and was out of the picture, he would have a change of heart. I couldn't take that risk, so I brought you into the equation."

"Wait a minute," Natalie said. "You staged your own kidnapping, and Benny has known about this all along?" Natalie asked, turning on Drew who simply stared back at her. Eventually, his gazed dropped and Natalie drew her attention back to Emma who seemed to be enjoying the revelation immensely.

"I had William hire Andrew so he could look after you while all this was going on. With all the media attention surrounding the kidnapping, we couldn't risk them finding out about you. It would cause them to look a little closer to what was going on. Convenient, you know, that just as the wife is kidnapped, the girlfriend moves in to console the husband. And when the wife never returns, questions would be asked about how badly the husband really wanted the wife back."

"So, your job was to keep me out of the way till this, this... charade was over?" Natalie said, addressing Drew.

He shrank back in his chair and looked at Natalie. Not a stare, but a doleful look. There was resignation in his voice. "It got messed up on the boat," he said.

"What boat?" Natalie asked.

"The tour boat at Hilton Head," he said. "We were supposed to meet that night. I was going to whisk you away on a holiday for a few days, enjoy the islands."

"And keep you away until after William paid the ransom," Emma finished.

"But the kidnapping went wrong. The boat wasn't supposed to sink. We all had to improvise. I hadn't intended spending the night with you."

"You slept with her!" Emma shrieked. Guests at tables nearby glanced over quickly. Emma didn't notice. "How could you?"

Natalie grinned. The perfectly coiffed, cosmopolitan matron was ruffled. It looked good on her.

"Actually, Drew has wonderful bedside manners," she said.

"That's my son you're talking about," Emma hissed.

Natalie leaned forward. "Oh, so I can screw your husband and that's okay. But if I go near your son, you're outraged? That seems a little twisted to me."

Drew threw back his chair and stood up quickly. "For God's sake, this is ridiculous."

"Sit down Andrew," Emma said forcefully. Drew stared at her for a moment, then his shoulders drooped and he slowly pulled his chair back and sat. But he stared out toward the harbor. Natalie shook her head and sighed. Emma's head spun to her.

"You…" her finger stabbed the air in front of Natalie. "You could ruin everything, you stupid, stupid girl."

Now it was Natalie's turn to stand up abruptly.

"Thanks for the drink Mrs. Benneton. Drew, have a nice life. I'll be going home now," she said. Then she turned and headed toward the patio doors.

"He'll kill you."

Natalie turned back. Something in Emma's tone had changed. She wasn't being catty now, just factual.

"Who?"

Drew was watching his mother with a questioning expression. She turned to him and nodded. His eyebrows raised but he shrugged and looked up at Natalie who was standing just a few feet from the table.

"The Dutchman," he stated. Natalie frowned. "You know him as Manfred DeVries," he added.

Emma sipped her drink, her sudden outburst forgotten.

"Diane's husb---ah, partner?" Natalie said, crossing her arms and settling on her left leg.

"Manfred is the one my mother hired to stage the kidnapping," Drew said. Natalie's arms dropped. "And he's not her husband or partner or anything. He's a reclusive billionaire criminal."

"More specifically, a kidnapper for hire," Emma added, then went back to sipping.

Drew stood and went to Natalie, gently pulling her arm till she unfolded them. He steered her back to her seat and sat again, leaning in and lowering his voice.

"The Dutchman--Manfred-- has kidnapped a lot of wealthy women over the years. It's a real cottage industry and he's the biggest player. But he's also a control freak. He plans things meticulously and when the plans go awry, he goes a little nuts."

"Is that why he knocked you off the yacht? Natalie asked, her own voice lowered to match the level of Drew's. She noticed Emma's head cock slightly at this news.

"You noticed that had been on purpose, huh?"

"Diane was sure he'd done it on purpose," Natalie stopped momentarily. "Who is Diane, anyway? I'm sure you hurt her back at the airport."

"Diane is a contract agent for the Dutchman," Drew said. "I'm pretty sure she was to be my replacement, or at least a threat. That's why he put me in the drink. It was a warning. He was telling me I was dispensable and he could replace me with Diane--acting as your consoling friend--anytime he chooses."

"Why is it so important someone look after me?" Natalie asked.

Emma put her drink down and pulled her chair closer to the other two. All three were leaning over the table now, conspiratorially.

"Because I was never sure William would go along all the way with my plan," she said. "So, you were always an insurance policy; security against failure, if you will. If William didn't pay up, then Manfred would use you as enticement. It would then become a real kidnapping; but you would be the victim, not me."

Natalie stared at one then the other. "But you said Benny had asked Drew to look after me while you were, ah... playing your little game. He would never agree to risk having me become a victim."

"Don't be so sure about that, my dear," Emma said, leaning back again.

"Mother, don't," Drew said quickly. Natalie looked at Emma who simply sighed. Drew grabbed her attention by putting his hand on hers.

"Look, I don't think Benneton really understood the extremes the Dutchman could go to in order to achieve his goals. This is all about money," Drew said. "Money for my mother to escape New England and live out her life somewhere else without worrying about how she would support herself. But more importantly for the Dutchman, twenty-five percent of the ransom money goes to him for, ummm, services rendered. The ransom was ten million which means the Dutchman's cut is two and a half million."

"Men will do pretty much anything for two and a half million dollars, my dear," Emma said stonily.

"And look what you're willing to do for the rest of it," Natalie said.

Emma crossed her legs, watching Natalie. She said nothing.

"The point is," said Drew, pulling Natalie's hand closer to him across the table. "The Dutchman is not going to be happy about me taking Diane out of the equation. He's going to want to know why I thought that was necessary."

"And we're going to tell him that you found out what was going on and want in on the action," Emma said.

Natalie stared at her.

"And we're going to tell him we made a deal with you. Say a quarter million to go along with the ruse. You go back to…" she grinned. "Benny--after the company's paid out the ten million--and everyone lives happily thereafter."

"One million," Natalie said forcefully, drawing her hand out from under Drew's quickly. She leaned back in her chair.

Emma laughed. Drew groaned.

"You're not quite that valuable dear," Emma said.

"I think I know Benny well enough to know that if he thinks I'm in jeopardy, he's not going to go along with the plan until he knows I'm okay. And he'll only know that if I talk to him."

"William is reasonably confident that everything is going smoothly," said Emma. "I've disappeared, the police have their ransom demands, and Drew here is making sure you can come home safely when it's all over. Just to console, ummm, Benny."

Natalie looked at Drew. "I don't think so."

"She's talked to him," Drew said to his mother. Emma's eyes narrowed. "That's what escalated things. Maybe I could have contained the problem but Diane knew she'd reached Benneton. And she would have told the Dutchman by now."

"And that's why you hit Diane and stopped me from flying home? Natalie asked.

Emma sat up straight. She obviously hadn't been informed of all of this. How could she? Drew had been with her since this all began and he hadn't had the time to go over every detail on the phone when he'd arranged this meeting.

"You hurt Diane?" Emma glared.

"Diane was taking Natalie somewhere else, where we couldn't control the outcome," he said. "I had to do something."

"Somewhere else?" Natalie interjected.

"You weren't going home dear," Emma snarled. "And I don't think Diane's accommodations would have been quite as pleasant as Sint Maarten."

No one spoke for a few moments and Emma looked to be deep in thought. Drew was watching his mother intently, as if waiting for some kind of parental wisdom. Natalie mulled it all over.

It was all a little overwhelming and Benny had been a part of it right from the start. But he had genuinely been surprised when she'd called him. He didn't know where she was meaning Drew had not taken her where he'd said he would. She understood now that he'd brought her close to his mother so they could control the situation. But what were they trying to control? If Benny paid the ransom, as they obviously had planned, then Drew would take her back to him and Emma would have her money to disappear for real. Manfred--she cringed at the memory of the malicious grin he had worn when Drew had fallen into the ocean--would have his fee. She assumed then that Benny's own company would pay the insurance eventually, and he would get his ten million back, in time. Meanwhile, she and Benny would be free to become a real couple. That would be what he wanted, wouldn't it?

"Nothing's changed," Emma said abruptly, interrupting Natalie's thoughts. "As far as the Dutchman is concerned, you just took the competition out of the picture. You're protecting your own interests, that's all. He won't know how much you've told Natalie but it won't matter. You're still looking after her until William pays the ransom."

"Manfred doesn't know she's your mother?" Natalie asked Drew.

"Of course not. I'm just an employee, like Diane," Drew said. "This is my third job. The first time it was a grown-up child. The last time it was a girlfriend."

"Did she skinny dip with you at Orient Beach?" Natalie said. Emma cocked her head but said nothing.

Drew sighed. "She wasn't as attached to her boyfriend as you seem to be. And she wasn't smart enough to figure out what was going on."

"It would have been nice if William had picked someone like that," Emma said, as much to herself as the others. "But unfortunately, he was looking for something a little more substantial."

Natalie wanted to punch the woman. But instead she just frowned.

"You see, we haven't really been a couple for quite some time," Emma said. "In fact, I was the first to have an affair," her gaze shifted to Drew momentarily. Drew looked away. "But that was a very long time ago," she continued. "There have been several others since. William has always been so focused on building his company that I don't think he notices anymore."

Natalie fidgeted. Benny had told her he'd never been with anyone other than her--not even his wife for the past several years--and Natalie had never known whether to believe him. She did now.

"He began talking about divorce," Emma said. "Which was about the same time Andrew had finished his first caper with the Dutchman. I could see it was coming together and all I had to do was get all the players in place."

Natalie shrank back in her chair. "Benny has known about this all along," she said, a low sniffle erupting from her nose.

No one said anything momentarily. Then Drew stood up, leaned in to peck his mother on her cheek, and turned to Natalie. "Of course he knows. He helped plan it." He took a step toward the hotel lobby then turned back. "Even my part," he said and continued inside.

Natalie's mind was reeling. Emma leaned in and touched her arm, drawing her attention. "Forgive Andrew my dear. He has never known a father and resents the fact that I never told William about him. He feels he could have been a son to both of us. But of course, he can't. Andrew is mine, not William's."

Natalie just stared at her. After a moment, Emma stood and reached out for Natalie's hand.

"Come, I'll show you to your room," she said. "We'll continue later. There is so much to talk about. And plan."

Chapter Twenty-Eight

Natalie lay on the bed fully clothed, watching her torso raise with every quick breath. She could still hear movement elsewhere in the hotel but it was slowly dying down. Staff and patrons were calling it a night. She looked at her watch. Despite it being two-thirty in the morning, she could still hear voices in the distance, but very little from the small downtown area fronting on the harbor. Since all the stores and most of the boutique restaurants rolled up the carpet by midnight or so, the exclusive vacationers who were able to afford this island seemed content to continue their holiday time amidst the luxury of their opulent villas and expensive hotel suites.

She had to leave. It was that simple. Up until now she may or may not have trusted Drew; she wasn't sure. But since their afternoon talk and the revelation that Drew and Emma Benneton were partners in all of this, she simply couldn't stay to see what happened next. She had to get back to

The Security

Benny; had to ask him why he had been a part of this convoluted, complicated kidnapping scheme. And she had to find out why he had never confided in her. Did she mean anything to him, as Emma had suggested, or was she just a play toy that he needed to remove while this extravagant plan unfolded.

She needed to hear it from him. And if the answers weren't satisfactory, she would leave them all. Disappear. And she wouldn't need a kidnapping scheme to do it.

She half expected to hear a knock on the door and was determined not to let Drew in for further discussion. They had all met again earlier in the evening for supper and Emma had continued to elaborate upon her plan. Natalie had to admit, the bitch had spent months preparing for this. But something didn't quite add up. She understood why Emma wanted to leave Benny. She even understood why someone so accustomed to wealth would obsess about the money she wanted to guarantee after leaving her husband. What she didn't understand was Drew's involvement. Emma hadn't needed an inside man to achieve her goals. Neither had any of the other women Drew had spoken about.

"This is my third time out," he had said during dinner. "My job is to look after the security." Natalie had realized that in this instance, she was the security; the guarantee that the money man--Benny--would follow through with paying everyone.

Emma had added: "Manfred only works with wealthy women in marriages where the husband is having an affair. I doubt you'd be surprised to know that's quite a few couples in our circle." Natalie hadn't acknowledged the fact though she wasn't surprised at all. Emma continued: "So Andrew's job is to take the floos-- ah, girlfriend out of the picture for the duration. Two reasons for this: One, the husband doesn't risk showing the authorities that he might have a motive for not paying the ransom," she grinned

164

at this; "and two: if for any reason the husband has a change of heart, Manfred ransoms the girlfriend instead of the wife."

"Of course, sometimes the girlfriend isn't as, shall we say, valuable to the husband as everyone hopes," Drew added. "In which case it is made clear to the husband that should the girlfriend disappear and never return, certain measures had been taken to ensure the husband is blamed for the disappearance."

"Disappear where," Natalie had asked, "and for how long?"

Emma and Drew had exchanged a quick glance. "It's never come to that," Drew said slowly. "At least not while I've been on board. The husband in question gets the message and straightens out. Everyone knows what the Dutchman is capable of."

Natalie thought it over for a moment. "He would kill the girl?" she exclaimed.

"Of course not, dear," Emma said reassuringly. "But the threat of doing so--and being framed for the murder-- is enough to scare the husband back to the script."

"How do you know he hasn't actually done it before?" Natalie asked. "You said yourself that men will do anything for ten million dollars."

"It's not how Manfred works, I assure you," Emma had said but her eyes had gone a pale blue. "Murdering someone everyone knows was alive and expecting everyone to be quiet about it would be silly, wouldn't it?" She hadn't seemed to be asking Natalie the question because she was looking at Drew when she had said it.

Drew averted the gaze and said to Natalie, "Benneton hired me--after Mother suggested it--to look after you. He knew what the Dutchman was capable of and wanted to be sure it didn't happen to you. "

"Why you?" Natalie asked

"Because the Dutchman has used me for this purpose for the past eight years," he said. "And because he has no idea that his current client is my mother."

"You said Benny doesn't know you're Emma's son either," Natalie said, "so why would he hire you?"

"Because William doesn't know Andrew works for Manfred, dear," Emma said condescendingly. "He thinks Andrew is a talented bodyguard who works for me."

Natalie had thought she'd followed the conversation well enough and both Emma and Drew had provided all the answers to all the questions she could think of at the moment. The problem was that now, a few hours later, she wasn't sure she'd asked all the right questions, or that she was getting straight answers. The fact that she was even more confused just proved how elaborate and convoluted the whole affair was. One nagging question that hadn't been answered was what Drew's connection to Benny's government friend was, the one who Drew had been talking to after the boat sinking in Hilton Head. But she hadn't thought of that till she'd been back in her room. Did it really matter at this point?

She looked at her watch. It was almost three and she'd waited long enough. She pulled out her bag, threw it on the bed, and began packing.

Escaping the island meant plane or boat. She needed to reach someone and she had seen old-fashioned pay phones in the lobby. Although a plane would be quicker, she doubted that could be arranged on short notice. And although there was an abundance of boats and yachts in the harbor, most of them were probably docked here long term. She may end up being a stowaway on a ferry or tour boat, if there was such a thing.

She got up off the bed and strode quietly toward the dresser. Moonlight illuminated its bamboo top creating a luminescence that would have evoked romance or at least a holiday vibe at any other time. But things weren't as they seemed on this island. Answers were elsewhere. Benny had been a part of the hoax since the beginning but she knew he would hold no secrets back once she confronted him.

But first, she had to get out of here. She pulled a card out of her pocket and placed it atop the dresser. Leaning in, she smiled as she read the cell phone number of Oliver, the taxi driver.

The Security

Chapter Twenty-Nine

"She is called the 'Me and Marley'," Oliver had said, his voice anxious but controlled. "It's a fishing rig and my second cousin Raymond will be there waiting. I will call him."

It had not taken Oliver long to understand Natalie's predicament and though he didn't ask detailed questions he seemed to sense the urgency in Natalie's voice. Then, due to the pure-hearted chivalrous nature embedded in him from years of being the family protector, he quickly detailed a solution for her.

Had it been for any other reason, and at any other time, Natalie may have enjoyed the scenic walk down the narrow street toward the harbor. But she was too intent on planning what she would say to Benny when she arrived back at Hilton Head.

Would he be confrontational, evade questions, try to calm her concerns? Or would he want her to leave again? If she was important to him, then once he realized she already knew much of the truth, then surely he would rescind and confide in her. Lurking in the back of her mind was the possibility that she was not that important to Benny, despite Emma's innuendoes, and he would, in fact, end their relationship once he realized how much she knew about the devious plot to bilk his own company out of millions. And for what? Just to get rid of his wife? It seemed ridiculous. She needed him to explain.

The ever-constant fact about late nights on tropical islands is that it is never dark and gloomy. Stars and a partial moon illuminate everything from the brightly painted stucco'd buildings lining the dockside street, to the gently lapping waves in the harbor. Even the water seemed warm and inviting, the usual turquoise hue more of a darker green except under the equally spaced lamppost lights where miniature white caps sparkled against a rippling patch of emerald.

Natalie stood directly in front of several yachts docked stern in along the concrete jetty, their multiple decks looming high, gently rocking from side to side in a manner that evoked a constant state of unbalance. Or maybe that was just her state of mind at the moment. She turned to search for the "Me and Marley".

Smiling at Oliver's depth of care and speed of contact, Natalie strode down the dockside where a waiting Raymond greeted her at the stern of a very sturdy-looking fishing boat. He resembled Oliver slightly, though much younger and leaner but the huge smile was definitely a family trait.

"You'll be warmer below Miss," he said. "We'll be on open ocean for about two hours. Got fresh coffee in the galley and a couple of sandwiches I rustled together along with some fruit. Help yourself.

Natalie thanked him, and inwardly, thanked Oliver for being willing and able to muster up a rescue excursion on such short notice.

The Security

When Natalie pushed the plane's window shade up seven hours later, she was blinded by the mid-afternoon sun streaming into the cabin. It had been a whirlwind trek over the Atlantic, beginning with a two-hour voyage from St. Barths to Sint Maarten, the constant throb of the fishing boat's motor steadily churning up water giving her a headache. Somehow, Raymond had managed to drop her off at a dock within walking distance of Princess Julianna airport and she had waited nervously for a couple of hours until her early morning Stateside flight was ready to board, swallowing four Tylenols and washing them down with terrible coffee from the only stand open at that time of the morning. She had nervously checked around the lounge until boarding time, thinking someone would surely stop her. But it was too soon. Even if Drew and Emma had discovered she was missing, they'd never figure out her escape route yet.

She had slept soundly during the flight north, waking briefly to traverse the makeshift airport corridors between her international flight to Charlotte, N.C.--the best she was able to get on standby--and the regional short hop to Hilton Head Airport. The sight of Port Royal Sound was like a welcome embrace as they descended over what was actually the Atlantic and onto the tiny airstrip on the northeast edge of the island.

It had been a gruelingly long trip, and after calling for a cab, she decided to call Benny and ask him to open up a bottle of wine.

She desperately needed a drink. Nothing fancy, but no umbrellas.

Chapter Thirty

As the cab slowly progressed through the canopy of trees covering the driveway, Natalie saw the huge front door swing open and a man rush out, his attempt at running resulting in a sloppy gait similar to a mature dog that had been sleeping on its legs too long.

William Benneton was disheveled and frantic. Natalie smiled. It was somehow reassuring to see that he wasn't as tailored, as prepared, as he usually was for most situations. She liked the effect her impromptu visit was having on him, though she wasn't sure why.

The cab rounded the center island and stopped opposite the door and as Natalie stepped out, he rushed up and embraced her.

"My God, you're okay, you're okay," he blustered. "I was so worried."

Natalie hugged him back and after a quick kiss, Benneton handed the cabby a fifty and told him to keep the change. The cabby tipped his baseball cap, dragged Natalie's backpack from the back seat and handed it to Benneton who took it, and with his other arm around Natalie's waist, led her into the house.

"You know where Emma is, don't you?" Natalie began. They had gone straight to the gleaming white kitchen with the huge window that overlooked part of the rear yard. Benneton had already opened a bottle of red and was pouring two glasses.

He put the bottle down very gently and stared at it for a moment.

"You don't understand," he said quietly.

"Damn right I don't understand," Natalie blasted, her hands on her hips, her hair doing a floppy dance as her head jerked with every word.

Benneton looked up and reached out for her hand. Natalie stepped back a pace.

"Can we talk about this a little later. I want to know what happened to you," he said, still in a low tone.

Natalie dropped her arms but she stood her ground, just beyond reach. Humbleness became him. "What happened is that I met your lovely wife and found out that I'm some kind of pawn in your sick game of kidnapping chess."

Benneton looked around quickly then shushed Natalie. "There's an FBI agent in the den watching TV. He's supposed to be monitoring the computer and phones, waiting for calls from the kidnappers but there's been no contact for a couple of days."

"You mean the Dutchman, don't you," Natalie spat. When Benneton cocked his head in surprise, she quickly realized her mistake. "You don't know who he is, do you?"

"Dutchman?"

"You planned this and don't you even know who the guy is on the other end?" she said.

This time Benneton stepped forward and grabbed her arm, and leaning in to whisper, he said, "I don't know who he is and the less I know the better." He pulled her out to the hall. "Come on, if we're going to do this, I cannot afford to have anyone overhear."

He led Natalie to the stairs and they ascended to the second floor. Natalie hadn't been up here the last time she had been at the house. A woman's touch was everywhere from the colors of the walls to the knick-knacks on various antique tables strategically placed along the corridor. Double doors at the end of the corridor exposed a very large bed and Natalie pulled her arm free and stopped.

"I'm not going in there Benny," she said firmly. He looked at her, then sighed and turned toward another room just before the end of the corridor.

"The spare bedroom," he said and pushed her through the door ahead of him. The room looked like the cover of a bed and breakfast brochure, complete with hard cover books on a small white desk and extra blankets folded neatly at the end of a double bed. Seeing no other chairs other than the one under the desk, she sat on the edge of the bed, her hands folded in her lap. Benny pulled out the desk chair, placed it in front of Natalie and sat down. He grabbed her hands and held them in his own.

"It was all Emma's idea," he began. "She thought it was the perfect way to move on with our lives."

"Without losing all your money," Natalie said defiantly.

Benneton winced. "It's not just about the money Nat," he said. She drew the corner of her mouth into a frown as if to say 'Sure it isn't'.

Benneton continued. "It's difficult for people in our position," he said, letting go of her hand and standing up. He began pacing. Natalie put her arms behind her, to brace herself against the mattress. "Getting a divorce isn't simple. It's not just the break-up of a family--"

Natalie snorted. *What family?*

"--It ruptures businesses, affects hundreds of people. The law considers assets gathered during a marriage to be of equal value, and that includes the family business. So, in order to accomplish an equal separation of assets, I would have had to put the company on the block."

"You could have paid her off," Natalie said. Benneton looked at her and sighed.

"It's not that easy Nat. I don't have the kind of liquid assets it would take to simply buy her out. The company is worth millions. Besides it's not her company to play with, it's mine."

"So, it is about the money."

Benneton continued pacing. "You don't understand Natalie," he said. "The business is everything. It's my life. Everything I've achieved is because of the company."

"Not everything," Natalie said quietly.

"You know what I mean," he said, dismissing her comment.

"So you came up with this crazy scheme to steal from your own company," she said, suddenly understanding a little more.

Benneton sat down again but he didn't reach for Natalie. He placed his hands in his lap. "It was Emma's idea, and I think she'd been planning it for a while. She had it all figured out. She didn't demand half the company. She just wanted enough to live the rest of her life the way she wanted to. She'd put a price tag on that and I knew I didn't have to sell the company to get there for her."

"But you would have to break the law," Natalie said.

"Maybe Natalie. But it *is* my company I'm stealing from. Nobody else gets hurt. At first I thought she was crazy. But after a while it began to make sense."

"How could kidnapping ever make sense Benny?" Natalie said, leaning forward and looking him in the eye. "And why did it have to include me?"

He shifted in his chair and nervously stroked his hair with one hand.

"She had it all figured out Natalie," he said. "I know it sounds insane now, but. back then it seemed to be an ideal solution. Emma would be gone from my life and I wouldn't lose the company in the process."

Natalie stared at him.

"And we could have kept seeing each other," he said sheepishly.

Natalie jumped up. "Seeing each other?" She leaned over him and pointed her finger at his nose. He flinched. "You weren't thinking of me Benny. No, this was about being able to keep things the way they are: Me in my place and you… you in your lap of luxury!"

"Natalie, please…"

"Don't please me Benny. You let that woman kidnap me as part of her plan to ensure you paid your kidnap ransom; the money that's going to allow her to live the way she's accustomed to. It's just like a divorce settlement, but not as messy, right?"

"You were never supposed to be a part of this," Benneton said. "I had a bodyguard assigned to take you away from any danger until it was all over."

"No Benny," she stabbed her finger at the air in front of his face again. "What you did was get me out of the way so the plan could be executed smoothly with no glitches." Benneton shook his head but Natalie didn't stop. "And I am a glitch Benny, aren't I?"

"Did you know Emma knew all about me Benny?" she said, her voice raising. "Did you know she's known about our affair, right from the beginning? And did you know that so called bodyguard you had take me away is Emma's…" she caught herself. Now was not the time for that revelation. "Emma's employee?"

"Drew Scanlon works for me now," Benny blustered. "And he was supposed to make it a holiday for you. When it was all over, he was to bring you back."

"And he wasn't supposed to touch me Benneton? Was that the plan?" she blurted. His eyes suddenly darkened.

"What did he do?" he said, his voice cold. Natalie laughed.

"What the hell does it matter what he did or didn't do Benny? You pushed me into the arms of another man and asked him to take me to a tropical island paradise and babysit me till you were ready to have me back. Just how loyal do you think your employees are Benny?"

He stood up suddenly, went to the window and stared out at the trees, bows swaying gently, as they always did due to the never-ending breeze coming in from the Atlantic just a few hundred yards to the north.

"What happened Natalie?" he asked quietly. Natalie heard a change in his voice. It was the corporate voice now, all business, cold, calculating. She'd heard it before when she'd overheard him talking to a business associate. It was the voice that controlled the Benneton empire; the voice of power and persuasion.

"What I found out William is that my whole life, of late at least, is a game," she said. "A game that I didn't ask to play. Hell, I don't even know what the rules are!"

"You're being melodramatic Natalie," he said without turning.

"I've had a lot of time on airplanes and boats to think of how this conversation was going to go. In fact, I played out all the possible directions it could take many times."

"When this is over, we can talk about us," he said. He turned and though his voice was pleading, to Natalie, his eyes were still a little darkened. Natalie hadn't called him William in years; it was always Benny.

"That was certainly one of the directions I figured the conversation could go," she said, standing and wiping down the crease in her jeans, "But regardless of when we discuss it, the conclusion is always the same."

"Which is?"

"Me leaving, Benny," she said. She stood still, hands in her pockets now, staring at him.

"You're overreacting Natalie," Benneton said. She noticed his voice wasn't soothing any longer. Something had changed.

"I need space Benny, at least for a while. Don't worry, I don't plan on getting in the way of your little plan; I wouldn't know what to do anyway. But I need to be away from you, all of you, for a while."

"Did you fall in love with Drew Scanlon, Natalie?"

The question floored her. She stepped back as if rocked by a physical blow.

"What?" she said.

"You've spent a lot of time with a young man I, ah, thought would be more professional, but naturally, he's more your age. He lives an exciting lifestyle, I'm sure. Perhaps he swept you off your feet and now you're confused and aren't sure about the great life we could have once this is all over."

Natalie stared at him. She then took her hands out of her pockets and headed to the door. Benneton followed. In the hallway, she turned quickly and Benneton jerked to a halt.

"This has nothing to do with Drew," she seethed. "No one has swept me off my feet, and I haven't fallen in love with anyone else. I thought I was in love with you."

Benneton didn't react so Natalie continued. "My confusion stems from your inability to understand that I don't want to be a part of this crazy, highly illegal scheme of yours. If we have any kind of a life together, we'll have to pick it up later. Much later. Right now, I'm going home." She turned back and headed down the hallway. "Can you call me another cab please," she said over her shoulder. When Benneton didn't reply, she turned to ask him again. He was standing still, in the middle of the hallway, his eyes glazing over. *Was he angry, frustrated, maybe even despaired, damn it?*

"I think you're making a mistake Natalie. I need you right now." He rubbed his chin and turned his head away as if to gain resolve. "I'll get Danny to drive you into town. We'll talk tomorrow."

"Benny, please. A cab will be fine."

"No Natalie, I don't think so," he said. This time his tone was a little shaky. She wasn't following his mood but at least she wouldn't have to wait for a cab if his driver took her right now.

"I need you to be safe," he added, turning his head again. "I don't know who this *Dutchman* is Natalie, but I have a fair idea of what he could be capable of. You've done well so far on your own. But please, If I hope to get any sleep tonight, I want to know that you are safe in your apartment in Savannah. Danny knows where you live and he can check out your apartment before you go up, okay?"

Natalie shook, an uncontrollable shiver that stemmed not from what Benneton had said but more the way he had said it.

"Okay Benny. Okay."

He nodded, stepped forward and taking her arm, led her toward the main foyer.

"And I want you to take one of my guns," he said.

Chapter Thirty-One

The gun scared the hell out of Natalie but Benny had insisted so, after a hurried lesson on turning the safety on and off, she had simply put it in her purse and walked out to the waiting limo.

Danny, the driver, had closed the door quickly behind her, and without another word from Benny, they drove away. As they slowly travelled the tree-lined avenue, Natalie considered her options.

She could go home, have a bath and wait for Benny to call tomorrow. But what then? Emma was still on St. Barths, and the police here were still waiting for the kidnappers to call and arrange for a transfer of money. She wasn't sure how it would be done but figured that if Emma had planned it, there wasn't going to be any bags full of cash being handed over in a back alley somewhere. More likely, it would be an internet transfer that would be not only untraceable but probably monitored from St. Barths.

The Security

The woman was a calculating bitch, but she was a smart one. Of that, Natalie had no doubt.

As the car slowed for a stop sign, Natalie heard a loud roar and a space-age looking neon green motorbike screeched to a stop directly in front of the front left bumper of the limo, preventing the driver from taking the turn. For a moment, Danny tapped his fingers on the steering wheel impatiently, waiting for the ignorant biker to take off. But instead, the biker turned and looked directly at the front windshield, his face totally obscured by the full-face, tinted helmet. Just as Danny looked to be shifting his hand to the center of the wheel--Natalie assumed he was going to honk the horn--the biker pulled a gun from his jacket pocket and pointed it at Danny's head.

Danny glanced at Natalie via the rear-view mirror and with a slight nod of his head, she knew he was going to try to make a run for it. He spun the steering wheel sharply to the right but before he had a chance to press the accelerator the biker lowered his aim quickly and shot out the front tire. Natalie felt the car sharply drop to the left. The biker then quickly raised the gun again, returning his aim to Danny's head. With his other hand, he motioned for Danny to lower the driver side window. Danny glanced in the rearview once again, his eyes glowering. Natalie shook her head. Whatever this was, it obviously had something to do with the kidnapping. Did they work for Benny? Of course not. Danny worked for Benny and he would have known. Was it Emma? But how could she know what Natalie was doing? She and Drew would know that she had left the island but they wouldn't know where she'd gone.

By the time Natalie realized the biker probably worked for the Dutchman, as Benny had feared, the dark leather-clad man had stepped off his machine and come directly to the driver's window, the tip of his gun tapping on the glass. Again, he motioned for Danny to roll down the window.

Danny took one last glance in the mirror at Natalie and then shook his head at the biker. As he did, Natalie saw a shadow quickly cross past her own window. Something hit the glass hard beside Danny's head and the window smashed, pouring shards all over his face and chest. Natalie screamed and instinctively Danny put his arms up to protect his face, but an arm pushed through what was left of the window and something was clamped against his mouth. He struggled briefly but very quickly his struggles lessened until his head finally slumped forward to his chest.

Natalie gasped and pushed herself backward and sideways across the rear seat, away from the driver's side. She heard the door behind open and tried to turn but a hand came into view and a sponge of some sort was pressed against her nose and mouth. She smelt a faint odor of sulphur and she made an attempt to grasp the attacker's arm but suddenly felt numb all over. Her vision blurred slightly and her eyes fluttered, but just before darkness overcame her the thought registered that she had completely forgotten about the gun in her purse.

Chapter Thirty-Two

Drew searched the grounds and found his mother sipping a coffee and staring out toward the ocean. A warm, early morning breeze swept her hair back gently.

"He has her," he said.

Emma Benneton turned and smiled, acknowledging his presence, then turned back to the ocean.

"He needs her for insurance," she said. "To make sure Benneton pays."

"He's likely to kill her once he has the money."

Emma reached for Drew's hand. "He doesn't need to. In fact, he would be better off sending her back to Benneton to ensure he is distracted enough to not think about me."

Drew pulled his mother's arm so she turned all the way toward him, "Leaving the Dutchman free to kill you."

Emma smiled. "Well, we certainly know he won't try that before he has his money." She placed both her hands on his shoulders for reassurance, looking into his eyes. "And he needs me to do the transfer, remember." She dropped her hands and turned back to the ocean again.

"I will be there when you do that," Drew said. "Because from that point on, the Dutchman no longer needs you."

Emma's expression didn't change, other than a slight twitch of her jaw.

"Yes, we've always known that would be the tricky part," she said. "But I have an ace up my sleeve."

"And now that Natalie's there, will that change our plans?" he asked, knowing his mother had plenty of secrets. Another *ace* wasn't surprising but would it be enough? "She may have already told him who I am."

"She probably has but it doesn't matter," Emma said. "He still needs me to complete the arrangement and he will think you're off somewhere trying to find her. He won't bother going after you until after he's taken care of me. But if everything works the way we've planned, it won't matter what he thinks. And he will never find us."

"He'll likely kill Natalie out of spite." Drew's voice cracked slightly but Emma either didn't notice or chose not to acknowledge it.

"There's no advantage in harming her. In fact, her fear of him is something she'll take back to Benneton and help ensure he fears retaliation too. If she is scared of the Dutchman, she'll convince Benneton to let it go and move on with their lives."

They said nothing for a moment, then Drew quietly said, "I can't see her staying with him."

"Of course not," she said, smiling. "Benneton has no compassion, no love of life. All he has is ambition. She'll tire of that, just like I did. Only she's younger, and not his wife. She'll tire of it faster."

"And then what?"

"By then we'll be long gone and even if Benneton tries to find me, he never, ever will."

"I was talking about Natalie," Drew said.

Emma turned to him. "Whether she stays with him or not is irrelevant. You'll be with me and we'll find you a nice, rich heiress to play with. Natalie will find another sugar daddy."

They had been quiet for a while, lost in their own thoughts, gazing in different directions. Far off seagulls and the swishing of branches bending in the gentle breeze were the only sounds to break the silence. Emma knew she would miss the serenity of this island paradise. She had talked Benneton into buying a floor in the boutique hotel fifteen years ago, before prices on the celebrity island skyrocketed. The owner had needed money to refurbish and had jumped at the chance, despite losing a full floor of rooms. Emma had remodeled and it now looked like any other high-rise condo--minus a kitchen. She ate in the hotel restaurant daily. William had only been there once so it had become her haven, her escape from the reality of being essentially an aging trophy wife. Benneton had sensed that and let her come here alone--or at least he thought she was alone--two or three times a year. Now, she would never see it again. She would never see anything she was used to again. Her whole life was about to become something else, something different. She smiled. Something better actually. And she would have her son. She turned to take his hand.

But he was gone.

Chapter Thirty-Three

As Natalie's eyes flickered open, her first realization was that it was too warm to be North Carolina.

Not hot, but warm, with no humidity. As her head slowly cleared, she realized the bird calls didn't sound right either. They did, however, sound familiar. And that was because she'd heard, and felt, all these sensations yesterday.

In the tropics.

She jumped off the bed and surveyed her surroundings. She was in a tiny room with a wardrobe a mirror and a small desk the only pieces of furniture other than the bed she had been lying on. There was a small window on one wall and next to it, a door. Looking out, she could see trees, lots of them, like her room was on the edge of a forest. She was fully dressed in the same clothes she had worn on the plane and at Benny's last night.

At least she assumed it had been last night.

She remembered Benny's driver, Danny, stopping at the intersection on Hilton Head and being threatened by a motorcyclist with a gun. She had watched as a second person had covered his mouth with a cloth and moments later, Danny slumping sideways in his seat. She shuddered as she recalled something being placed over her own mouth seconds later and the sudden drowsiness that had swept over her.

And that was it. Her next memory was this one; waking up in the tropics somewhere. Had she been kidnapped, transported back to the Caribbean again? What for, and by whom? She feared she knew the answer to the last two questions.

She reached for the door handle, expecting it to be locked, and was surprised when it turned in her hand. She opened the door a few inches and stuck her head out. She saw a long corridor with other similar doors on either side. In one direction, the corridor curved, leading in and around another corner. In the opposite direction, she saw sunlight shining on the floorboards at an intersecting corridor at the end. The light would be coming from outside meaning an entrance, she hoped. She stepped out and slowly tiptoed down the corridor toward the light.

Natalie stopped thinking of why she was here or even how she had been brought here, wherever here was. She just thought about getting out. She knew that whoever had done this certainly hadn't asked her permission and that meant the odds were it wasn't a good thing. She briefly wondered why the door hadn't been locked, but as she turned the corner and saw a screen door at the end of a smaller corridor, her thoughts focused on escape.

The door opened up to a lush walkway that seemed to cut right into the forest. Just a few feet from the door on her right, a thick jungle of tall, green trees beckoned to her. On the left, she could make out rugged stone steps that lead downward in a spiral from the walkway, thick bushes on either side of the trail. She heard water gently lapping against a shore and assumed there was some kind of beach or dock in that direction. If there were people around, that's where they were likely to be. A tropical jungle in the daytime didn't scare her as much as the possibility of being caught and sent back to the room, this time with the likelihood of it being locked to prevent her escaping again. Without another thought, she stepped off the path and began working her way through the dense growth.

After ten minutes of trudging through bush and ground cover, gently stepping over shrubbery she not only didn't recognize, but debated whether they were poisonous or not, she second guessed her choice to venture into the forest. Even though this was the tropics, surely she would come to a resort or native village or something soon, she thought.

Then, as abruptly as the thickness of the jungle had enveloped her it suddenly stopped as she stepped out into a clearing. It wasn't manicured like a front lawn but the grass was shorter and the plant life wasn't as dense. The clearing sloped upward gently and after walking a few meters, she turned to see that she had emerged from a distinct tree line. The ground cover was rough, rocky even, and the greenery was nothing more than a few inches tall as she slowly ascended what was turning out to be a hill. A dull roar that had been in the back of her subconscious was getting louder and more identifiable as she rose. Soon she heard waves crashing heavily against a shoreline and assumed she was heading to the top of small Caribbean mountain. She was excited in the hope that she would be able to see for a distance and either recognize something or be able to see a town or resort and head in that direction, looking for help.

As she approached the crest of the hill, the noise from the waves crashing below was deafening. Natalie looked out toward the horizon but saw nothing but azure blue water. She edged closer to the crest and peered over. The shoreline, such as it was, consisted of jagged rocks. The sea seemed to be eroding a hole in the bottom of the hill since she couldn't see any land directly below her, just rocks. The land was indented from the assault of the sea and there was likely a cave down there but that wouldn't help Natalie now.

In desperation she looked in each direction, following the shoreline and realized she was actually standing at the end of a narrow peninsula with sea surrounding her on three sides. When she looked back in the direction she had come, she saw nothing but trees, as far as her eyes could see; nothing but green. She knew there could be civilization hidden underneath--including the building she had escaped from--but nothing could be seen, even from this vantage point.

As she was staring at the forest a movement at the tree line caught her eye, not far from where she had emerged from the forest. It was a small vehicle of some kind and as she watched she realized it was following a man-made trail that lead upwards toward her.

She waved frantically and began running down the slope toward the vehicle which now looked to be a golf cart or something similar. One figure was driving, the brim of a Panama hat blowing in the breeze but low enough to disguise any facial features.

Part way down the hill, Natalie realized she had discovered the trail the cart was likely following and she slowed to a trot. She briefly wondered if she should be running toward or away from this person as it seemed that so far, the only civilization she'd seen was the room she had escaped from. Could this person be looking for her?

As the cart closed in, Natalie saw the driver was a tall, older man and there was something vaguely familiar about him. The cart stopped and the man stepped out, his head tilting up allowing Natalie a clear view of his craggy face. She gasped.

"Hello again Miss Grainger," said Manfred DeVries, stopping directly in front of her. His voice had an airy lilt to it but his grin turned the encounter into something menacing. "I had been wondering where you had gotten to."

The Security

Chapter Thirty-Four

Natalie got in the golf cart, perching herself as close to the outside edge of the seat as possible. Manfred's crooked smile was unnerving. Drew and Emma had referred to him as the Dutchman, but to Natalie, he was Diane's partner, the sailor, Manfred.

"You're free to go wherever you wish," he said as he engaged the forward throttle and began descending the hill following the trail that led back into the jungle. "It's an island and that is the Caribbean Sea out there. You can try to swim somewhere but you'd better be good. The nearest landfall is at least a few days swim, assuming you survive the predators, of course." He laughed. "You could try the Tom Hanks thing--great movie by the way--but once we knew you were gone, we'd hunt you down and bring you back long before you got too comfortable."

The way he used the phrase "hunt you down" made Natalie squirm and Manfred noticed.

"Don't worry," he said. "If you behave and enjoy the facilities, everyone will leave you alone. Once my little transaction is complete with our mutual friend William Benneton, then you'll be free to go."

Go? Go where? The fact that he hadn't mentioned how she would leave the island once his transaction was done bothered her but that would come later. "Why am I here?" she asked.

"Normally you wouldn't be," he said staring straight ahead. "But it seems my associate mislead you into believing you had a little more freedom than we would like. We can't have you running around influencing people's decisions with emotional outbursts and complicating what is normally a very straightforward transaction."

"You keep saying 'we'," Natalie said. "Who is we?"

Manfred slowed the cart a little and turned to stare at her. His eyes were dark and luminescent in the shadows of the jungle. It was like looking into a cat's eyes… or maybe a leapord's. Natalie knew there was something going on back there but the eyes and face held no indication as to what that something was.

"It's a habit of mine, I apologize." he responded. "I have staff and one or two associates but this is my island, my operation, and I control everything that happens." His voice was monotone and resolute. He winked and grinned again, then turned back and pressed the accelerator again.

"Everything, Miss Grainger. I control everything."

Chapter Thirty-Five

After a few minutes of travelling the rough-hewn trail, bounding right, then left, missing huge tree trunks by centimeters, and shearing off small sprouts of new vegetation on the edge of the path, Natalie saw water.

As they approached, the jungle diminished and was eventually replaced by a manicured lawn. They turned a corner and Natalie was caught by surprise as she saw that the water was, in fact, an inlet right out of a travel magazine. Soft white sand met the water, its flat carpet stretching toward a perfectly landscaped lawn which in turn spread out to accommodate a beautiful one-story building, much like a cottage but spread out ranch-style. Glass windows adorned the side facing the inlet and Natalie noticed a covered outdoor patio, and in several places on the lawn, seating areas made up of wooden chairs, small stone tables and even a wrought iron fireplace. It reminded her of upstate New York but with palm trees instead of spruce or pine.

As Manfred drove toward the front entrance where two other golf carts were parked, Natalie noted a long wooden dock that disappeared behind the side of the home. Extending well out into the inlet, she figured it must have been dredged for large vessels because the sailboat she had been on with Drew, Manfred and Diane was tied up to one side.

Manfred parked and jumped out without saying a word, and headed to the front entrance, a covered porch with no door. Looking around, she recognized the stone path curving up beside the house. At the other end, she knew, was the back entrance to the corridor that lead to the room she had been in.

"There is a library at the back of the house, and the kitchen is that way," Manfred said, standing in the doorway and pointing in the general direction of the dock. "Dinner is served on the patio at seven. I usually dine alone but I trust you will join me this evening. I am intrigued as to how you managed to turn your minder, Drew Scanlon, into a traitorous idiot." And with that, he turned and disappeared into the interior.

Natalie looked around her, noticing the serenity and seclusion of the setting. She suddenly felt very alone.

As if on cue, a white clad, dark skinned woman of about fifty walked around the corner and headed toward her. She had a broad, genuine smile on her face and was carrying an overflowing basket of what appeared to be white linens.

"Ah Miss," she said, her low-pitched voice accented with a Jamaican twang. "I was worried you might have been lost in the jungle. Mr. DeVries didn't seem to be concerned but I urged him to go and find you. Please, I will show you around the villa. Then, we put new sheets on your bed. I think you--how you say? --sweated a lot last night. Everyone sweating when they first arrive. Give it a few days, you'll be calm as pineapple."

193

A few days! Natalie sighed. Not if she could help it. This place was gorgeous but Manfred--the Dutchman--was a scary dude. She wouldn't want to be spending much time around him. She smiled, despite the tension she felt. The woman's smile was genuine and her attempted use of western cliché's was amusing.

"I'm Natalie," she said, extending her hand. The old woman looked at it, confused, then grinning, remembered her manners and grasped Natalie's hand and pulled her toward the dock.

"Natalie, Natalie," the woman muttered as she led the way toward the back entrance. "Good Jamaican name, that, like mine: I am Emerald."

Natalie smiled. Her name was short for Natalia and she was pretty sure it was Eastern European but who knew? The Caribbean was an eclectic mix of many generations of Europeans and natives. Regardless, she let the woman lead her through a huge kitchen, appointed with gleaming stainless-steel appliances and cooking surfaces. Several other dark-skinned staff turned and smiled as they passed. Natalie got the distinct feeling that either Manfred brought a lot of guests here, or they had no idea she was, in fact, a prisoner.

Chapter Thirty-Six

For the next two or three days, Natalie tried to act like a guest more than a prisoner. She found her room was only locked at night. Around 10:30 on the nights Manfred was here--he had left once on his catamaran and returned early the next day on a smaller launch-- he would look in on her, smile and bid her good evening, then lock the door. She awoke around eight or so without an alarm and found the door always open. Did Manfred ever sleep? Or was someone else in charge of morning rituals?

On the fourth day, she sat quietly on a lounge chair on the deck reading and watched as the small motor launch left around ten in the morning. It returned early in the afternoon with supplies and groceries. This was the second time the boat had made the trip this week. That meant some kind of mainland was nearby; perhaps Philipsburg, since Manfred had said his island was close to Sint Maarten.

She noticed Emerald the housemaid lugging produce and got up to help.

"You don't have to do this Miss," the amiable women said. "You are a guest. You should be sunbathing or taking long walks in the woods."

"Please!" Natalie exclaimed. "If I don't do something useful around here I'm going to go crazy."

Emerald raised her eyebrows slightly, then her permanent smile returned. "As you wish Miss Natalie. Please, there is one other bag," she said, pointing into the boat.

Natalie stepped on to the launch, grabbed the bag and turned to step back up onto the dock. She stopped short as she noticed Manfred standing on the patio of the house. He had a coffee cup in his hand and he was staring at her. A cold chill swept her spine. It was the reaction she always got when she saw the man from a distance. Something in his manner, his gaze, was disarming. Danger lurked behind those eyes, she knew. She waved nonchalantly but he didn't acknowledge her. She stepped up and followed Emerald and the others through the kitchen entrance. When she glanced at the patio just before going in, Manfred was gone.

The kitchen was bustling with people emptying bags, putting things on shelves and in the refrigerator. And they were all chattering away, talking of family, things they were planning for their day off, even how they were looking forward to seeing their spouses again.

Natalie's ears perked up when one man mentioned the name of a street that she recognized as being in Philipsburg. So they were close after all. If she could figure out a way to get off this island, she could contact Oliver again and escape for a second time. But this time she wouldn't go straight to Benny. She would call her sister, borrow some money, and get away till everyone forgot about her.

The boat was the key. If she was to get off this island, the supply boat was her best bet. So she would have to ingratiate herself with the staff, get them used to her helping unload the boat. Then it wouldn't be unusual for her to be jumping on and off the dock.

The following day, Manfred approached and sat beside her. He had brought a couple of colorful drinks and offered one to her.

"You seem to be making yourself useful here Miss Grainger," he said, handing her one of the glasses. His gaze wasn't malicious, but it wasn't friendly either.

She smiled and took the drink. "Your staff are very friendly. Besides I have to do something. I can't sit around doing nothing all day. The staff make me feel at home. Do they know I am a prisoner?"

Manfred grimaced. "A prisoner? Not at all my dear. You are my guest," he said, sipping his drink. "It is true, you cannot leave, but I think of it more of an unplanned vacation for you. Actually, my staff think you are a relative, I think. They will continue to treat you well." He shifted in his seat, stretching his legs out on his own chaise. "You seem to have accepted that I need you here until the transaction is complete. That is good. I was rather hoping you had concluded that I mean you no harm. You are a form of insurance, that's all."

"Well it's nice to be needed," Natalie jeered.

Manfred smiled thinly. "Your time here will be most enjoyable, as you have already experienced," he said. "But it must be clear that you cannot leave until William Bennington has fully completed his obligations. I'm sure you understand."

"What I understand, Mr. DeVries," Natalie said, putting her glass down on the small glass table that separated them. "Is that I am a pawn in this fantastical chess game you are playing with the Bennetons." She put up her hand to ward off an interruption from Manfred. "Although I don't understand all the ins and outs, I'm quite used to deception and accept my role... and do, indeed, thank you for your hospitality. But once this is over, I'm hoping you'll release me immediately. I see my future elsewhere."

Manfred shifted his head sideways, a frown forming. "You do not see yourself with Mr. Benneton once this is all over? After all, once he has paid my fee, he will be free of his wife and you will be welcomed in his home, I'm sure."

Natalie guffawed. "I'm sure that's what he thinks. But I don't think my future lies with Benny," she said, turning her attention away from Manfred and gazing out into the lagoon.

"Hmmm," he said under his breath. "That is interesting Ms. Grainger. And food for thought."

Natalie didn't notice Manfred's lurid gaze. The island was a tropical paradise and she had taken to lounging daily in her bathing suit which she had thankfully packed before flying to Hilton Head. Most of the clothing in the one bag she had smuggled with her from St. Barths was a combination of evening wear and casual beach clothing. The bathing suit, with a scarf as a wrap around her waist, had become her daily fare.

As she continued to stare out into the gentle waves of the lagoon, she ignored Manfred as he slowly stood and stared at her one last time before heading back to the villa. His face was a mask of consternation. Had she known even a tenth of his thoughts at that moment, she would have shuddered in utter fear.

Chapter Thirty-Seven

The best way to utilize the boat for a getaway vehicle was to get to know the driver. He wasn't Caribbean like most of the others, but some kind of eastern European. His accent was heavy but his English was fluent. He was a dark, brooding man in his late forties, Natalie guessed. About five foot five, he was shorter than Natalie and with slicked back hair, reminded her of a Russian bad guy in a B-rated movie. She knew he occasionally stayed over in one of the guest suites just down the hall from her own. But he was always gone before she woke up. He must take the boat back to the mainland very early in the mornings.

Natalie watched him as he maneuvered the boat in reverse alongside the dock for the third time this week. She caught him stopping now and again to watch the rear ends of the younger female workers as they bent to pick up bags from the hold. A letch. Of course, he would be.

But Natalie knew how to deal with his type, had done since adolescence when her own body had betrayed her to men as something they could stare at incessantly, sometimes touch if they felt the desire, and only if they were willing to pay her price.

In time, she had learned not to hate how men looked at her but to use her looks to her advantage. She could get men to do anything for her, once she had captured their attention. She knew the driver had watched her a couple of times but she had turned away and had no idea if his leering gaze continued once she'd disengaged, or if he had turned his attentions elsewhere.

Regardless, it was time to turn it on. She needed to get on that boat and if she had to go through the driver to get to it, she knew exactly how to start the process.

He wasn't particularly chatty though as she found out later that afternoon when she had placed herself on the dock prior to his departure. He had watched her carefully, perhaps wondering if she was going to jump on. *Does he have orders not to let me on the boat?*

She offered to release the bow line and threw it lazy into the side as he drew away. He nodded his head slowly, then turned his attention to maneuvering out into the lagoon.

Two days later, when he arrived late in the afternoon, she hurried down to the dock to help tie off the bow. The driver nodded as she gestured for him to throw it to her. Once moored, she stepped into the boat and grabbed a couple of the bags.

"I'm Natalie," she said. He turned and gave her an appraising look.

"I know."

"Do you work for Mr. DeVries?" she said, turning and stretching more than usual to step up to the dock. She had removed her towel and knew the fabric of her bathing suit bottom would be tight across her ass.

"No, I work for the local co-op," he said. "A taxi driver, kind of. Mr. DeVries owns the company."

"Like in Venice," Natalie was poised on the dock in what she considered one of her best model poses, the two grocery bags hanging from her arms on either side.

He squinted, looking puzzled.

"You know, no cars or buses. Just boats along the canals. Even the taxis are boats."

"Ah, of course," he said, the beginning of a grin forming, ever so slightly. "Yes, something like that, yes. But not canals, open ocean." He swept his hands in front of him, as if to take in the entire Atlantic.

Natalie smiled. And waited. The driver grabbed a box and adroitly jumped onto the dock from the side of the boat which swayed sharply as he leapt. He landed close to Natalie.

"I am Yuri," he said, nodding slightly. "Please, after you."

Natalie sashayed toward the kitchen, passing the other staff who were coming to meet the boat.

They dropped their bags on the counter and Natalie followed Yuri down the hall past her own room. Yuri stopped and looked up at her as he entered his room.

"If you don't have to rush back, would you like to join me for a drink on the patio?" Natalie asked. "I can make a mean Rum and Coke."

Yuri opened his door and Natalie watched as he dropped a set of keys into a small bowl on the desk right inside the room.

"I would like that very much but Mr. DeVries wouldn't like it," he said. "But I have a bottle of vodka here. Perhaps after supper, you could meet me here and we could have a nightcap."

Oh boy. How predictable.

"As you say, Manfred wouldn't approve. But perhaps another time, on the dock maybe, before you leave tomorrow? "There aren't many people here to talk to, you know. It would be nice to talk to someone different." Her emphasis on people and someone different told Yuri she meant a man. At least, she hoped he got it. His grin told her he had.

"I leave very early in the morning, around six am. But perhaps you could come before I go. We can talk quietly in my room, so as not to disturb anyone, yes?"

"Okay then," she said and continued down the hall. "Later," she said, waving her hand over her shoulder and wiggling just a little more than she normally would. It would have been better to have been in heels but she'd look like a hooker in a bathing suit, so the flip-flops would have to do. Her bum would do its job. She could feel his eyes boring into her as she turned the corner out of the hallway.

Early in the morning. What an idiot!

Chapter Thirty-Eight

That night, Natalie set the tiny alarm clock radio in her room to four-thirty figuring that would be early enough to roam around the house before anyone else got up, especially Yuri. It was still dark out but once her eyes adjusted, there was enough light from the three-quarter moon filtering in for her to quietly get out of her room and make her way down the hallway.

She was in bare feet, carrying her flip-flops. The flooring was some kind of poured concrete so there was no creaking of floorboards. As she approached Yuri's room, she didn't see a light under the door. Good, he was still asleep. If she could grab the keys, race to the boat and leave without being seen, no one would think anything of the motor noise. Yuri said he left early in the morning; the staff were used to it.

She gently tried the knob and to her surprise, it turned. With the door open a crack, she could hear heavy breathing and leaned in till she could just make out the top of the desk beside the door. She reached in and searched for the bowl where Yuri had dropped his keys the day before.

She found the bowl. But no keys.

Just then the heavy breathing stopped and she heard a rustling. He was getting out of bed!

She quickly pulled her arm back and was about to shut the door slowly when a hand reached around and gripped her wrist. Then the door flung open and Yuri stood there, hair mussed, shirtless, in jeans.

"I didn't think you were coming," he said, his voice husky and alert.

Had he really been sleeping?

He began to pull her into the room, his grin evidence of what he was thinking.

"No, this was a mistake," Natalie said, trying to free her arm.

"But I thought you wanted to talk to someone different," he said, opening the door wider with his free hand.

Natalie grabbed the door jam and was stretched out as Yuri pulled her arm. "No Yuri, I don't think so. Another time, ok?" she yanked but his grip was strong. His eyes were a little glazed she noticed. He'd already had some vodka no doubt. That wasn't good.

"I think I know what you need," he said. "Something different, right?" And with that, he let go of the door and grabbed his crotch, his other hand still firmly holding Natalie's wrist.

Natalie flinched. "Oh my God, no. Not now. Not here!" she said, hoping her resistance was seen as a short-term problem and not some kind of permanent rejection. She wasn't really afraid. All she had to do was scream and everyone would be alerted, Manfred included. Yuri knew that and she could tell he was thinking that very thought right now. He was watching her closely, his leery grin edged with just a tinge of wariness.

He loosened his grip just enough for Natalie to pull her hand away. She backed out of the room quickly.

"Another time Yuri, another time," she said coyly, then purposefully checking both ways in the hallway, she quickly tiptoed back to her own room. As she stepped in and pulled the door behind her, she glanced down the hallway. Yuri was leaning on the door jam, his grin a full smirk now. His other hand was around his crotch and he was hefting it and squeezing, his tongue licking the edge of his lips.

Natalie rolled her eyes, closed and locked the door from the inside. There would have to be a better way. Seducing Yuri would mean she would have to go all the way. But he was probably demented, so it wouldn't be a simple roll in the hay. If she became desperate, it was still an option, but definitely a last resort.

She wasn't that desperate yet.

Chapter Thirty-Nine

Natalie went back to bed and slept past her usual wake up time, her brain taking a long time to settle after the run in with Yuri. She knew now that if she was going to sneak on the boat with Yuri's help, she would have to give him what he wanted. He was attractive in a European way, but vulgar, and...well, short. She smiled to herself. She couldn't possibly contemplate sleeping with the guy; she'd given up that lifestyle after meeting Benny. No more one-nighters, no more dead-end relationships. That had been the deal she had made with herself five years ago.

Oh, she knew she was capable. It was just that it seemed like some kind of a betrayal to the promise she had made to herself.

No, she would find another way.

She eventually made her way out to the kitchen where some of the staff were preparing lunch.

"You missed breakfast Miss Natalie," Emerald said as Natalie strode in.

"I was up late last night, thinking," she said. "Is Yuri gone?"

Emerald raised her eyebrows and gave Natalie a hard look. "What you want with that one?" she asked.

Natalie smiled. "No, nothing like that Emerald. I was just going to ask him to get me some shampoo on his next trip. I've missed him?"

She frowned, unconvinced and turned back to the dishes in the sink. "He left at his usual time, around six this morning, I think. You can ask him day after next. He'll be coming from the mainland again." She turned back to Natalie, her smile returning. "Can I make you some eggs?"

Natalie shook her head. "Thank you, I can wait till lunch." She turned, grabbed an apple from the bowl in the middle of the counter, and left the kitchen.

Chapter Forty

The next afternoon, Natalie was waiting for Yuri to return, all the while thinking of a way to sneak onto the boat at night and hide under a tarp or something. As the boat closed in on the dock, she noticed he had a passenger.

Emma Benneton stepped out onto the dock, shielding her eyes from the sun, and noticed Natalie staring at her.

"Hello my dear," she said as she approached, reaching for Natalie's drink and taking a sip. "Hmmm. Delicious. Perhaps I'll have one before dinner."

"You have to get me out of here," Natalie said, grabbing the older woman's forearm. Emma stared down at it until Natalie let go.

"No, this is working just fine dear," she said, a grin right out of *The Wives of Beverly Hills* on her face.

"Where's Drew?" Natalie asked.

Emma's face clouded. "I don't know," she said putting the drink back on the table and frowning. "That's one of the things I want to ask Manfred."

She turned and walked toward the house.

Natalie usually ate alone or with Emerald in the kitchen. But with Emma's arrival, the staff were busy preparing for a formal dinner and Emerald told her that Master DeVries had asked for her to join them at six.

"I don't like that woman," Emerald said.

"That makes two of us," Natalie replied, drying dishes Emerald washed.

"I say she up to no good," the older woman continued. "You see in her eyes. Very cold, very--how you say, snister?"

"Sinister," Natalie smiled. "Yes, that's a good word for her."

"You know her?"

"She is doing business with Mr. DeVries," Natalie said. "We've met before."

"Like that other woman he brings here," Emerald said. "She has cold eyes also." Her gaze wandering in thought.

"You mean Diane? I thought she was his partner?"

Emerald snorted. "She might want it, true, but Master DeVries see through her. He no marry a witch like that."

Natalie had suspected Diane was Manfred's mistress or something similar. But she now knew the woman was a part of this whole Emma kidnapping caper somehow, but couldn't figure where she fit into things. And where was the woman, anyway? Natalie had seen no one other than Manfred and the house staff since arriving.

"Is Diane on the island often?" Natalie asked.

"No, she visits once in a while and she and Master DeVries have dinner and talk till well into the night," Emerald said. "She always leaves the next morning. As will this one, I hope."

Perhaps, Natalie thought. And I'm going to be on that boat with her. Somehow.

Chapter Forty-One

Natalie hadn't packed much in the way of dinner wear, but she threw on a loose t-shirt over her bathing suit bottom and tied a light towel around her waist so it resembled a skirt.

Emma, of course, was impeccably dressed in a flowered summer dress that hugged her figure. *How does this woman always make me feel second rate?*

Manfred was in khaki's and a button-down shirt with leather sandals on his feet. He made them both a drink at the dining room bar and then led them out to a patio that Natalie hadn't seen before. It faced the forest and was about twenty feet square. In the center of the space was a six-person table set with white tablecloth and shiny silverware. A canopy protected the table from heat and rain and the chairs had plush matching cushions. Manfred pulled out one of them and motioned for Natalie to sit. Emma stood at the side of the table waiting and once Natalie had sat, Manfred repeated the process for her.

At least I was first.

Emma and Manfred chatted idly about the island and how it compared to St. Barths. Natalie sat quietly, listening and watching their engagement. They acted like neighbors at a street party, both amiable but with an underlying lack of real interest in what the other was saying.

"Where is Drew?" Natalie said during a lull in the conversation. Both of them turned to look at her. Emma grinned. Manfred took a sip of his drink.

"Diane is looking for him," he said finally. "When we find him, we will all have a discussion."

Natalie caught a nervous grimace from Emma but didn't acknowledge it.

"He fell in love with you, you know," Manfred said. "That's why he went rogue."

Emma looked at him, then at Natalie, her brow furrowed.

"He'll come to get you, I think," Manfred continued. "Eventually. So, while Diane is out there looking for him, I think he will come here looking for you."

Emma crossed her arms and leaned back.

"How would he know I am here?" Natalie asked, glancing at Emma.

"He knows Mrs. Benneton is here to receive her payment," Manfred said. "Normally, Scanlon would be here to return you home once the transaction is completed."

It was if he was reading her mind, though her idea had been to smuggle herself out. Perhaps Emma was prepared to take her along anyway.

"But I think we'll wait and see if he shows up," Manfred continued. "If he doesn't, then Diane will take you back."

"What if Benny doesn't pay?"

"Then you won't be leaving," he deadpanned.

Natalie looked at Emma but the latter's face was expressionless. Emerald was right. She was a witch. Natalie didn't think she really cared whether Natalie left the island or not. But if Benny didn't do his part, Emma might not be leaving either.

"You think that's enough incentive to make him pay?" Emma asked, apparently reading Natalie's mind.

"You had better hope so because if I threaten to harm you, I have a feeling it won't alter the man's demeanor."

Emma was speechless. Natalie could see that last remark had surprised her. The calm, calculated bitch had misplayed her hand.

"You're disgusting," she finally said.

"But accurate," he answered.

Natalie understood now that it was more important for her to be a prisoner here than Emma, which only made her want to escape even more. She could leave Emma to her fate here with Manfred. But she didn't fully believe him either. She didn't really think he was going to let her simply leave, with Diane or Drew.

Emma pushed back her chair and stood erect. "I see no point in further banalities Mr. DeVries. I will retire to my room and read if that's alright with you. William will be depositing the money in your account tomorrow at precisely four o'clock. I will be in your office with my computer at that time. We will make the final transfer and I'll be on my way the following morning. I see no point in staying here any longer than I have to."

Manfred didn't seem perturbed by Emma's sudden outburst and without looking up gave a short wave of his hand, as if to dismiss her.

She grunted, stamped her foot, and left in a huff.

Manfred leaned back and stared into the forest. Natalie wondered whether she should excuse herself or stay.

"I understand she planned to go to South Africa when this is over," he said quietly. Natalie wondered why he was telling her. Besides, Emma had told Drew and her that she would be going to Greece, not South Africa. Had Emma lied to Manfred? Of course she had. She didn't want the man to know where she was.

"How do I know you'll let me go when it's over?" she asked quietly.

He turned to look at her. Cocking his head slightly, his eyes looking over her face as if analyzing it, he said, "Because if you go back, Mr. Benneton won't waste time looking for his wife. He'll have you. And once you assure him that all is well at this end, he won't pursue me either." He reached for his drink and took a long sip. "That's how it always works. The mark gets what he wants. I get what I want. And the wife gets to disappear. With more of the mark's money than she would have ever got in a divorce."

"So that's how this scam works?" she said.

"It has been working remarkably well for several years now, Miss Grainger," he said. "You'd be surprised how many rich wives are aging and feel they may be traded in for a younger model. They want to cash out without going through a messy, unpredictable and very public divorce." He leaned back and crossed his arms. "But this is the last time. I am getting tired of the work involved. And it appears some of my employees are also getting bored with the current arrangement."

"You mean Drew?"

"I knew it would happen sooner or later," he said, placing his drink down again. "Falling in love with one of you, I mean."

Natalie tossed back her head and smirked. "I don't think that's why he's disappeared," she said, then immediately regretted it.

Manfred rubbed his chin and looked at her. "You are a very beautiful woman, Miss Grainger. Don't short change yourself. Mrs. Benneton is a charming and sophisticated woman in her own right, but there is no comparison. Scanlon will come for you. Of that, I am quite certain. And then, one way or another, you will be going back to the Carolina's."

Natalie's stomach had knotted up but she realized Manfred had misinterpreted her meaning. He thought she meant that Drew had fallen for her. Of course, if he knew the truth, he'd change that way of thinking immediately, and certainly wouldn't let Emma leave the island. She smiled. He had also paid her a compliment though, one she was prepared to accept, regardless of its source. Manfred DeVries was dark and dangerous. But he didn't seem to be a letch: He hadn't approached her even once the entire time she'd been on the island. And he thought she was beautiful.

Perhaps he intended to let her go after all.

Chapter Forty-Two

Dinner had ended abruptly when Manfred had excused himself, saying he had to prepare for Benny's pending ransom payment.

"I suggest you have an early night. After all, you may be leaving tomorrow," he said.

And with that, he had left, refreshed wine glass in hand, presumably for his office.

Natalie sat for a minute or so, wondering what to do and who to believe. She needed to think things over. But she wasn't going to sit in her room and wait it out. She could start by asking Emma why she had lied to either Manfred or her about where she was going. It didn't really matter of course, but it would pass time and help keep her mind off what was going to happen next.

After quickly checking Emma's room and the other common areas, including the outside patios, Natalie decided Emma had taken a walk into the woods. She didn't think Emma was the hiking type, and the woods quickly became jungle behind the villa, so she figured the woman hadn't gone far. Grabbing a sweater from her own room, she headed to the trail at the back of the villa and was about to enter the woods when Emerald yelled.

"Miss Emma said she was going to the beach, my dear," she said, pointing into the woods. "It's on the other side of the island," she added. "Just follow the trail."

Surprised that Emma would venture that far, Natalie quickly followed. After about a hundred yards, the trail changed from a paved walkway to a stone path, and eventually little more than flattened foliage. The unfamiliar large plants and tall grasses seemed to close in on her as she continued. She looked behind her now and again and kept reassuring herself she wouldn't get lost. Occasionally, the trail would wind close to the water's edge and the forest would open up to a haphazard clearing where she would see small stretches of sandy beach. This truly was a tropical paradise, reminding her of the Tom Hank's movie Manfred had referred to: *Castaway*. It was secluded and deserted away from the villa. The surroundings felt so wild, so primitive and untouched. And although Manfred had tamed a small portion of the island, creating a small swath of civilization, Natalie realized the island was still essentially jungle. She had seen several species of multi-colored birds, and rustling in the tree tops made her nervous. Monkeys? Snakes? She could only imagine. A person could easily get lost here.

Just then, Natalie heard a louder rustling and from pure instinct, she jumped behind a large tree trunk just off the trail. She stood, her back to the tree, as the rustling grew louder, now sounding like footsteps hurrying down the trail. As the person reached her hiding spot, she peeked out to see if it was Emma. It wasn't but she recognized who it was and stepped out.

"You came to rescue me," she said. It wasn't really a question but she was curious. After all, she wasn't really sure who's side he was on.

Drew Scanlon cocked his head and grinned, stopping just in front of her. His hair was disheveled and his pants had dirt stains on them, as if he'd crawled through some mud.

"Actually, I'm here to get my mother off the island once the money transfer is completed," he said.

Natalie sighed. Manfred considered Drew a traitor, and now so did she. "You don't trust Manfred?"

"I've never talked to the women after a transfer. I don't really know if they disappear on their own terms... or his."

Natalie felt a shiver race up her spine. "But the girlfriend goes home?"

"Up till now, yes."

"So, what do you usually do?" she asked. She meant in normal situations, assuming he and Manfred had done this before. Drew misunderstood.

"Like I said, once Benneton makes the transfer, I grab her and we get out of here."

"And you figure I'm safe," she said.

"He's never harmed the security before," Drew said. "It's sort of a guarantee that the mark never comes looking for him. The wife gets what she wants and the mark gets his security back."

"He'll just send me back to Benny, is that it?" she asks, her hands on her hips. "Don't you usually do that?"

Drew's puzzled look demonstrates that he hadn't really given that much thought.

"And what if I tell him I don't want to go back to Benny?"

"Why wouldn't you?"

"It's not going to work."

"Because of me?" he said, his puzzlement deepening.

"Don't flatter yourself. I don't need *any* man to rule my life anymore. Not Benny, not Manfred, and certainly not you."

"So you want me to leave you here then?" he said, his smirk an expression Natalie had never seen before on Drew.

She gave him an incredulous look. "If Manfred finds out you're here and what you're planning, he'll kill you and Emma. Then he won't let me go; I'll know too much."

"I'm waiting till the transfer is complete and he ships you home," Drew said. "He never lets the wives go until every contingency is accounted for."

"You'll wait till I'm gone, then rescue your Mother?"

Drew didn't answer and Natalie realized that once the money was safe, he planned to take Emma immediately and leave her to whatever Manfred had in mind. But if Emma escaped, would Manfred let it go or chase after them? *And will he send me back to Benny first, or just kill me so he's free to chase Drew and Emma? Shit!*

A few seconds later, it became clear to Natalie that she had been right in thinking she had to get off the island soon. Watching Drew, his eyes narrowing at the same speed her mind was working, it was obvious he knew that was a possibility too. She had to assure him she was demure and willing to play along. She decided to change the subject. "Where are you going to hide?"

"This is the tropics," he said, cautiously, his eyes gradually returning to normal and his demeanor changing to nonchalance. "A tree will do just fine."

Natalie frowned. Drew shrugged.

If he wanted to be macho and spend the evening in a tree with slithering species, bugs, and other crawling surprises common to jungle surroundings, he was welcome to it. After a few moments, she realized he would most likely go back to the boat that must have brought him here and hide out. She would follow him and see where it was hidden. Then later, when he went to the villa to find Emma, she could go to the boat and get the hell out of here.

Drew was staring at her. She had the uncanny feeling he could read her mind. But there was nothing more to say. She needed him to head to his boat, get supplies, whatever.

She shrugged, turned, and headed back the way she had come, back to the villa. She would have to come back later, after dark, and search nearby this spot to find Drew's boat. Escape was paramount now. Of course, traipsing around this clearly unused portion of the jungle at night was not appealing. But waiting to see what Manfred would do once Drew took Emma away was a fear she couldn't put into words. She was still debating whether to tell Manfred that Drew was on the island. But then, that might thwart her own escape plans. One thing she knew for sure was that she couldn't be here if Drew succeeded in getting Emma off the island.

She briefly wondered what would happen to Emma and Drew if she escaped before them and her stomach tightened at the prospect of Manfred's rage. Then she sighed. She had to figure out a way they could all escape together. She knew Drew wasn't worried about leaving her in Manfred's clutches but she couldn't do that to them. However twisted Emma was, and no matter how devoted to his mother Drew was, Natalie just couldn't leave them to face the wrath of the calm, unpredictable, and eerily scary Manfred, the Dutchman.

Chapter Forty-Three

Drew couldn't decide whether he'd been happy to see Natalie, or frustrated because of the obvious complication. His mother had warned him that getting too close to her would make it more difficult to treat her as negotiating chattel if push came to shove. And she had been right. Natalie wasn't the first of his charges--the security--that he had tried to bed during the vacation period of the kidnapping. She was the first failure, however. The Dutchman had told him he was good at his job: confusing the security, making them question whether in fact they wanted to go back to the husband or not; standard Stockholm syndrome with a minor variation. Manfred had insisted that, short of getting them to fall in love with him, he wanted them to be so shattered when he sent them back, that they went running to the husband, demanding comfort. This, of course, distracted the husband from the possible attempt at following the wife, at least for a while. Often, the security was so hurt from being dumped by Drew that when they were shipped back to the husband, they demanded marriage, or at the very least co-habitation. It helped them get over Drew. And it kept the husband occupied while everyone else disappeared.

But Natalie was different. Although Drew had gotten off to a good start at the hotel on Hilton Head the first night with his shy act, she had effectively sidestepped any advances he had made since. He knew she was doubting her relationship with Benneton, they all did that. But she wasn't ready to have an affair with him either which had made her more difficult to control. Figures that this, the most important kidnapping, the one that he and his mother had been working on for months, was the one that involved a mistress who wasn't easily seduced by Drew. A little ironic really: Natalie said she didn't want to go back to Benneton now. And his mother had given up on the old man years ago. What an insane fool he must really be. And what a complication that had become.

Throughout all their planning, neither he or his mother had counted on Benneton being in love with Natalie in the beginning. Still, it was better he was, because with Natalie safely trapped on this island, having just been snatched literally from Benneton's grasp, the old man would be ready to finish the deal with no hiccups. The poor sap was probably ready to send the money right now and get his little girlfriend back. In future jobs, the Dutchman would do well to actually plan for the mistress to take a visit back to the husbands, just to remind them what was waiting once the ransom was paid.

A rustling in the long grass brought his thoughts back to the present and, thinking Natalie had returned, he turned toward the path.

"You need to deal with that girl, son," Emma Benneton said wryly. "She needs to be back at the villa where Manfred can see her. We can't have him distracted looking for his security. We're too close to finishing this."

Chapter Forty-Four

Natalie stared at the boat. Bobbing gently in the low, lapping shoreline waves, it was partially hidden by a rocky outcrop on one side, and a small outward curve of the land which, when combined, created a tiny inlet that protected the small vessel from the open ocean.

She had driven ski boats during spring break at a friend's cottage and this one didn't look too much bigger, about twenty feet or so. It was a lot wider though and she briefly worried about how she would dock it when she reached Sint Maarten. *Shit, what am I thinking. If I make it that far, I'll throw the anchor out near shore, jump off and swim the rest of the way.*

"You need to stay here Natalie," Drew said, stepping out from some bushes.

Natalie spun her head to see Drew standing directly on the path behind her. He'd read her mind, and he'd followed her.

"No, I need to get off this island," she said.

"If you go, my mother's life will be in danger. You're her security."

Natalie turned back to the boat. Was this how he had gotten to the island?

As if reading her mind, he stepped closer. "Sint Maarten is quite a ways away," he said, grinning.

She knew that already. "I'm going Drew. What happens here now is your problem, not mine." She started toward the bow, her jaw set, her eyes focused on the boat, anchored just a few feet out in the inlet. Could she just wade out? Were her arms strong enough to pull herself up and over the railing? Maybe she could swim to the back. If there was a swim platform, that would be easier.

"He'll hunt you down," Drew said. His tone had changed. She stopped and turned to look at him. His eyes seemed to have darkened. "He can't let you get away Natalie," he continued. "You know where he is, you know where my mother is. He can't risk you telling Benneton. or worse, the authorities."

She continued staring. He was saying Manfred couldn't let her go but his tone made it sound like it was he who was going to prevent her escape.

"Even if you make it to Sint Maarten, you'll never get off that island. He owns people there. They'll stop you and bring you back."

"That's a chance I'm going to take," she said, all bravado, though what Drew had said shook her to the core. After all, the Dutchman had brought her back once already.

"You know I can't help you." he said.

"Does that mean you'll tell him?"

"Of course not. He doesn't know I'm here. And he can't know I'm here yet." Drew said.

She stared at him for a few moments, his dark eyes flatter than she'd ever seen them; cold, almost colorless. After a moment, he continued. "If you're not here when the ransom money is transferred, there is nothing stopping him from killing my mother right away."

"And you think me being here will prevent that?" she said.

"I do. He needs to send you back to Benneton and have him acknowledge that the deal is complete. That's the Dutchman's assurance that Benneton will never come looking for my mother. By sending you back, he is verifying that he has given my mother her share of the profits and she has gone. The whole deal hinges on Benneton never searching for my mother."

"And if no one looks for her, everyone will assume she's living happily ever after in some obscure pre-determined location, known only to you and her, is that it?"

"You understand then."

She turned and stepped into the water. Though not cold, the sudden wetness surrounding her ankles jolted her senses. "Sorry Drew. It's a nice plan, and well thought out. But you've missed one important aspect," she said over her shoulder, reaching for the bow line that led to the anchor loosely buried in the sand near the shore. "I'm not going back to Benny. I'm disappearing myself; from him, from you, and certainly from Manfred. I'm leaving...now!"

"Okay, okay, you win," he said, his voice sounding resigned.

She turned, surprised. His eyes were brighter. And he was smiling; well, grinning anyway; the same mischievous look he'd had at Orchid Beach that first day on Sint Maarten.

"Look, I get it, okay," he said, walking toward her. She was wary and held tightly onto the rope as if it were a lifeline. Knee deep in water, she felt vulnerable.

"I understand how you feel and I get why you have to go. So okay, go. I can deal with things here without involving you. But he will come after you. You need a weapon just in case. You will have to protect yourself. Do you think you could shoot someone, to save yourself I mean?"

The turnaround was so too quick and transparent but the idea had merit. "You have a gun?"

He nodded. "Back at my camp. Come on, I'll show you how to use it."

This was stupid. She would follow him, he would overpower her along the way, tie her up or something, take her back to the villa, and his problem would be solved. Natalie stood her ground.

"Okay, look, let's search the boat first," he said, stepping into the water. "I rented it from a fishing crew. Maybe there's something on here you can use as a weapon." He stepped by her, grabbed the edge of a stanchion and hoisted himself easily up and over onto the deck. He leaned over the bow and held out his hand.

"Come on, we have to be quick. The boat can't stay here for long. Someone will see it and report it to the Dutchman. You don't want to be here when that happens."

She grabbed his forearm and he clenched his hand around hers. She wasn't sure why she knew how to do that but then remembered. She'd seen Manfred do it that way when he'd pulled Drew out of the ocean during their sail.

Drew easily pulled her up and deposited her beside him on the deck. The fiberglass was slippery and she inched her way slowly to the edge of the windshield and hoisted herself around it and dropped down into the cockpit.

Drew followed and headed into the cabin so Natalie went to the back of the vessel. There were storage bins along each side and one large one she assumed would be under the huge cushion at the stern.

She found some coiled rope, a couple of flares and four life vests; nothing she could use as a weapon readily. There were a couple of wooden oars at the bottom of the rear compartment and she supposed she could use them to hit someone with. That was some assurance. But not much.

She could hear Drew rummaging things around in the cabin and wondered whether he would tell her if he found anything. If there was a weapon on this boat, it would be in the cabin. She started down the stairs.

Drew was underneath the cockpit in the narrow space between the deck and the hull at the rear of the boat. His legs were sticking out and he was stretched deep inside the cavity.

"What are you doing?" she asked.

His legs jerked a bit and in a muffled voice, he said "Jesus, you scared me." Then, "If someone wanted to hide something, this would be the best place to conceal it."

"What's back there?"

"The engine compartment," he said. "And I rented it from a not-so-legit fisherman." He rummaged a bit more, his rear end shifting as he adjusted his weight. It's watertight and there are a few places people can hide things. I know, I've done it myself."

She moved out of the way as he began sidling himself backwards out of the tight space. It was hard not to admire his butt as it continued to wiggle to and fro while he worked his way back out. She shook her head for clarity and held out her hand as his torso emerged.

"Thank you," he said as he slowly stood straight, leaning backwards a bit, hands on hips, stretching. "Man, there must be a better way to get in there."

"Probably from the back of the boat, on dry land," she said.

He grinned. "I'm sure you're right. Anyway, there's nothing of any use in there. Did you find anything?"

"A couple of oars. I used to play baseball as a kid. Might come in handy," she said.

The Security

"Come on, let's go and get you hooked up with something a little more, ah, effective."

He gestured for her to go up the steps. She took a quick look around and saw no real compartments for storage of any kind, other than some plastic dishes and a shelf with maps. She was about to start slewing questions at Drew when he jumped off the side of the boat into about a foot of water. He reached out with his arms willing her to jump. She was immediately flustered and seeing no other way to get off the boat gracefully, stepped out and into his arms. The water was chilly compared to the warm air and she hung onto Drew a little longer than she'd wanted to as he guided her over some submerged rocks and back onto the shore where he released her and began sloshing into the jungle.

After about ten minutes of winding through what must have been a path, though it certainly wasn't obvious, they came upon a small clearing. Drew went up to a fallen log and reached inside the cavity at one end. He pulled out a knapsack, unzipped it, and pulled out a small, silver pistol.

"What is it?" she asked, not sure if she wanted to hold it until she knew how it worked.

He handed it to her, holding the barrel and extending the hand grip.

"A Smith and Wesson .44. Accurate up to about five feet. If your target's farther away than that, there's a good chance you'll miss him."

"I thought bullets went long distances?"

"They do, but if you want any kind of accuracy, you need to practice. And since we don't have time for that, you'll just have to wait till your guy is very close."

His eyes bored into hers. Hands on his hips, she thought he was being a little arrogant.

"I'm sure I can hit the target, but I don't want to kill anyone."

"Then don't aim for the chest. Wait till he's closer and aim for his leg. It'll stop him from coming any closer but it won't kill him. Don't aim for the arm. You might miss and hit him in the heart."

Natalie winced.

"Or you could miss him altogether," Drew said. "If I had a silencer, you could practice. But I don't and if you shoot it now, someone will hear it and come looking for us," he said.

Natalie looked down at the gun in her hand and wondered what the hell she was doing. It was the second time this week someone had given her a gun and the last time she'd forgotten she had it when it might have come in handy. She figured her assailants had taken it.

"The safety's on?"

"Of course." Drew leaned toward her and with his forefinger, pointed out the small lever that turned the harmless piece of metal into a deadly weapon. She eyed it carefully, making a mental note of where it was on the gun's body.

"It's loaded," Drew said matter-of-factly.

"That's good. I guess"

"Yeah. Listen, if you use it." he hesitated and looked away momentarily. "Keep it behind your back with your arm straight down. Remember, your aim will be considerably better the closer your target is." He moved closer to her and took the hand holding the gun and gripped it in his. He stood inches away from her and pointed her hand, and the gun, toward his leg.

"Wait till he's this close," he said, his mouth so close, she could smell a fruity aroma. Had he been eating oranges? "Then slowly bring it around and touch his leg with the barrel like this." He placed her hand, now gripping the gun tightly, against his leg, the barrel pointing straight down just above his knee.

"Then squeeze gently. Don't jerk or it might do this." He pushed the barrel quickly and she could see that a bullet would have gone into the ground. "Hold your breath and squeeze slowly but decisively. He won't know what hit him until his kneecap is shattered and he can't stand up anymore."

Natalie shuddered and stepped back quickly. The gun hung down at her side. Drew stared at her, his eyes narrow and dark.

"Do you think you can do that?"

She didn't say anything, but her breathing got heavier.

"Don't pull the gun out unless you intend to pull the trigger. Unlike the movies, the sight of a gun doesn't necessarily stop people from attacking you. Most professionals will figure you don't have the guts and keep coming at you."

She nodded, her mind a little foggy, partially because of what he was saying, partially because he'd been so close again she was sure she could feel his heartbeat. *Could I shoot Drew?* She remembered his coldhearted attitude toward leaving her on the island just to save his mother. She thought about the dark look in his eyes when he'd stared at Manfred as the other man had pulled him out of the water. Then her mind quickly went back to how his shoulder muscles rippled as he stepped out of the shower back in Hilton Head.

Damn it!

Natalie made sure the safety was in the "on" position and slipped the gun into her pocket. Maybe it should be in the small of her back, in her waistband. She didn't know. It seemed more secure in her pocket. Drew watched but said nothing. She took a couple of steps backward and started to turn. Drew was watching her.

"Don't turn the boat around until you've backed well into the lagoon," he said. "You might get stuck in the sand."

She nodded her head. She couldn't think of anything to say. She just had a sudden urge to get off the island. She nodded, then turned and walked back into the dense foliage.

"Thanks" she yelled over her shoulder. There was no reply.

Chapter Forty-Five

Getting back to the lagoon was easier as the trail she and Drew had forged to get to his camp was still visible, though trampled foliage was slowly starting to spring back to its upright position, arching upwards as if magnetized by the sun's rays.

As she pushed back the last few branches at the edge of the lagoon beach, Natalie saw the boat and immediately realized there was something wrong with how it was sitting on the water.

Actually, *on* was the wrong word. The boat was sitting *in* the water. It had sunk about a foot and a half and was resting on the sandy bottom of the lagoon, listing toward the beach.

"Drew!" Natalie screamed, her tightened fists pounding the side of her legs. "You asshole Drew!"

She stared at the useless vessel, watching as sea water slowly seeped in over the port side and made its way down the hatch into the cuddy. He had sunk the boat. She wasn't sure how he had done it but thinking back on how easily he had let her come back alone, she was sure he had. He had coerced her into searching the boat for a weapon and then talked her into returning to his camp with him.

"Shit!"

Somehow he had opened a valve or even punched a hole in the hull while he'd been in the engine compartment and knew it would eventually sink low enough to render it useless.

With one last scream of annoyance, she turned and stormed down the same path yet again. She'd had it with him.

As she purposefully rammed herself through the semi-erect jungle fauna once again, she reached into her pocket and pulled out the gun. Was she mad enough to use it on Drew? She didn't think she could kill anyone. But Drew had shown her how to maim a man with a bullet to the leg. She fumed momentarily. Why the hell had he given her the gun, and worse, shown her how to use it? It didn't matter. Could she maim him? Yes. Well, maybe. After he'd ruined her best chance of escape from this ridiculous situation, yes, she could definitely consider it.

There was nothing at the clearing. She looked up into the trees but saw no sign of bedding or other camping items. She quickly went to the fallen log where Drew had hidden his backpack. Nothing.

She moaned and looked at the gun in her hand. What's the good of having a weapon if there's no one to shoot?

That's it, I'm done. I need a boat. She started toward the path she had followed earlier that morning, the one that lead back to the villa.

Fifteen minutes later she pushed passed the familiar palm that was like a doorway to the cleared villa property. Her shoes made a squishy noise as she stomped down the stone pathway leading round the villa to the front.

"Where have you been?" Emma stepped out from the verandah and stood firmly in Natalie's path.

"Where's Manfred?" Natalie said, her eyes blazing.

"He's inside, making phone calls," Emma said, stepping back slightly in reaction to Natalie's obvious fury. But she still didn't let Natalie pass. "Don't disturb him now. What he's doing is vitally important."

"I'm getting off this island," Natalie said, trying to push Emma out of the way. "And he's going to help me."

"I don't think so," Emma said, her eyes squinting. She grabbed Natalie's arm, preventing her from getting past her.

"Let go of my arm."

"Stop and listen," Emma said, her stern voice causing Natalie to hesitate.

"You're going home," she said, looking straight into Natalie's eyes, only a few inches apart. "Tomorrow morning."

"What are you talking about? And where is that idiot son of yours?"

Emma's eyebrow arched at the mention of Drew. "William is transferring the money, as we speak. Once that's verified, the Dutchman will want you on a plane, back to my darling husband." She smirked and let go of Natalie's arm. "To comfort him and assure him that all has gone according to plan."

Natalie was unsure what to think. Should she storm in on Manfred, tell him Drew was here, and convince him to search for him? Then when everyone was busy, steal a boat and try to find Sint Maarten in the middle of the Caribbean?

Or, should she do nothing and gamble that the Dutchman would send her back to Benny? A picture of Benny's face during his final outburst at the house on Hilton Head, popped into her head. No, she wasn't going back there. But she couldn't give up Drew. The odds of getting away at some point after landing back in Savannah seemed much more feasible than Plan A, the extended escape adventure from this island.

But Drew sank the fucking boat! She was mad and not thinking rationally and she knew it. But damn him. She wanted badly to smack his face. Or worse. She felt for the reassuring bulge of the gun in her pocket.

"Forget about my son," Emma urged. "You're going home now; in style I might add. Don't screw things up." She put both her hands on Natalie's shoulders and stared straight into her eyes.

"I need Drew for my part of this to work. You'll be safely on your way home first thing. If you don't want to stay there, fine. William can't hold you. Once this is over, you can go your own merry way." She gripped Natalie's shoulders tightly. "But until then, you need to play by the rules, so that everyone gets what they want."

"So you get your money and disappear?" Natalie said.

Emma nodded. "And I need Drew to help me set up my new life. We've been planning this for a long time." The last word was strained through clenched teeth. Natalie looked at the hands on her shoulders, then into Emma's eyes. Emma released her grip and stepped back.

"It's all up to you now," she said. "You can destroy everything, and probably get us all killed. Or you can relax and let the plan unfold as it was supposed to. And by the way, William will lavish you with gifts and money when you return."

Natalie stared at her. This was so screwed up. All she wanted was to get away from all of them: Emma, Manfred and this island, Drew, and yes, Benny. She suddenly realized that all she really wanted was a chance to be free of all the lying and cheating; free of the destructive nature of the people surrounding her. Free of the life she had been living for so long. She wanted to control her life, a normal life, whatever that was going to be now. Mostly, she wanted off this island, the sooner the better.

She stared at Emma momentarily, then forced her shoulders to relax, breathing from her lower stomach, controlling the stress, slowing her breathing.

"The plan calls for me to leave after Benny has transferred the money, correct?" Natalie said, her voice softer, calmer.

"Yes. Once the Dutchman acknowledges receipt of funds and divides the shares, you go home and Drew and I go... well, elsewhere."

"And you wait here until I leave?"

Emma smiled, though the effort didn't make it to her eyes. They nodded at each other in confirmation of their unspoken understanding of each other's goals, and what it would require for each of them to reach them.

Emma turned and briskly walked back to the verandah. Natalie watched her, head high, nose upright, hips swinging jauntily. She continued to stare even after Emma disappeared around the corner. She thought about going home, on an airplane. Which made her think of airplane food, and how hungry she was.

Chapter Forty-Six

It took about a half hour for Natalie to be sure no one was around. Emma and Manfred were dining in the living room and so she figured they'd be there for at least an hour or so, even if Emma eventually got angry and stormed off again. Manfred had sent an invitation for her to join them but Natalie had told Emerald she had a headache and was going to rest. Let the two of them reconcile or desecrate each other. Whichever route it took, she didn't care; she wasn't going to be there to witness it, either way. That would give her time to play detective.

Natalie purposefully strode down the corridor, then checked both directions before closing the door quietly, turning to take in the mostly teak and leather furnishings adorning the office belonging to Manfred. An oversized brown leather couch and matching chair dominated one end of the office, strategically placed just in front of floor to ceiling teak bookshelves. The end closest to the door was taken up by a huge teak desk. If the adage *'a clean desk shows an organized mind'* was true, then Manfred was in trouble because the top of the desk was covered with papers, pens and pencils, strewn everywhere, and Post-it® notes haphazardly stuck to pieces of paper all over. At one side, a new-model Mac dominated the desk and Natalie recognized the screensaver to be a picture of the Elysee, currently docked in Sint Maarten.

To the left of the desk and covering nearly the entire outside wall was a huge picture window facing a quiet edge of the lagoon. She figured this was so the Dutchman's view wasn't disturbed by passers-by. Perfect. No one would see her either. On the one wall remaining there were a series of black and white as well as some color photographs of oil rigs on water.

It had occurred to her that since Yuri hadn't kept the boat keys in his room, and there was no official place for them to be kept, like a hook near the back door or on a wall in the boathouse, then Manfred would keep them in one of his rooms. He could have kept them in his sleeping quarters but she wasn't sure she had the courage to go in there yet. Besides, the office was more logical, so it was her first choice.

She figured she had about an hour to find the keys, get to the supply boat, and put out to sea. There were no other boats at the dock so it wasn't probable Manfred could chase her. He had used the supply boat a couple of times also which was why the catamaran was only here once in a while. Drew had sunk the only other boat that was likely on the island. That left Sint Maarten. If Manfred did have someone waiting to head her off, what were the odds of them finding her amongst all the small vessels coming in and out of all the various harbors, not to mention all the quiet beaches that she could simply drive up on to the sand? Sint Maarten may be small by Caribbean standards but it was still over thirty miles of coastline to cover. She had thought about that while she was waiting in her room and decided not to head for Phillipsburg or even the marinas near the airport. She would follow the coast north until she saw something she recognized, say Dawn Beach or Orient Beach.

Surely I'd recognize those rocks and all the people kite surfing.

After beaching the boat somewhere, she would head to one of the restaurant shacks that dotted the various beaches and make a quick call to Oliver. He would get her to the airport. He'd know where to drop her off so she wouldn't spend much time out in the open.

Maybe he'll even buy the ticket for me so I don't have to be exposed in the departure lounge again.

She could hide in the washroom or something and rush through customs at the last second. She felt her stomach tighten.

I hope I've memorized Oliver's number right.

The top drawer wasn't locked and she began rifling through its contents, looking for the familiar blue float key fob. The guy was definitely unorganized; it was a veritable flea market inside.

"Excuse me sir." The voice came from right outside the door. Natalie recognized it as Emerald's.

"We're out of several staples since Mr. Yuri didn't take Olivia to the market today," Emerald continued.

"Why are you bothering me with that now?"

Natalie froze. It was Manfred and his voice was getting louder as he spoke. He was coming here!

"I just wanted you to be aware sir," Emerald said. "I was hoping you could tell me if a boat will be going tomorrow. I don't want to run out of things for you and your guests, sir."

Natalie frantically searched the room for a hiding place. How would she explain what she was doing there? Had Emerald seen her sneak in and was trying to buy her time to hide? The knob began to turn as she stared at it mesmerized. The couch. She could squeeze behind it, between it and the bookshelves. But if he walked around, to get a book or something, he would see her right away.

There was no other choice. She quickly scrambled round the couch and slid onto all fours, pushing herself up against the backside of the couch. The smell of the leather filled her nostrils. Normally she loved that smell. She could only hope it's reassuring odor was a sign that it would keep her hidden from view until Manfred left again.

She had missed whatever else Manfred had said to Emerald and when the door opened, he was alone. She heard his footsteps as he entered and stepped behind the desk. Then some papers shuffling. His breathing was heavy and that reminded her not to hold her breath but breathe slowly and as quietly as possible. She didn't want to take in a sudden breath of air and risk being heard. Luckily, the shuffling of papers was significant enough to cover her shallow air intakes. She wondered how long he planned to be here. Not that she was going anywhere.

"There you are," another female voice suddenly broke the semi-silence. "We need to talk."

Natalie recognized the voice. It was Diane! What the hell was she doing here?

"You're late," Manfred said, still shuffling papers. "You said you'd be here by three. The transfer is coming through today. You need to set up the next operation. Drew will be finished by tomorrow night and be ready to go with the next client.

"He's here," she said. Her voice sounded strained, a little higher pitched than Natalie recalled.

"Who?" said Manfred.

"Drew Scanlon. He's on the island. And we need to find him and do something about him," she said. The shuffling stopped. Her voice had moved further into the room. She was probably standing in front of the desk facing Manfred.

"Of course he's here. He'll take the girl back stateside tonight," Manfred said. "Once I've had a little...ah, word with him."

"He's FBI."

"That's ridiculous," Manfred said indignantly. "He's been with us for five years. "

"Then why is he hiding on the other side of the island?" she said. There was silence for a moment. She continued, "Besides, my source in Washington is positive. Drew Scanlon is a federal agent and is still very much on the government's payroll. And he specializes in kidnapping."

"Specializes?" asked Manfred.

"He has quite a reputation for finding victims and bringing them back alive," she said. "That's what he was doing when you recruited him."

"That's insane," said Manfred, his tone clipped. "He's been with the girl the whole time. And he could have rescued the Benneton woman anytime. "

"That's what worries me," Diane said. "Whatever he's doing, it's not about one kidnapping case. He infiltrated our operation intentionally. He's not trying to rescue anyone. He's trying to shut us down."

There was momentary silence. The blood was rushing to Natalie's temple. She wasn't sure if it was the position her body was in or the revelation that Drew was a Federal agent. That didn't make sense. He was here because of his mother, wasn't he?

"We need to get him off our trail" Diane said. "Before we start the next operation. Once he takes the girl home, we'll simply not contact him about the next client. He won't know where we are or who we're dealing with."

"No," Manfred said, his voice calm, his tone a little lower. "If he's hiding on the island, as you say, then he must have no intention of finishing his task for us and taking the girl home. He must be eliminated."

"We can't do that," Diane said quickly. "He's a Federal agent. We don't need that kind of attention."

"He will simply disappear," Manfred said, his voice eerily calm and assured. "Let me worry about that. We'll find out first if he's alone and if he's in contact with anyone nearby. If so, we will simply sever ties."

"And if he's alone?" Diane asked.

"Then he won't be leaving here alive."

Chapter Forty-Seven

The two spoke for a few minutes longer as Natalie tried not to squirm behind the couch. She still worried that either Diane or Manfred would wander behind and discover her, but it was secondary to her fear that she wouldn't be able to get to Drew and warn him.

What did it mean that Drew was an FBI agent? And if Emma was his mother, why would he be mixed up in her kidnapping caper, especially if he was, as Diane said, a specialist in preventing kidnappings?

It was too confusing, too much to think about right now. Diane eventually left and a few seconds later, she heard Manfred's footsteps head toward the door and then the door close. Then there was just silence.

She waited a few moments longer and then slowly crawled forward until she could glimpse around the edge of the couch and be sure both had left.

She then jumped up quickly and looked out the window. Nothing. She put her ear to the edge of the door, listened for a second or two, and slowly opened it.

The corridor was empty in both directions. She headed to the side door, the closest exit from the villa, sprinted across a small expanse of cut grass and disappeared into the cover of the jungle.

Ten minutes later she was pretty sure she had found the main trail to the other side of the island, the one she had used several times now. The foliage was flattened somewhat, showing a path of sorts leading more or less straight ahead. She half jogged--it was impossible to run quickly because of exposed roots and meandering growth--but remarkably, she recognized certain tree formations and shrubbery shapes and knew she was heading in the right direction. When the deep blue of open water peaked between the tree branches, Natalie knew she was reaching the western shore of the island. Almost immediately, she came upon the small lagoon where Drew's boat lay half submerged and was now listing even farther to one side. A brightly colored bird was perched on the outer edge of the boat and its large, red eyes followed Natalie as she jogged past.

It was a good job he burned his finger and cursed or she would have run into the clearing and fallen over him at full speed, or worse, tripped and fallen headlong into the small fire he was trying to put out. As it happened, Natalie stopped short, just as she entered the clearing.

"Hey," Drew said out of the side of his mouth. He was sucking his finger and quickstepping around the fire in obvious pain.

"Hey?" Natalie blurted. "That's the best you can do? You sank the damn boat. Now nobody gets off the island."

"I figured you'd come back sooner or later," he said, stooping down to pull a semi-burnt twig out from the burning embers. Natalie moved around so she would be facing him when he stood up. "You want some coffee?" he asked.

"Manfred knows your FBI," Natalie said.

Drew stared at her, his eyes narrowed slightly. "And how would you know that?"

"Because I just overheard Diane talking to Manfred about *'not needing you here anymore'*," she said.

Drew stood up and his stare intensified. His eyes moved away from hers and she realized he was looking just over her shoulder.

"Actually, what he said was that he didn't need you anymore; here or anywhere else."

Natalie turned to where the voice had come from. Diane looked like she didn't run much. Her face was flushed and with one hand, she brushed loose hairs from her forehead. Her other hand held a gun and it was pointed directly at Drew and Natalie.

"You followed her," Drew said, not as a question but with resignation.

"Ah, no kidding," she said, pointing her free hand at Natalie. "She made as much noise as a herd of elephants. I'm surprised the Dutchman isn't right behind me." Diane's facial expression suddenly changed, as if she had given up trying to play a tough broad. She dropped her hand and the gun pointed down to the earth. Drew turned toward the fledgling fire and ignored her. Natalie wasn't sure what was going on but any animosity seemed to have dissolved, almost instantly.

"What the hell were you thinking?" Diane said. "Letting her escape and go back to Benneton pretty much screwed up any trust the Dutchman had left in you."

"I wanted her out of the way before things got dangerous," Drew said, his attention on the fire, his voice quiet and calm. "When the Dutchman realized we were on to him, I figured he'd panic and disappear, eliminating any evidence in his wake."

"Well, he did just the opposite," Diane said. "He brought her back. And even though he knows you aren't who you said you were he still wants to

The Security

finish the operation as normal. He figures he can take care of you along the way." She shifted her weight and crossed her arms. "Actually, I think he's surprised you came back to the island. I'm sure he thinks it's out of character for you to fall for the security."

"I didn't fall for the security," Drew said, his head raising as he stepped closer to Diane. "I just wanted her out of the way."

Natalie felt like she was intruding. She knew they were talking about her. She was the security.

"Obviously, the Dutchman thought it imperative he bring her back. " He shrugged. "There's nothing I can do for her now. We'll just have to finish this the way I had planned," he said.

"The way you planned?" Diane blurted. "Your idiotic planning has put everything at risk."

"Hey, just what the hell is going on here?" Natalie blurted. They were talking about her life as if she wasn't here to provide input. Both of them turned to look at her blankly. Then they turned back to each other, Diane now with arms crossed, chin raised in defiance.

"You blew it," Diane said to Drew, ignoring Natalie's outburst. "Now leave it to those who know how to deal with phsyco's like the Dutchman."

Drew laughed. "If you're such a pro, how come I could achieve in six months what you've been trying to do for two years?"

"Will someone please explain to me what's going on?" Natalie said, stepping closer to both of them. She would step between them if she had to. "I thought you hated each other. You attacked her on the plane Drew!"

A grin formed on Diane's face and she stepped back a pace. "Yes, that was a bit harsh, I agree. You see, Drew seemed to think you would be easy to handle. So much for his renowned charm, huh?" She looked around the clearing as if searching for something. Then, eyeing a clump of thick tall grass, she went over, scrunched it down so its crushed density would allow her to sit, and perched herself on top of it. She looked at Drew and nodded her head toward Natalie but said nothing. Natalie turned to Drew who had watched Diane walk away and started to turn back to his fire. Natalie pushed her arm into his stomach, stopping him from bending over. He looked up.

"How were you going to handle me?" she asked. "Was I supposed to fall in love with you or something?"

Diane snickered. Natalie continued. "Was rescuing me off that boat, taking me to that hotel, was it all part of the plan?" Just thinking about how chivalrous she'd thought he was, how sexy he had looked in that shower, how romantic he had been after, only to find out it was all part of the elaborate plot. She was fuming. "And what about that day at Orient Bay? Was trying to seduce me part of the plan too?"

"Say, this is getting really interesting," Diane said from her perch.

"My job was to keep you away from Benneton, any way I could," Drew said. "I didn't plan for it to get personal--"

"Personal!" Natalie pushed her finger into his chest. Not expecting it, Drew stumbled back a step. "How could it not get personal. You were protecting your own--"

"Machismo," Drew interrupted. His eyes blazing into hers, his head dipped down as if to say *be careful what you say."*

Natalie drew a deep breath and looked at Diane. She had been about to say *your own mother* but decided against it now. Clearly, he hadn't told Diane of the connection. Still perched on her shrubbery cushion, Diane wasn't smiling or grinning anymore, just staring at the two of them. "You knew I was with Benny," Natalie said, changing the subject.

"That's why I thought it would be just another routine job," Drew said, nodding at Diane. "But then you told me your life story and I realized there was a chance you might not want to go back to him when all this was over."

"I thought the old coot was rich," Diane said, standing up and coming toward them. Her quizzical eyes bored into Natalie. "Not like Drew here, who is intent on protecting his, what did you say, machismo?"

"Believe it or not, there's more to being a mistress than just spending money," Natalie said.

"You're kidding, right?" Diane said. "Why do you glorified sluts always think the married dude will leave his wife and marry you? Diane asked.

Natalie reached forward and slapped Diane's face. Shocked but unhurt, Diane balled her fist and started to raise her arm but Drew grabbed her wrist.

"There's no time for this?" he said.

"The security doesn't get to hit me," Diane seethed, talking to Drew but facing glaring at Natalie. "I'm going to teach you how girls fight when this is over.

"You called me a slut," Natalie said, hoping Diane couldn't hear the fear in her voice. "I was never after Benny just for his money."

Diane laughed and stepped back and turned to Drew. "No wonder you couldn't control her, she's insane."

"Enough," Drew said, stepping between them, his arms in front of his chest protectively, just in case either of them decided to start slapping the other. "You have to go back to Benny, Natalie," he said. "Even if you leave again after a few days."

"She's not going back with you obviously," Diane said. "Manfred knows you're a Fed and he knows you're here," Diane said.

"Of course he does, you told him!" Natalie exclaimed. Drew stared at Diane.

"Yes, I did," Diane said, stepping away. She addressed Drew. "You need to either step back out of the way or join forces with us to get the job done right."

"You know I can't do that," said Drew. "I've worked a long time for this and I'm taking him down. He doesn't get out of a trial just because you have another agenda. He's committed multiple kidnappings. That's a federal offence and I can put him away for a long time."

Natalie wasn't really listening to Drew. She understood that he was a federal agent, though she knew she'd have to think about what that meant later when she had time to mull this mess over. She looked at Diane, the unknown entity.

"Who is us?" she asked.

Diane stared at Drew for a few seconds, then sighed and turned away. Drew watched her take a few steps toward the edge of the clearing.

"She's CIA," Drew said.

Natalie looked at him to be sure he wasn't trying to be funny. Then she looked at Diane's back. Suddenly she felt tired and dropped to her haunches in front of the now slightly burning embers.

"You two are fucking crazy."

Chapter Forty-Eight

"Come in Mrs. Benneton"

The Dutchman sat behind his desk, staring at a laptop, the forefinger on his right hand steadily tapping the mouse. He smiled and stood, sweeping his hand across his desk indicating for Emma to take a seat facing him.

"If I am to call you Manfred, then I insist you call me by my first name at least once before we conclude our business here," Emma said, her smile shallow but meaningful as she sat in the one chair facing him. She had every reason to be excited. Today was the day she would receive her share of the Benneton fortune. After years of being William's attractive trophy wife, then aging and eventually being deemed unsuitable for even that figurehead role, Emma felt she was finally being rewarded for many years of second-rate existence. Oh sure, William had provided the best homes, the best furnishings and toys, the best vacations, and yes, even a decent attitude towards her. But they had never been a happily married couple.

"And what are your plans once we are finished here, Mrs Ben...ah, Emma," Manfred said, staring at his screen.

Emma shifted in her seat. She wasn't accustomed to men not giving her their undivided attention. Yet she had learned while in this man's company social etiquette was not a priority. Smile maintained, she answered him.

"I will be disappearing Manfred. After all, that is part of the requirement for this endeavor, is it not?"

Manfred eyebrows raised slightly but he continued to stare at his screen, momentarily tapping the mouse and moving it around slightly.

"Has William signed on?" she queried, assuming that was what Manfred was fiddling with. Why else would he continue insulting her by working while she sat in front of him?

Suddenly, Manfred smiled, a huge grin from ear to ear. He gave the mouse a final tap, pushed his chair back and relaxed into it, looking at Emma for the first time since she had entered the office.

"It appears your husband is true to his word my dear," he said, smacking his knees with both hands and jumping up from his chair. He quickly walked around the desk and reached out to Emma who stood and allowed him to take both her hands in his. "The funds are deposited in my Cayman account and in a moment I will be transferring your share into your Swiss account, as you requested."

Emma grinned. "That is good news Manfred."

"Why don't you change into something a little more...say, "beach-ish" and we'll celebrate our mutual good fortune by having Emerald whip us up a late picnic supper."

Emma frowned. Although she was thrilled that the ordeal was finally coming to an end, she had no desire to spend any more time--especially social time--with this Neanderthal of a man. Manfred mistook her expression for one of uncertainty.

"Please," he said, shaking her hands up and down merrily. "Just a few moments of personal indulgence before parting ways. I have a favorite spot at Shell peak, the highest point on the island. The view is mesmerizing and a perfect place to celebrate the beginning of your new life."

Emma's eyebrows lifted. Perhaps a little wine and sandwiches overlooking the magnificent Caribbean would be a soulful moment of reflection before the whirlwind next stage of disappearing into the unknown.

"I would like to speak with our guest before she leaves Manfred."

Emma turned to see Diana come into the office and reach for one of Emma's hands. Manfred's eye twitched and he reluctantly let go of Emma.

"Just a few moments," Diana said. "You know, to go over some of her travel plans. I had a couple of ideas that may help."

Manfred stepped back and cocked his head, his eyebrow rising.

"I can then bring her up to meet you at the peak in a half hour or so. That would be alright wouldn't it?"

Manfred's confusion slowly turned into recognition and finally a devious grin. "Yes, of course," he said. "That would be fine. It will give me a chance to transfer your funds. I will, of course, bring you a printout of the exchange."

Emma looked from Manfred to Diana. She had hoped to see the verification of transfer on Manfred's computer personally. But then, he had already dismissed her so she would have to wait for confirmation regardless. She had no idea what Diana was talking about but knew there was likely a good reason for her to want to speak with her right now.

"If that is alright with you Manfred, that would be fine. She turned to the door. "I will look forward to seeing your transaction verification in a few moments."

"Of course," Manfred said and went back to his chair.

Chapter Forty-Nine

Special Agent Josh Burelli didn't like boats. He stood with his feet as wide as he could without it being obvious to the others that he had no sea legs whatsoever. The water was a beautiful dark blue and the waves were nominal at the moment--not like the whirlwind waves they'd experienced on the short trip from St. Barths to just off the coast of Shell Island. Although technically the Caribbean Sea, he knew he'd really been in the middle of the Atlantic on a boat not much bigger than his Escalade back home.

"Sir, Special Agent Scanlon is on the radio, sir," a voice yelled up from the cabin. The radioman had been manning the communications devices for the past hour while Burelli had been literally cooling his heels in the sloshing sea water that now trickled all over the small deck of the 35' cabin cruiser. He tore his gaze from what appeared to be a lush, natural island near the horizon, and slowly stepped down into the cabin, grabbing the microphone from the radioman.

"Jesus, Scanlon, where have you been?" he said, reaching up for a ceiling stanchion to steady himself. He didn't like being down here for long, not that bouncing around up top was any better, but he didn't like the feeling of knowing he was actually half underwater down here. A quick look out the elongated cabin window and he could see the menacing sea lapping against the hull just inches below the window line, and that was about the level of his chest.

"Minor change of plans," came a static-laden voice over the radio's tiny portable speaker. "My boat is inoperable. I have to wait until dark when I can steal the launch that the Dutchman's staff use for quick trips to Sint Maarten."

"How did that happen?" Burelli asked.

"It's a long story but we'll rendezvous sometime around eleven and I'll tell you all about it." Drew Scanlon said. "When is the landing scheduled for?"

Burelli looked out the tiny window, his eyes boring into the nearby island. "Just after midnight, so don't be late; I don't want you caught in the crossfire."

"I'm bringing the girl too," Drew said, his voice crackled over the airwaves but his determined tone was discernable.

"Like hell you are," Burelli said. "There's no room. Your job is to get the Benneton woman out of harm's way, then we go get the Dutchman."

There were a few seconds of silence, accented by the crackling, then, "Burelli, don't be an ass," Drew said.

The radioman snickered and Burelli gave him a hard look which didn't stop him but forced him to turn away so the lead agent couldn't see his smirk.

"She's an innocent and my job was always to get her back Stateside--"

"That was your job with the Dutchman," Burrelli snapped. "You're FBI. And in case you forgot, this is a government-sanctioned operation and there are always casualties in an operation like this."

"There won't be if I bring her with me," Drew said. "How many are in the landing party?"

Burelli knew Drew was purposely changing the subject but he glanced at the other men in the small cabin: two on the tiny couch, one sitting on the steps, and another edged into the head. They all stared back, their faces expressionless.

"Enough to do the job, Scanlon," he said.

"Then you do your job and I'll do mine," Drew answered. A couple of the men grinned. Burelli blew out a heavy breath.

"If you're not here by midnight, we're coming ashore," he said.

The line was quiet momentarily, aside from the constant static. "There's something else."

Burelli sighed.

"CIA is here," Drew said.

"Fuck!"

"One operative. A woman. But she's been infiltrated for a long time; longer than me actually," Drew said. "I can't control her so she might need to be neutralized."

Burelli slapped the microphone against his leg which caused feedback in the speaker. He quickly returned it to his mouth. "Goddamn CIA. We know why they're on the island."

"Doesn't matter," Drew said. "She's his right-hand man, so if she doesn't choose sides quick, she'll be in your line of fire and it'll be justified." One of the men cocked his head and raised an eyebrow.

"She knows about our invasion? Burelli said."

"Yeah, so you need to get to her before she has a chance to kill him," Drew said. "Something has held her back from doing it already and I'm not sure why but if she sees you coming, she may re-schedule and take him out before we can capture him."

"I don't want to mess with CIA, Scanlon," Burelli said. All the men were watching him intently. "I don't care if she's got a different agenda; they always do. But she's still an American. I won't take her out intentionally."

"Then the mission may fail," Drew said. "And after all I've been through to get us this close, failure isn't an option." Static pervaded for a couple of seconds. "I'll see what I can do to neutralize her."

"Just watch your clock, man," Burelli said. "It has to be tonight. The money's changed hands. He'll be leaving soon. We have to take him before he becomes mobile or we risk losing him."

"10-4. We'll be there."

The static continued but Burelli knew Scanlon had turned off his mobile unit. He dropped the microphone on the desk and slowly edged up the stairs again to the deck. The sun gleamed and the azure water glistened. Even the trees on the island gently moved with the tropical breeze. Peace pervaded.

Capturing the Dutchman would be an immense feather in his cap, he knew. Sure, he'd have to share some of the glory with Scanlon but Manfred DeVries was a huge win that could catapult his career up a notch or two. The plan was simple which was always the best. Not much could go wrong when you didn't plan too much in the first place. Get in, grab the perp, get out. Simple.

"Fucking CIA!" he exclaimed, but his expletive was carried off with the breeze.

Chapter Fifty

"What was all that about?" Emma asked, as Diane dragged her quickly down the corridor, away from the Dutchman's office, back to her room.

"We have to leave, now!" Diane responded, pulling at Emma to make her move faster. "Manfred has no intention of giving you any money."

Emma stopped in her tracks making Diane lose her balance momentarily. Emma's tone was stony.

"What are you talking about Diane?"

Diane dropped the other woman's hand and looked past her to see that no one was within earshot. "We need to talk Emma," she said, nodding her head toward Emma's room. "And then we need to escape."

"Be quiet Emma," Diane urged, reaching for her hand again. She then stepped closer, caressed Emma's cheek softly with her other hand, and gave her a kiss on the lips. "You have to trust me."

"Hmmm," Emma replied, her frown softening slightly. "You know I trust you Diane," she said. "I would never have had the strength to do this without your encouragement and... your inside information."

They reached Emma's room, stepped inside and closed the door behind them.

"Well, I see you have the right idea anyway," Drew said, standing up from the single high-back chair by the patio door.

"Drew!" Emma exclaimed, dropping Diane's hand and running over to give him a hug. Drew loosely responded but eyed Diane over his mother's shoulder.

"I gather William has sent the money?" Drew said to his mother, though he didn't remove his stare from Diane.

Emma stepped back, still holding Drew's arm. "As far as I know he has, yes. I'll get a verification shortly when I meet the Dutchman at Shell peak."

"You're not going to Shell peak Emma," Diane said firmly.

Emma turned, bewildered. "Why not? It's a small gesture of kindness, I think. The man's horrid I know but he's trying to conclude the transaction civilly. I really shouldn't disappoint him."

"Actually, he plans to kill you," Diane said.

Emma's eyebrows furrowed.

"You're sure?" Drew asked.

"Of course I'm sure," Diane said, stepping closer. "No woman has ever left this island alive."

"You must be mistaken," Emma said, turning to Diane. "How could you know that?"

"Because I watched him take the last woman up there," she said staring first at Emma, then at Drew. "And he came back alone."

"Why didn't you tell me this before...before we planned this thing?" Emma said, hands on hips, her bewilderment turning to anger. "I thought you loved me! How could you put me in danger like this?"

Drew frowned at his mother, then stared at Diane, suddenly understanding. No wonder his mother had lost any feelings for Benneton months ago. "Because she has an ulterior motive," he said, turning to the patio window and looking out. "You see Mother, you are lucky Diane seems to like your company because if she didn't she may have let you go with him today."

Diane said nothing.

Emma stared at the back of her son's head, and then at Diane. "You would have let him kill me?"

"Of course not," Diane said, stepping closer, placing her hands-on Emma's shoulders reassuringly. "Drew thinks he understands me but he doesn't know about us. I love you Emma. I could never let any harm come to you."

"And yet, here we are," Drew said, still staring out the window.

"Yes, you could have warned me sooner," Emma said. "And we could have escaped together."

"Without the money?" Diane asked.

Emma hesitated for a moment, then lifted her shoulders back. "Yes, without the money. We had a plan Diane. It will still work. We don't need the money. It will be harder, of course, but we will have each other and that would be enough."

"Diane can't leave yet, Emma," Drew said, starting to turn.

Diane stepped past Emma quickly and reached out to Drew's neck and squeezed. Half turned and not ready for an attack, Drew fell into the side of the chair, and then slumped to the floor, unconscious.

"What are you doing?" Emma cried, bending down and touching her son's chest.

Diane bent down, checked Drew's neck for a pulse, and stood up again. She pulled Emma up to her and stared into her eyes, which were just inches from hers. "He was here to take you from me," she said, her eyes slightly glazed.

"Of course. And you would have met us later," Emma said. "I was going to wait for confirmation from the Dutchman and then Drew was going to whisk me away."

"Straight into the arms of the FBI," Diane said. "They're waiting offshore and once you were safe, they were going to attack the island and arrest the Dutchman."

Emma's eyes narrowed. She thought about that for a moment, not fully comprehending why her son would want to complicate things by involving the FBI, but recognizing the merits of the plan. "And what is wrong with that idea? We would have our money and we could all finally fulfill our dreams and begin new lives, my son included." She turned and knelt down beside him. He hadn't moved. Diane kneeled beside her but turned her head to look at her again.

"Drew is an FBI agent, Emma," she said. "His job was to arrest the Dutchman and take him into custody. He took advantage of your kidnapping scheme to get close to the man." Emma's eyes showed miscomprehension. Diane continued. "When you first told your son about your plan, he was torn. He wasn't sure whether to stop you or to tell you of the coincidence that he had been working the Dutchman case for several years. He took your idea to his superiors and they immediately saw the value in having Drew stay undercover and use you and your kidnapping as a means to get close enough to the Dutchman to trap him."

Emma's gaze faltered as she tried to formulate her thoughts. Diane didn't want to let her stray.

"The FBI concocted an elaborate plan and created a persona for Drew that would make him out to be a valuable asset to the Dutchman. Then they arrested the man who had been the Dutchman's actual recruiter and set up Drew to take his place."

"A recruiter?" Emma stammered. It wasn't the first question forming in her mind amidst the confusion, just the one that popped up at that moment.

"Drew has protected the mistresses of two other rich men over the past year and a half, Emma," Diane said. "He has been infiltrating the Dutchman's operation ever since you divulged your plan to him."

"But he would never put me in danger," Emma said, shaking her head. She looked down at her son, still lying still; innocent, loving, a little estranged perhaps, but loyal nonetheless.

"He didn't think you would be," Diane said. "He doesn't know about Shell Peak." Diane grabbed Emma's arm and turned her body so it faced hers directly. "Those two women who faked their kidnappings over the past eighteen months, just like you did?" She placed her face as close to Emma's as she could. "They have never been seen again."

Emma stared into Diane's eyes. "Drew would never put me in that much danger."

"Drew doesn't know," Diane said. "He thinks they escaped and are living in luxury somewhere else in the world. His job is to take the security back to the husband and ensure everyone at that end is happy and no one comes looking for the kidnapped wife. He did his job well. No one is looking for those two women."

"The Dutchman...Manfred killed them?" Emma mumbled.

"He pushed them off the peak, into the rocks and sea below."

Emma's face registered shock and she stood quickly, beginning to pace. Suddenly she stopped and turned to Diane who was slowly getting off her knees. "How do you know all this?" she asked, her head cocked slightly.

Diane sighed. She then came over and reached out for Emma's hand. Emma pulled back.

"Who are you, Diane?" she asked icily.

Diane's lips curled downward as she pursed her lips. "I know because I've been sent to eliminate the Dutchman," she said and stared at Emma, waiting for a reaction. When none came, she kept going. "My people aren't as concerned about bringing a criminal to justice," she said. "We just want his operation to stop. He's hurting the wrong people and exposing important associates to unwanted financial discomfort."

"Who the hell is *we*," Emma asked.

Diane stared hard. "It doesn't matter who we are, Emma. Suffice to say my job is to kill the Dutchman and then get off this island before the FBI get here and mess things up. If they do anything illegal during their invasion, the Dutchman's lawyers will have him walking out of custody, or at least serve a lesser sentence and be back in business within the decade. We can't allow that to happen. His influence is getting dangerous to the wrong people."

"You're a killer too?" Emma said, taking a step backwards. "I thought you loved me. I thought we were going to escape our world and discover a new one... together."

Diane stepped closer, trying to keep the gap between them small. "I do love you Emma. And we *are* going to escape and live a life of freedom and happiness." She reached out and grabbed Emma's arms, firmly. "But first, I have a job to do. Unless I kill him Emma, he will always be chasing us. I can't let that happen. Besides, it's the only way I can leave the Company and not have them chasing me too. I do this one last job. They'll let me out."

"The Company?" Emma repeated. "I've heard William talk about that. That's another name for the CIA. You're a CIA agent?"

Diane pulled Emma toward the door. "We have to go. Now."

Emma resisted, turning to look at Drew, still lying on the floor. "I can't leave him."

"He'll be fine Emma. When his colleagues realize he hasn't got you they'll assume something is wrong and will come ashore. We don't want to be here when that happens or it's all over. No money, no escape, nothing."

"You said the Dutchman isn't giving me the money anyway," Emma said.

"He doesn't need to," Diane said, grinning. "I have access to his Cayman account. We don't need his payment to you. We can have it all; everything he's amassed over the past five years. It's millions, Emma. Millions!"

When she reached the door, Emma in tow, she whipped it open and stopped cold.

"Oh Diane," the Dutchman said. "And I had such plans for us. I thought you were one woman who understood me. "He shoved her back into the room and quickly surveying, noticed Drew on the ground by the patio door. Emma had retreated back to stand over him. "But now I understand everything, don't I?"

Chapter Fifty-One

Natalie knew there was something much bigger than a simple kidnapping going on here. With the revelation that Drew was an FBI agent and Diane was CIA, there was obviously something more important, more sinister at play. And when you added Emma--Drew's mother and the official kidnap victim--to the mix, the whole thing got really complicated.

Without a doubt, it was time for her to leave. If the FBI and CIA wanted the Dutchman, they were welcome to fight over him. As for Emma, she was the deranged and damaged ex-wife of her supposed lover.

Natalie thought about that for a few moments. No, she definitely wasn't Benneton's lover any longer. That ship had sailed, so to speak. Once she was back in the U.S. she would say her goodbyes and get on with a normal life.

She snickered. Anything would seem normal after the past nightmarish few days. Maybe she'd get a job in Savannah again, try going out on normal dates, with normal, single, men. No more sugar daddies, no more playboy FBI agents. *Give me an accountant, a grocery store manager, anyone who hasn't got a hidden agenda!* Deep down, she didn't really believe that, she knew. But for now, her determination kept the fear at bay.

She entered the villa from the back door and walked toward the kitchen. She needed the keys to that supply boat and get the hell off this island. Her friend, Emerald the housekeeper, might have an idea where they were kept. If it wasn't Manfred's office, then it was likely in the servant's section of the house somewhere. Maybe one of them kept the keys in their room, maybe even Emerald.

There was no sign of Emerald in the kitchen and Natalie was about to ask one of the other ladies where she was when the older woman rushed in, wiping her hands on her apron as she hurriedly came up to Natalie.

"Miss Natalie, Master Manfred be looking for you," she said, one hand brushing loose strands of her curly black hair from her forehead. "He says it be impo'tant and that I fetch you to his office."

Natalie grabbed the older woman's hands and tried to calm her. She knew that Manfred could be a hard task master and if he had given Emerald the task of finding her, he would want it to happen instantly or Emerald would likely receive a harsh talking down.

"It's alright Emerald, I'll go and see what he wants," she said, noticing the woman's nervous expression ease just slightly. "But when I'm finished, there's something I need to ask you, okay? Will you be here?"

Emerald nodded, and then pointed to the main corridor. "You go now," she said. "I make tea for when you return."

Natalie smiled, then turned and headed down the corridor to the office that she was supposed to have never been in before.

"It appears your time here is coming to a close," the Dutchman said when Natalie appeared at his open office door. "Please, sit down." He was shuffling papers and didn't seem too interested in whether Natalie sat or

265

not, but she did anyway. Just the way he said the words sounded sinister, like coming to a close was not an altogether positive development.

"The funds which enable Emma Benneton's departure from the island have arrived and it is my pleasure to say that your services are no longer needed."

He sure had a way with words. Was it her knowledge of what he was capable of, or just his sinister aura that made every positive line he spoke reek of hazardous intentions?

"You're letting me go home?"

The Dutchman stopped shuffling papers and looked up, cocking his head slightly. "Was there ever any doubt?"

They stared at each other for a few moments, Natalie not wanting to say anything that may provoke a rebuke from the man. After a few seconds, the Dutchman grinned.

"I appreciate that it may have felt as though you were being held against your will," he said. "And I suppose that is true. However, there was never any doubt in my mind that your benefactor, Mr. William Benneton would do anything to ensure your return."

Natalie continued to stare. the Dutchman continued.

"It is quite an effective system we have here, I assure you," he said, putting his hands on the edge of the table as if preparing to get up. "And it wasn't even our idea in the beginning, you see."

Natalie must have frowned because the Dutchman stood, walked to the front of his desk and leaned against the front, his arms crossed. He stared down at Natalie.

"You see it is the wives who begin the process. They want some of their husbands' money and after exhausting various other routes, such as affairs or attempted divorce, the idea of arranging for their own kidnapping comes to mind. Surprisingly, we are not that hard to find. A question here, an inquiry there, and next thing you know, one of my associates manning the dark web gets wind of the request and investigates."

Natalie wasn't sure why he was telling her all of this but she didn't want to do anything to change his current mood. Perhaps bragging about his exploits was an important process for him and the security would naturally give him their undivided attention at this point.

"Most extremely rich men eventually find their wives do not satisfy their needs sufficiently and therefore find alternative sources of pleasure." He swept his one arm out to point at Natalie. "And for all intents and purposes, it is a marvelous solution. Except the wife usually doesn't want to go along with it. In most cases, divorce is not an option as it would either destroy the man's business, or force him to part with more than half of his worth. Again, most rich men abhor such a solution."

Natalie listened intently. The Dutchman was rambling but it was interesting. Most of it she knew from Drew, but some of it was fascinating. Something in the back of her mind was nagging at her but she couldn't put a finger on it.

"Initially, most men aren't immediately receptive to the idea of a kidnapping scheme but once one of my people interviews them and provides them with all the information, they usually come to terms with it being the best solution all around. The wife is eliminated, without the legal procedure of divorce, chapter eleven, whatever, and she only takes a fraction of his worth. For a short period, his friends and family surround him with support when it seems evident the kidnappers killed their victim and she isn't coming back. And throughout the ordeal, his loving girlfriend acts as insurance that he will continue to play along until the very end. Because, my dear, the whole reason he goes along with all of this is because ultimately, he wants you." He pointed at Natalie again. "Without you, none of this would work. So, you see, you are very important to the process and I only choose the rich patrons who have a lovely young girl in the mix. It just wouldn't be possible without you."

Why was he telling her all of this? That nagging feeling was getting stronger. Was he planning to kill her? Why else would he tell a stranger, a stranger he's about to release, the ins and outs of how his criminal activities worked?

"And now it is very important that you go back home, back to your lover, and tell him all that went on here. You need to tell him that if he comes looking for his estranged wife, for me, or for any of my associates, we will kill…" he stood quickly and unfolded his arms, staring intently at Natalie. "…you."

Natalie flinched.

"And when we come for you, we will make Mr. Benneton watch as we snuff out your life."

Natalie gasped. She pushed her chair back and gripped the edges. The Dutchman stepped forward, just inches from her, his towering figure dominating her view.

"And then we will make Mr. Benneton also disappear, though not as eloquently as his wife's departure, I assure you."

Natalie's throat was very dry. She could feel the sweat dripping from her forehead into her eyes, mixing with the tears that were starting to form.

Now it made sense. She suddenly realized she had never been in any real danger here. The danger would be evident once she left. The Dutchman needed her to go back and convince Benny that both their lives depended upon him not looking for anyone, not his wife, not the Dutchman, not Drew, no one. And the Dutchman was counting on her to be enticing enough to keep him happy at home, so he would have no desire to come looking for anyone in attempt to recover his money.

The Dutchman turned and went behind his desk again, the removal of his physical presence providing instant relief to Natalie who felt herself shaking. He sat, looked up at her and smiled.

"But none of that will happen will it Miss Grainger because you are going to go back to your room, pack your bags, get a good night's sleep, and be ready to go home first thing in the morning, correct?"

Still shaking, Natalie just stared at the desktop. What about Drew and Diane? What did they have planned? They wanted to stop the Dutchman, take him to prison, maybe even kill him. But what if they tried and failed? Would the Dutchman think she had been part of that plot? If they didn't kill him, sooner or later, he'd come after Natalie if he thought she'd had something to do with it.

She stared across at the Dutchman. He was obviously waiting for a response. She simply nodded her head.

"Good evening then, my dear. I will see you off at ten tomorrow morning. Yuri will be escorting you."

She wasn't sure what to do but realized he had dismissed her. She slowly rose and headed to the office door.

"It was a pleasure meeting you Miss Grainger" he said, his eyes travelling up and down her body for the first time since she'd arrived at his office. "Perhaps we will meet again. And be careful of young Yuri. He feels he's a bit of a ladies' man. Normally, I wouldn't entrust the security to him but Mr. Scanlon is nowhere to be found, I'm afraid."

She turned to see him give her a quick wink, his expression no more sinister than at that moment. She quickly walked out.

Her plan to escape was still the best option. She couldn't go with Yuri, back to Benny. She didn't want to know what Benny would do when she left him right away, which she was determined to do. Would he try to follow her? Would he look for Emma or the Dutchman? Surely, if Natalie didn't go back, Benny would want revenge of some kind.

And the Dutchman had said he would come for her first. She couldn't put herself in that position. And if Drew and/or Diane failed in their attempt to stop the Dutchman, then one way or another, she would be the first target. And they'd know exactly where to start looking.

No, she needed to get that boat key, and escape the island tonight. Then she could disappear forever. No Benny, no Drew, no Dutchman. A new life, a fresh start. And to hell with everyone!

Chapter Fifty-Two

When Natalie returned to the kitchen, Emerald handed her a cup of tea. She appeared nervous and Natalie was about to assure her that she had gone directly to the Dutchman and that she needn't be concerned about him, when Emerald grasped her arm.

"There are noises below," she said, her eyes boring into Natalie's.

At first, Natalie wasn't sure why that was something important to Emerald but apparently it was. "What kind of noises, where?"

Emerald looked nervously around the kitchen. There was no one else in the room. "I think there is someone down in the cellar," she said. "Locked inside."

Natalie stared at the older woman for a moment and then she realized what that could mean. Drew had been caught and the Dutchman had locked him away until he could figure out what to do with him. "Show me," she said, touching the woman's hand on her arm, reassuring her that it was okay to do so.

The cellar was an appropriate name for the lower level, under the villa. The entrance was reminiscent of a mid-western hurricane shelter, dug under the main house and accessed by stairs leading down from flat doors placed just above the surface. Emerald unlatched the doors and pulled them back to lay against the ground. Natalie shuddered. She wasn't claustrophobic but something about going down the five or six steps to another heavy wooden door leading underneath the villa wasn't appealing.

"I don't hear anything," Natalie said.

Emerald looked at her and then shrugged. "I pass by while you were with Mr. Manfred and I heard tapping noise. I think maybe an animal got in somehow and was stuck in stairway. So I opened doors and looked down there." She pointed to the door at the bottom of the stairs. "As soon as I opened them, I hear loud tap-tap-tap noises from other side."

Natalie nodded and started down.

"They not animal sounds," Emerald added, standing at the entrance, not following Natalie.

Suddenly the tapping sounds came again: Definitely not an animal; too organized, too purposeful. Then she realized. It was Morse Code: three short taps, two slow ones with space in between, then three short taps again. She leaned close to the door. "Drew?"

"Jesus, Natalie, it's you!" a muffled voice came from the other side.

"Why aren't you yelling and screaming?" she said. "Someone would have heard you a lot sooner."

"I can't risk the Dutchman hearing us and then coming to shut us up. Besides, there's no one here that can do anything about getting us out of here."

"Us?"

There was a pause. "Diane is here too," he said. It was hard to tell because of the muffling effect of the thick door but Natalie thought Drew sounded frustrated. "The Dutchman caught us planning to escape."

"Are you okay?" Natalie said. "I mean, both of you?"

"Yeah, yeah, we're fine. But Natalie, you've got to find my mother and get her off this island."

"What are you talking about?"

"Natalie, the Dutchman knows about our plan," he said. "He took my mother and Diane thinks he's going to kill her and take all the money."

Natalie thought about that for a minute. It made sense of course. But had the Dutchman decided this after he'd caught Drew and Diane, or was taking all the money the plan all along? It didn't really matter.

"I have to get you out of there," she said. "You and Diane are better equipped to save her than I am. How can I get you out?"

"Natalie! Listen to me," Drew was yelling. "We've tried everything. This door might as well be iron. We can't get out without the key on your side."

Natalie looked at the huge metal lock attached to the door. It was heavy duty and there was no way she could easily break it, even with a wrench or crowbar if she could ever find such a thing. She sat back on one of the stairs, her head in her hands.

"You okay, Miss Natalie?" Emerald asked from above.

Natalie nodded. "I'm fine Emerald but we need to get these people out of this cellar. Do you think any of the men would have any ideas?"

Emerald stared at her, then a grin formed on her face. "I have idea," she said. "I be back." And with that, she grabbed her skirt and ran out of view. Natalie wasn't hopeful but the woman had lived here longer than she had so maybe she did have some insight into getting someone out of the cellar. She stood and looked at the door, her resolve growing as she stared at its solid construction.

"I have to leave Drew," she said finally. "Emerald will fetch the men to help."

"Find my mother Natalie!" he shrieked.

Natalie didn't answer but bolted back up the stairs, looked around to see if anyone was watching, then she ran into the jungle.

Chapter Fifty-Three

The sun had set three hours ago and there was still no sign of Drew Scanlon.

Agent Burelli wasn't going to wait much longer. The plan was to hit the island at midnight. He checked his watch. It was already 11:15. He was about to order the men to suit up when the radioman yelled up from the cabin.

"Unknown vessel at four o'clock, Sir," the man said.

They were on a boat, bouncing around all over the place. How was he supposed to know which way was four o'clock?

The radioman had apparently anticipated this reaction and when Agent Burelli peered down in the cabin, the man was pointing out the starboard window just off the rear of the boat.

Burelli looked out and could just make out a red and green light bouncing in the darkness. It was about five hundred yards away and appeared to be stationary.

"They're anchored?"

"Must be sir," the radioman said. "They've held that position for the past ten minutes. That's why I thought it may be important, sir."

Burelli thought for a moment. This assignment had been exceptionally weird from the start. And he knew he hadn't been told everything. The higher ups never explained all the details; just enough for the grunts like him to get the job done. It was sometimes just enough to get the grunts compromised too.

"Any ideas?" Burelli asked.

The radioman stared up at him. "Could be a local fishing boat off the coast," he said. "Could be one of the Dutchman's security too, I guess, though reports from Agent Scanlon didn't elude to any sophisticated security on the island, sir."

And exactly how much could he trust any information coming from Agent Drew *fucking* Scanlon? The guy was a loose cannon as far as Burelli was concerned. And if this didn't go down right, they might lose the best chance they've had at the Dutchman in ten years. Not to mention the fact that someone could get killed in the process.

"Sir, there is one other possibility, sir," the radioman said.

Burrelli peered down into the cabin again. "And that is?"

"Well sir, Agent Scanlon said the CIA had someone on the island, right?" When Burelli didn't respond, he continued. "Well, though it's a little unusual for the CIA to provide back-up, sir, it is possible that boat is offering similar support as we are to Agent Scanlon. After all, the Dutchman is a big prize for everyone, sir."

Burelli stared at the lights in the distance. The kid could be right, on either count. It could be CIA here to back up their agent on the island. Or it could just be a local fishing crew, bedding down for the night. He didn't know how likely it was for a commercial fishing vessel to stay out overnight, and after he thought about it, he really did doubt it. So who were they? Seemed a bit far-fetched that it could be CIA. He grinned. Of course, he was here for his guy, so why wouldn't they be here, for theirs? Like the kid said, the Dutchman was definitely a big prize.

"Let me know if they move, or change position, whatever," he instructed the radioman. Regardless of who was on the other boat, it didn't change his plans. They were going in. It was their job to capture the Dutchman and take him into custody. He knew the CIA wouldn't have quite the same agenda.

Which begged the question: If it was CIA, why exactly were they here?

The Security

Chapter Fifty-Four

It had gotten dark about four hours ago and Natalie felt a little nervous about running into the jungle with no flashlight or any other form of illumination. But she'd toured the island several times over the past couple of weeks and as long as she stayed on the roughhewn trail, she'd be okay. Besides, it was almost a full moon and its eerily white light flickered through the trees occasionally and lit the path for a few yards ahead as she walked.

She'd decided to head toward the makeshift campsite Drew had fashioned in the middle of the jungle and found that he wasn't there. She'd hoped to find some kind of weapon she could use.

The scream stopped her cold.

It came from the other side of the island, closer to the Villa than where she was now. She couldn't recognize who it was of course, except that it had sounded female to her. She quickly turned and headed back to a cut-off she knew would take her behind the villa and up to the hilly side of the island. She didn't hear another scream and that made her wonder what was going on. No one screamed just once if they were in danger. Unless something, or someone, stopped them from repeating their cry.

The ground slowly rose as she began the steady climb up one of the hills that seemed to dominate this side of the island. She was heading toward the largest hill, the one the Dutchman had taken her to when she had first arrived at the villa.

Was that where the scream had come from?

It was as good a place to aim for as any. Natalie knew there weren't that many pathways on this side of the island and if someone wasn't familiar with it, they would likely stay with the trails and not stray into the jungle.

After a few minutes of fast-paced walking, the jungle density eased and she could make out flickering lights in the distance. They appeared to be in a row or even a circle. She peered through the last few bushes onto a clearing she recognized. It was the manmade pathway up towards the cliff where the Dutchman had taken Natalie on her first day. All along the edge of the cliff were tall torches, blazing red and yellow light into the sky, some of the long, thin flames being bent by the breeze.

Natalie heard another scream, this time muffled, and squinted to see past the stream of light into the darkness beyond the torches. Near the edge of the cliff she saw the Dutchman, holding Emma's arms behind her back tightly as she teetered on the edge, her gaze riveted out into the cold, open space ahead.

The combined noise of the pounding waves below the cliff and Emma's muffled screams, prevented them from hearing Natalie approach. Not until she was less than ten feet away did the Dutchman's head perk up and he turned to see her. He had one hand over Emma's mouth but let go to hold her tightly against him. His eyes were black and even though it was dark, Natalie felt they were two bottomless holes in his head. His cheeks were flushed and his stare was expressionless.

Natalie was torn between racing to them and pounding him with her fists, or turning to run for help.

Who was there to help though?

"What are you doing, Manfred?" she said, as calmly as she could, trying to match his casual, controlled demeanor, so as not to instigate a violent action. Emma was a few inches from the edge. One quick shove and she would fall to the jagged rocks below.

"Natalie!" Emma exclaimed. With the Dutchman's release of her mouth, she screamed louder. "My God, Natalie. Help me!"

The Dutchman slapped her face abruptly and clamped his hand back over her mouth.

"Leave us," the Dutchman grizzled. His tone was low and menacing, reminding Natalie of the low, guttural growl of a guard dog.

"You can't throw her off the cliff, Manfred."

He cocked his head, his face still expressionless. "Did you know they scream, all the way down. It is the most magnificent sound in the world." He shook Emma and she screamed into his hand again. "Then suddenly it stops, and the ocean swallows." His eyes glinted slightly and he edged Emma a little closer. "It is highly gratifying."

"No!" Natalie screamed, knowing she could never overpower him. Even if she tried, he would likely just push Emma over the edge in order to deal with her.

"I think you should..." The Dutchman didn't finish his sentence because of the loud swooshing sound, then what must have been the impact of something hitting the ground hard. They turned to look down the hill toward the villa and saw a flash of bright light followed by an orange glow that was unquestionably a growing fire. The first noise must have been some kind of explosion.

Natalie turned back to see the Dutchman pull Emma back, ready to hurl her into the abyss. Without thinking, Natalie took advantage of Emma being momentarily away from the edge, and hurled herself at both of them. The impact sent them perilously close to the edge again, all three of them landing hard on the stony ground forming the crust of the cliff. Natalie rolled away and shaking the dirt and mud from her face, turned to look at the other two figures sprawled on the ground beside her. Emma was moaning and Natalie went to her, lifting her head. She looked over at the Dutchman. His head lay at a strange angle and a dark liquid was pouring from a wound somewhere in the back of his head and pooling around a jagged rock beside him. He must have hit it, she thought. She watched for a few seconds and saw no movement. He was dead. She turned her attention back to Emma who had been dazed but seemed otherwise unharmed.

"We have to get away from here," Natalie said. She grabbed under the older woman's arms and dragged her to her feet. Emma mumbled incoherently but draped her one arm around Natalie's shoulder. With one last look at the unmoving figure lying near the cliff's edge, Natalie slowly lead the hobbling woman down the pathway toward the villa that was now glowing brightly.

Chapter Fifty-Five

Agent Burelli didn't like jumping out of moving boats but since his adrenaline was running at an all-time high, he didn't ponder over the two-foot leap from the edge of the hull to the wooden dock. Four of the men had jumped already and were racing down the dock toward the villa and what looked like a blazing fire somewhere behind the structure.

Rifle aimed in front of him loosely as he ran, he watched as the other agents surrounded the villa, ready to enter from three different points: the kitchen door, the patio door, and what looked like a sliding door off a bedroom on the far side. Suddenly, a dark figure exploded from the kitchen door and ran toward them, firing short bursts from what sounded like an old army M1 Garand, like those used in WWII.

The agent who had been heading to the kitchen, let out a quick burst from his MP5 and the man dropped in a heap upon impact. The agent jumped over him and kept going. Agent Burelli did the same, briefly noticing the man had worn shorts and a torn t-shirt. He was some six or seven steps behind and followed his colleague through the door.

"Clear!" the first agent shouted. Burelli dropped the front of his weapon and looked around. All he could hear, just above the now whooshing noise of the fire just beyond the kitchen, was whimpering, lots of whimpering.

"Stand up, arms first!" an agent demanded. Nothing happened and the whimpering continued until one shaky black hand reached up, followed by the rest of the body.

"Who are you?" Burelli asked.

"Em...emm...ah, Emerald, Sir," the older black woman stuttered as she slowly came from behind the kitchen counter. "Just house staff here, Sir." she said. "The one ran out be Mathias," she said, pointing to the door the men had just come through. "He Mr. Manfred's guard, dumb sum'o bitch. Got hisself killed, right?"

Burelli looked at the other agent who had worked his way around the kitchen island and was herding the others out where they could be seen. Burelli counted eight in all.

"Mr. Manfred?" Burelli said. "That would be the Dutchman?"

Emerald nodded. Apparently she'd heard that reference before. "He locked some people--his girlfriend--in the cellar..." she pointed behind her to where the orange glow was filling the view from the back window. "Then he take Miss Emma up the cliff. She no come back you know."

"The cellar? That's back there, back where the fire is?" Burelli asked. Emerald nodded.

Burelli pulled his collar mic closer to his mouth. "Search the villa quick, clear it, then find water taps... and a hose," he said. Then he pushed past the old housemaid and rushed out the back door.

Three black men were already hosing down the fire, but it was raging since everything in the vicinity was made of old wood.

"They're in there?" he yelled.

One of the men looked up, cocked his head, then nodded. Emerald had come up beside him.

"That where Mr. Manfred, he put Miss Diane and another man. Don't know him."

"Fuck!" Burelli exclaimed. Was the other man Drew Scanlon? And Miss Diane? Was that the girl Scanlon had been ranting about?" He stared at the flames which now engulfed what looked like a heavy wooden door, as well as the rail ties leading down to what must be the cellar. "If we don't get them out soon, they'll die," he said.

"I'll get the extinguisher from the boat," the one agent said, and took off back through the kitchen. By then, two of the other men had arrived. Burelli glared at them.

"All clear, Sir," one said. No one else in the building." Burelli turned back to the old woman.

"Who started the fire?" he said.

Emerald stared at him. "Miss Natalie say we had to get them out."

Who the hell is Miss Natalie, Burelli thought. "So they started a fire?" he asked, incredulous.

"Of course," she answered matter-of-factly. "It's wood. It burn down. They come out."

"No, they won't come out," he scolded her. "They'll die of smoke inhalation first, especially if there's no window or anything."

"No window," Emerald said. "Cellar." Her eyes shone in the firelight and Burelli could see she was questioning something.

"What?" he yelled.

She jumped back, then answered. "Miss Natalie. I think she go after Mr. Manfred and Miss Emma. She be hurt. We need to fetch her."

Burelli brushed his hand through his hair quickly and sighed. This was turning into one giant clusterfuck. Where was Scanlon? Assuming he was the guy in the cellar with the girlfriend, they had to get them out, now. He turned to one of the other agents. "Find some baking soda, flour, anything powder," he said. "We've got to douse this fire!"

Emerald's eyes widened and she turned and raced back to the kitchen. "I show you," she said as the agent followed her.

Burelli watched the black men aiming slow flowing water at the base of the door and hoped the couple were still alive. There was no screaming, so they were either overwhelmed by smoke and unconscious, or covering their mouths hoping for rescue.

"Come on!" he yelled, to no one in particular.

Chapter Fifty-Six

Turned out Drew Scanlon wasn't a complete fuck-up after all, Agent Burelli mused. Scanlon and an attractive older woman he called Diane had slowly emerged from the doused flaming entrance covered in a soaked jacket. There had been a full jug of some kind of clear fluid on a shelf in the cellar and Scanlon had been smart enough to douse his jacket with it and cover their heads, cowering in a corner, until one of the agents had jumped in to get them. Burelli wasn't sure what the liquid was; it had no smell. But thankfully, it hadn't been flammable and the soaked jacket had served to filter out enough smoke to allow them to breath until rescue arrived. The explosion had been a propane tank in the corner of the room, behind a half brick wall that had protected them from any shrapnel.

Burelli led the woman to a rock on the far edge of the lawn, and came back to Scanlon, still coughing repeatedly.

"Where's the Dutchman?" he asked, then coughed, turned and spit out some dark flem.

Gross, Burelli thought. "Don't know," he said. "But he has to still be on the island. No vessels have left in the past hour. Dutch Coast Guard is standing off about a mile and they report only our boats approaching. He didn't explain that the FBI task force only had one boat. The other one was CIA he figured, though they were still stationed out past the lagoon in open water, according to his Coast Guard contact.

"And the girl, Natalie?" Scanlon sputtered.

"Don't know who that is," Burelli said. "Which one's your girl? That one over there--"he pointed to the woman on the rock--"or this Natalie person?"

"Neither now," Scanlon said, grabbing Burelli's sleeve with both hands. "My mother, you have her, right?"

Burelli shrugged off Scanlon's hands. What the fuck! This got weirder and weirder. "Your mother! What the hell is going on here, Scanlon?"

Instead of answering, the sputtering agent pushed Burelli aside and sprinted around the side of the house.

"Where you going?" Burelli yelled after him. He was about to give chase when one of his men called for him from the kitchen doorway.

"Sir, we have two people coming from up there," the man pointed in the general direction Scanlon had run. "Two women, sir. And they might be hurt." He turned back into the house and disappeared.

Does this get any stranger? Burelli thought, watching Scanlon disappear around the end of the house. He shrugged. He'd deal with that fuck-up later. He glanced over at the woman sitting on the rock at the edge of the clearing. There was no one with her but she looked ok, head in her hands, coughing a bit. She'd be fine, whoever she was.

Chapter Fifty-Seven

"Emma, Natalie!" Drew yelled as he stopped short on the patio at the end of the villa. He had been focused on running up the hill to Shell Cliff when he'd seen the two women. Natalie seemed to be holding his mother up as they limped across into the clearing toward the commotion at the villa. He turned and ran to them.

Agent Burelli emerged from the kitchen door, along with his men and they all ran toward the struggling women.

Drew arrived first and grabbed his mother's arm, pulling her out of Natalie's grasp, placing her arm over his own shoulder, taking her full weight. Natalie didn't complain but stood still, shaking her arms.

Burelli and his men loosely surrounded the group, staring at the two women. "Scanlon, who is this?" he demanded.

Drew was too concerned about getting his mother to safety to worry about anything else. He needed to get to the boat and get Emma out of here. "I need to get my mother off this island, now!" he said to no one in particular.

Burelli seemed to be unsure of what to do so he turned to Natalie. "You okay?"

Natalie was breathing heavily and didn't seem focused but she managed to look up at Drew and Emma, then changed her gaze to Burelli.

"The Dutchman is up there," she said, pointing behind her, up the hill. "He's dead. Can I go home now?"

Drew turned to look at Natalie, then turned back and began edging his mother toward the boat. Burelli stepped out of the way and moved closer to Natalie. "You're sure he's up there?" he asked.

Natalie nodded, shuddered and began to follow Drew and Emma. Burelli turned to his men. "Let's go," he said, leading them up the hill, guns drawn. He turned after a few yards and yelled; "Wait for us on the boat, Scanlon."

Drew either didn't hear or didn't care to respond. He just kept dragging his mother toward the dock.

"She's fine, just shook up," Natalie said as she caught up.

"You killed the Dutchman?" he asked

"He was going to throw Emma off a cliff," she said. "I knocked him over and he hit his head on a rock or something. We left him. He wasn't breathing."

Drew squinted. "You're sure?"

"I didn't do mouth-to-mouth if that's what you mean," she said, brushing past him.

Drew wanted to ask her more questions about their ordeal but he could see Natalie was just as dazed as his mother, she was just a little more with it at the moment. Questions could come later.

"Let's get out of here," he said, following, dragging Emma along.
"That's the smartest thing I've heard you say all day," Natalie said.

Chapter Fifty-Eight

"Diane, where's Diane?" Emma's voice was strained but firm. Drew had eased her onto the boat as it swayed gently at the end of the lagoon dock. Natalie had jumped on first and was seated on the long stern couch. He knew he owed her an escape and didn't like the idea of leaving her to the debriefing Agent Burelli no doubt had in mind. In fact, he wasn't really sure how much she knew now. Yes, he'd take Natalie with them. But damnit, he didn't need Diane.

He gave his mother a furtive glance and was about to tell her to forget about Diane, they needed to escape, but the look on his mother's face told him she'd never forgive him. "I'll get her," he sighed, then pushed Emma toward the stern. "Look after her please. I'll be right back. "Natalie stared at him dumbly then nodded. Drew jumped onto the dock and ran to the villa.

Emerging from the kitchen on the other side of the villa, he immediately saw that Diane was no longer on the rock where he'd left her. He scanned the rear area seeing nothing other than gently swaying trees drawing attention to the jungle they edged. Had she run into the jungle? Why? His boat was underwater and the only other escape was on the FBI boat. Maybe she was grabbing personal things in the villa.

He doubled back and began searching each room, starting with the kitchen and heading down the corridor toward the bedrooms. Some of the rooms looked unused, others were obviously inhabited but nothing was in disarray. He turned and headed back the other way, across the kitchen and along a corridor that contained common rooms, rather than bedrooms. He passed a library, a small dining room, and came to an office. Someone had left this room in a hurry and it had been overturned. The Dutchman? Or had Diane been here and taking evidence that would have helped them all figure out exactly what the Dutchman had been up to?

No matter. His main priority was to get his mother away far away from here, so that Burelli and any other FBI reps couldn't interrogate her. He suddenly realized his career with the FBI was over. Then after a few seconds of thought, it dawned on him that it had been over the second he'd agreed to participate in his mother's crazy plan to leave Benneton and take a great deal of his wealth with her.

He raced back to the dock and stepped onto the side of the boat. He noticed that Natalie was seated at the stern, her face worn and stressed. There was something else about her eyes, though he couldn't figure out what it was.

"Where's Emma? I can't find Diane. We have to leave without her," he said as he waited for the boat to steady before taking his other foot off the dock.

"That's unfortunate. Because I would have liked to have finished her properly."

The voice came from the cuddy and Drew recognized it immediately. He peered into the cuddy and watched as the Dutchman pushed Emma out in front of him. The older man held a small serrated knife to his mother's throat, his other arm wrapped around her chin, holding her head back, Emma's neck protruding forward as he bent her head backwards towards him. His face was dirty and bloody, his eyes glazed, and his shirt torn. There was a trail of dried blood starting somewhere above his hair line, and extending down to his neck. A dark reddish, purple bruise adorned his cheek.

"Cast us off Mr. Scanlon," he growled.

Drew shook his head and tried to rebalance himself so he could pull his one leg back onto the deck but he lost his balance and pitched forward toward the Dutchman.

The old man pushed Emma out of the way, and as he reached forward to stop Drew from falling on him, the knife blade buried itself into Drew's upper torso.

He screamed as his legs buckled and he fell forward between the boat and the dock. As he reached out his head hit the edge of the boat and he lifelessly plopped backwards into the water.

"Andrew!" Emma screamed and rushed to the edge. The Dutchman pulled her back and since he had somehow pulled the knife out of Drew's body before he'd slipped into the water, he pointed it at her again.

"He's gone," he said. "Sit down."

Emma stared at him as she backed away from the knife. Natalie reached out and took her hand, guiding her to the seat beside her. As she sat, Emma threw her hands to her face and began moaning like a wounded animal. Natalie put her arm around her and watched as the Dutchman reached over the floating body and untied the bow line. He then moved past them and did the same at the stern. Then, with a quick glance at the two of them cowering on the stern backseat, he went to the controls and started the motor.

As the boat reversed quickly in a tight turn and the Dutchman gunned the motor forward, Natalie caught a glimpse of Drew's body floating face down in the shallow water near the dock. A stain of dark floating liquid surrounded his upper body and as they pulled away, she felt nothing. Drew was gone but she didn't feel remorse or even loss. Maybe that would come later. Right now, she had to get herself away from the Dutchman. Drew couldn't help anymore and Emma was wallowing in sorrow at the moment and wouldn't be much good for anything.

She watched as the Dutchman carefully steered the boat out of the lagoon, and hugging the coastline, aimed toward the open Caribbean. Every few seconds he would glance back to see that they were still seated. Natalie said nothing. She just stared at him blankly. He seemed satisfied they were no threat for the time being.

And they weren't.

For the time being.

Chapter Fifty-Nine

Natalie could faintly hear yelling in the distance. No doubt the FBI agents realized that the boat was missing, along with herself and Emma. Drew would be self-explanatory, floating in the lagoon.

Would they think she had done it, or since they obviously hadn't found the Dutchman's body, put two and two together and realize he'd escaped with the boat, and perhaps Emma as a hostage? It didn't matter. All she had wanted was to get away. And that, at least, she was doing. The problem was the Dutchman. When he reached land, presumably Sint Maarten where he had dockage, would he just leave them, or would he try to get rid of them along the way. Clearly, he didn't need them anymore.

A bright light suddenly shot across the bow. It was to the port side, not the shore side, so it was coming from out in the water somewhere.

"Stop your engines," came a booming voice from behind the light. It was amplified by a megaphone and bore a menacing tone.

Natalie watched the Dutchman as his hand hovered over the throttle lever. She knew he was thinking about outrunning them but even she knew the boat would capsize once they hit open water at full speed. It was simply too small to try to race over four-foot waves that fast.

The Dutchman turned to her and was about to say something when the voice boomed again. "Agent Burelli, we wish to board and confer. Please set yourself adrift."

Natalie didn't know who they were but they seemed to have them confused with some other vessel, but it was likely friendly at least. The Dutchman pulled back the throttle and turned to face Natalie.

"If you surrender now, you'll get a fair trial," she said.

The Dutchman's face contorted in anger. "You!" he blustered. "I knew it had to be an insider. How else would they know where to come?"

He shifted and moved closer to her. "Come here," he said, gesturing to the port side of the boat, where the light was coming from. She slowly stood and he reached out and grabbed her, pulling her around, forcing her back close to him. She could feel his breath on her neck. She could also feel the coolness of the steel as he pulled her up, the knife to her throat this time.

"I don't know what you two have done, or who you are, but they won't let an innocent suffer just to get to me," he said, pulling her tight to the front of his body. They were facing the light that was now illuminating the whole boat as if it was daylight.

Neither of them noticed Emma staring into the light and edging her way down the rear seat to the starboard side, as far away from the Dutchman as she could get.

The boat was drifting, moving sideways so that the port side was receiving the waves as the vessel was pushed closer to shore. Natalie stretched her neck sideways as far as she could and figured they were about a hundred yards offshore. In the illuminated shadows, she could just make out a rocky shoreline.

The Dutchman was forced to hold the knife to Natalie's throat with one arm draped around her shoulder, while his other held onto the windshield for support. The waves gently rocked the boat but he was struggling to hold her close and balance simultaneously. Although Natalie wasn't trapped in his grasp, she wouldn't be able to escape him easily, shy of jumping in the water, which she was still considering, if she could get away from his grip somehow.

The other boat was now only twenty or so feet away and she could make out the edges of its hull. It wasn't much bigger than the one they were on but the huge light mounted on the bow obstructed anything behind it other than vague human shadows on either side of the light.

Oddly enough, the only thing going through Natalie's mind was that Manfred had never physically threatened her before. There had always been that underlying sinister nature about him but he had always conducted himself as a gentleman since she'd arrived on the island. Watching him try to push Emma off the cliff had caused her to see the much darker, controlling side of the monster. She had no doubt he would kill her if it became necessary but somehow she thought she was safe as long as these new intruders didn't try to board their boat.

She stared into the light though she couldn't see anything other than shadows. Manfred's one arm was draped loosely around her shoulder and though she was aware he held a knife in that hand, she didn't think he'd do anything to her since she was, once again, the official security. As long as he was threatening to harm her, whoever was on that boat wouldn't do anything to risk her life.

At least she hoped so.

She heard a splash and felt Manfred turn quickly toward the other side of the boat. He let go of the windshield and grabbed her waist, pulling her over to the starboard side.

Emma was dog paddling in the water just a few feet out and heading to shore. She must have slipped over the edge while they had been focused on the approaching light.

Manfred growled and waved his fist at her as Emma turned slightly, her eyes looking huge and the whites bright as they were reflected in the light. She then turned slightly and began to side stroking purposefully. For a moment, Natalie thought Manfred was going to throw the knife at her, but then he seemed to think better of it and pulled her back to the windshield, wrapping his arm around her once again, the knife dangling in front of her chest.

"You can't go anywhere Dutchman," the voice boomed again. "We have several guns trained on you. If you harm the girl, we'll have no choice but to shoot you down, so keep her alive. It's the only way you get out of this in one piece."

Well that was reassuring, Natalie thought. They could clearly see the Dutchman, and apparently, the knife at Natalie's throat.

Out of the corner of her eye she saw a red dot travel down the edge of the boat. It reminded her of a laser cat toy. And of course, she instantly knew what it was. They were training laser guided rifles at them. She'd seen them on *Seals*.

Manfred had stepped back slightly, edging himself behind Natalie. His arm loosened around her shoulder as he shifted and she tensed.

Chapter Sixty

The Dutchman must have seen it too because he gasped. They watched in stunned silence as the red light danced along the side of the boat searching for its prey.

Sensing the Dutchman's pre-occupation, Natalie slammed her elbow into his stomach as hard as she could. With a grunt, he crumpled but as he went down, he slashed out and caught her arm with the tip of the knife. A warmness engulfed her, though she felt no immediate pain. She was free and tried to fight him but they both saw several lights trying to find a target. He moved back, away from the tracking light, to the starboard side and sat on the edge of the boat. The pain was coming now but Natalie caught a reflection on the floor and saw that the Dutchman had dropped the knife. She grabbed it and noticed the Dutchman's eyes follow her every move. She didn't know what to do with it but somehow, having it in her hand seemed to give her strength. She moved toward him. His eyes seemed glazed and she could tell he was deciding something. Then she knew and she lunged forward as he pushed backward. As his legs flew up, she managed to slash his lower leg muscle. Blood spurted everywhere as he flew over the side of the boat. His scream was cut short when his head dropped under the water. She hadn't been thinking really; it was just all the pent-up anger of being held captive, being treated like chattel, watching Drew die, and then watching Emma escape so easily. She just wanted payback, and had lunged at the one thing that represented all her pain and frustration. Had she thought about it longer, she would never have attacked anyone with any weapon, let alone a knife. But he couldn't get away. It just wouldn't be fair.

And so, she had acted. Now, as she watched him kick frantically away from the boat, heading toward shore, she noticed the thickening trail of dark liquid--just like the pool around Drew--follow him as he swam noisily back to the island.

A sharp bump caused her to lose her balance and she quickly turned to see that the other boat had touched hers. Matching men in black t-shirts and jeans were on the bow and stern, lashing lines to tie the two boats together.

Natalie dropped the knife into the water and turned with her hands up.

Chapter Sixty-One

"Where is he?" a booming voice came from the other boat. As if in answer, the bright light, which she could now see was affixed to the windshield, began moving around the immediate area, illuminating the water for twenty yards or so.

"Overboard," she yelled to no one in particular, and pointed in the direction the Dutchman had swam. The light immediately searched the area she was pointing too.

She thought she vaguely recognized the voice, the Bostonian accent, but she couldn't place it. Then he stepped across onto her boat and reached out to take her arm. Natalie flinched. Despite being in similar attire as the other men on the boat, she recognized him as the guy that Drew had been talking to at the hotel on Hilton Head; the same government guy that Benny had introduced her to at dinner several months prior.

"I'll have someone look at that," he said, gently turning her arm so he could see better. "Overboard you said? Toward shore?" He leaned down to untie the bow rope so his boat could give chase no doubt, when they heard an ear-splitting, terrifying scream in the direction of the shore. It sounded male to Natalie's ears, though it was hard to tell really.

"Go!" the man ordered, and stepped to the stern to release the rope joining the two boats, staying aboard with Natalie. Once the boats were a few feet apart, the pilot of the other boat quickly drew away and the man turned back to Natalie.

"What about Emma Benneton?" he said. "He take her with him?"

"No, she slipped off when you were approaching," Natalie said. "The Dutchman was distracted, so she jumped overboard. To escape."

He nodded and watched as the other boat slowly circled something in the water about twenty yards away. It circled the object a couple of times, then the engine was gunned and the boat swiftly came back to where they floated idling. This time, they didn't tie up but came by close enough to talk.

"Shark," a black-shirted man announced. "He must have been bleeding. They don't usually attack that close to shore."

"Dead?"

"Couple of limbs floating, lots of blood," the man replied. "I'd say so, yes."

The man turned as Natalie lurched to the side of the boat, leaned over and threw up. He turned back to the other man. "Any sign of the woman?"

"What woman?"

"Never mind," he said, then turned to Natalie who was now leaning over the stern railing, her hair dangling in front of her face.

"She must have made it," he said flatly.

Natalie wiped her mouth with the back of her hand and turned to face him. "It could have gotten them both." She shuddered and brought her hand to her mouth as she gagged.

"Sharks attack one target at a time and if he was bleeding, that would have made him the first choice. Other sharks will come now but if she had a head start, then she probably made it before the sharks were attracted. The FBI will find her if she made it. She'll be fine."

"So what now?" Natalie asked. "It's all over, isn't it?" The last part was a statement more than a question.

The man looked at her. "Why don't you see if there's a first aid kit aboard," he said. He waved to the other boat, gave them a thumbs up sign and the boat took off without him.

"We'll clean you up, then we get you back to Sint Maarten," he said.

Natalie cocked her head, confusion masking her face.

"The FBI can handle things from here," he said. "The Dutchman's gone. That's all that matters to us." He stepped over to the controls and revved up the idling engine. "My name is Frank Daro, by-the-way. I'm with the CIA."

Natalie laughed half-heartedly. Of course he was. This adventure couldn't get any stranger.

"It's time to go home Natalie," he said softly. As Natalie headed into the cuddy to find a first aid kit amongst all the bags in the hold, the CIA guy steered the boat away from the island and out toward open sea. He called down into the cuddy: "While you're down there, see if he stocked any beer, will you?"

303

The Security

Chapter Sixty-Two

Three months later

"It's beautiful isn't it?" Emma Benneton said.

It definitely wasn't the U.S.A. Colors seemed more vibrant, the air cleaner, and the buildings were considerably older.

"I think it's a great place to start over," the man sitting beside her said.

Emma put her arm around her son and squeezed.

"Urgh," Drew Scanlon exclaimed. Emma withdrew quickly.

"I'm so sorry. I keep forgetting it will take a lot longer to heal than the scratches and broken bones you used to get as a little boy."

Drew stood up and began pacing the patio. The knife wound had taken a full two months to heal and his shoulder would always feel tight. Since the knife hadn't actually penetrated any muscle, only the rotator cuff had been damaged, meaning he wouldn't be playing tennis or baseball for a while. And he'd probably know well in advance of any thunderstorms. Other than that, he'd likely recover and his injuries would be unnoticeable.

The owner of the Tuscan Villa had been a Spanish IT entrepreneur who cared little for the nostalgia and history that enveloped the property. As a result, the main house and two outbuildings had begun to show signs of neglect. Drew and Emma had picked it up for a song at an auction a couple of months back when the Spanish millionaire had finally realized he would never live here. They had since been going over restoration drawings and Emma's dreams for a perfect retirement palace.

He didn't like it when his mother spoke of his youth. He had not actually forgiven her for her neglect, though he knew she thought he had. He had been happy without her; his foster parents giving him a home and a life that more than compensated for her lack of maternal instincts. He wasn't about to become the son she didn't have and never wanted. She had given up that right years ago. He was only here because of her idea. It had brought them together again. And it had failed. So now he would help her get back on her feet. And then he would disappear.

His life savings were funding the project but he didn't care. The money wasn't important. Not really. If it set his mother up after losing her husband, her money, even her lover, then he'd gladly give it all to her. He wanted a life. A new life. He'd burned all his bridges at the FBI. But he'd realized somewhere along the line--playing the game of being the Dutchman's gigolo recruiter--that he hadn't been cut out to be a straight, by the book, fibbie anyway. It was just too fucking boring. Jet-setting was much more fun.

And although he was giving most, if not all of his funds to his mother, he wasn't worried. He had a plan.

He turned back to his mother, his own inner assurances allowing him to smile at her. "I'll be fine Emma," he said. "But will you be?"

She frowned. "I was rather hoping you would be a part of this, you know, the restructure. Of the building. Of our lives."

He sat down again and took her hand in his, staring into her eyes. "Emma... Mother, I am happy to help you start over. But I have my own dreams. In a few months, I'd like to move on, pursue the next stage of my life." He laughed at her mock disappointment. He knew she wasn't a loner. She'd have a new girlfriend, or sugar-daddy husband by year's end. What she needed Drew for was his money. "I am not ready for retirement. I've seen too much, experienced too much. I want more."

"But you're spending all your money on this," she opened her arms to take in the crumbling stone facade of the main house. "How will you support your dreams?"

Drew leaned in and kissed his mother's cheek. "I have to make a phone call," he said. "I'll go into town. Should I pick up some fresh vegetables?"

"Actually, I brought you a basket full," a voice came from the patio door. "Sorry, your front door was open. I left the veggies in the kitchen."

Drew stood and stepped back from the table where his mother sat, enjoying a late afternoon cocktail. He wasn't sure whether he should shake the man's hand, or run like hell.

Emma saved him the trouble of deciding.

"Frank, so good of you to come," she said, extending her hand to his. He pulled it to his lips and kissed the top of it gently. He then reached to shake Drew's hand.

"I'm sorry Andrew," she said. "I forgot to tell you Deputy Director Daro called earlier and asked if he could drop by. Her lips curled coyishly.

"Drop by?" Drew said, his tone wary. Frank Daro didn't just fly to Italy on a whim. He would have had to plan this excursion and therefore, had an ulterior motive.

"Sit down Agent Scanlon. I come in peace," Frank said.

Drew cocked his head. Frank handed Emma an envelope. "As promised my dear."

Emma took it, sat down, and after taking a big gulp of her drink, ripped open the top. Frank walked around the table, behind the flabbergasted Drew, and sat down beside her.

"The Dutchman files are closed. Everyone's happy," he said, looking at Emma, then when he realized she was pre-occupied, to Drew.

"Even the FBI?" Drew asked, knowing now that he would be forced to face them sooner or later or he'll always be on the run. If Frank had found him, they certainly wouldn't be far behind.

"Sure, we told them you died in the crossfire. Your Agent Burelli was more than happy to let my people handle the body removals. They were more pissed about not getting to interrogate the Dutchman."

Drew dropped down into one of the remaining chairs, a sigh escaping his lips. After a moment he said, ""You didn't want that to happen, did you?"

Frank smiled. "Start a new life or go home to face the music. You're choice. We won't interfere either way. We got what we wanted: one less Dutchman."

Drew stared at him. The "we" he spoke of was the CIA. And if the FBI thought he was dead, maybe things were okay.

They both looked over at Emma whose eyes were watering.

"I hadn't expected to linger," Frank said, getting up quickly. He reached out to take Drew's hand. "I'm sure you'll be glad to see the back of me Scanlon. Regardless of how it all came down, it was, in the end, a job well done." He grinned as he shook Drew's hand. "Even if you don't work for me."

After Frank left, Emma's sobbing turned into open crying and she dropped the envelope and its contents onto the table, staring out over the forgotten vineyard. Drew reached over, picked up the papers, and began to read.

Eventually, Emma stopped crying and pulled a handkerchief from her pocket to wipe her eyes. Drew put down the papers and joined his mother in staring out across the fertile but currently overgrown land.

One of the papers was an apology letter from Diane. When she and Emma had parted ways after Agent Burelli had deposited them on Sint Maarten, she had explained that she would have to report back to Langley and, hopefully, hand in her resignation. They were to meet again in Tuscany by the end of the summer. But that hadn't happened. Part of the deal she had made with her superiors upon her return was to take on another assignment in South America. Although she had intended to retire and live with Emma, the Company saw things differently. She had gone on to explain that in exchange for leaving Emma and Drew alone, she would have to make amends for almost letting the Dutchman escape from their grasp. Luckily, he had aided in his own demise and all was well with the world. But she hadn't been given the golden handshake she desired. Rather, they had shackled her to a diplomat in Bogota, the goal of which was to find out how much money he was skimming off the Columbian government's rebuilding and relocation initiative. No one left the CIA, as they say. Or at least she had said, quite decisively.

However, she had managed to convince the powers that be that since Emma had helped end the reign of the notorious killer/kidnapper, the Dutchman, she should get some kind of reward. At the bottom of the stack of papers were an American passport and Italian driver's license in her maiden name: Emma Richardson. Emma's country was thankful for her assistance but a passport and license were sufficient thanks in their minds. Diane had disagreed, albeit without anyone's knowledge. Thus, the last item in the pile: a five-million-dollar bank draft, also in her maiden name.

Diane had somehow removed funds from the Dutchman's Cayman accounts prior to handing over the ledgers to her superiors.

Drew reached out and took his mother's hand once again. "It appears you might not need all my money after all."

She touched his cheek and rubbed it gently with the palm of her hand. Her eyes were glistening but she nodded.

"We all have dreams dear. It's just that some work out better than others."

The Security

Chapter Sixty-Three

Even at ten in the morning, the street was lively and vibrant.

Natalie sat at a sidewalk table on the narrow serving space separating art deco restaurants and hotels from Ocean Drive, the most prominent features in her view being the world's most expensive, luxurious and rarely-seen automobiles, slowly pacing, engines throbbing, along the boulevard like models strutting along a runway. South Beach had always been one of her favorite places, where money was more important than power or even status. Drug dealers, questionable import/exporters, politicians, and legitimate businessmen all mixed with tourists along a roughly two mile stretch of Miami Beach that had become the epitome of South Florida opulence.

Across the road, the beach was filling up, first with locals who knew all the best spots, then as the tourist set finally arrived after sleeping off the previous evening's hangover, the rest of the wide, newly scraped sand became obscured by multi-colored umbrella's, bathing suits, and towel bags.

Off to the left, a giant party tent was being set up at the edge of the beach, close to the road. A corporate event no doubt, close enough to the road to be ogled by passersby but in clear view of the beach, thereby providing the perfect ambiance for moneyed schmoozing.

Natalie thought back over the past three months, how her life had changed, and how much it was yet to change. The flight Frank Daro had put her on from Sint Maarten to Savannah had included a layover in Miami and Natalie had simply grabbed her carry-on luggage and walked out of the airport's main doors into a different kind of sunshine. She had appreciated the islands, despite her circumstances for being there, but she much preferred a more civilized, lively, and luxurious place to the touristy equivalents in the Caribbean. And she hadn't been ready to go home yet, if indeed, home was in Savannah. Miami was where the action was for the young and beautiful. Besides, she needed to work and once she'd spoken to Benny last night, the Carolina's were no longer an option.

"Can I buy you another coffee?"

Natalie looked up to see a well-dressed older Latin man staring down at her, his smile attempting to be genuine, but his gleaming teeth betraying his true intentions.

"Refills are free," she said, opening her mouth wide, so her own teeth glimmered in the sunshine.

The man's smile intensified. Although he wore a beautiful mauve silk tie, his top button was undone; he likely wasn't used to sporting suits every day. Men began amassing weight easily after fifty.

"Well, I have a meeting to attend shortly but I would be happy to return and share lunch with you," he said, his Spanish accent only marginally evident. He spread his arms to encompass the abundance of high-end restaurants adorning the boulevard. "Your choice."

"Can my boyfriend join us?" Natalie asked.

The man frowned. "I fear that is a standard rejection line, correct?" he said, his smile faltering. "You are a tourist, yes?"

Natalie thought about that for just a second. "At the moment, yes. My boyfriend hopes to change that."

"Then perhaps a boyfriend does exist, after all?" he said, bowing and backing away. "I apologize for any inconvenience miss. But if I return in an hour and you are still awaiting your companion, I will no longer take no for an answer. The Avalon boasts the finest shrimp bisque and, alas, the bowl is too large for just one person."

He tipped his panama hat and Natalie watched as he strode over to a gleaming turquoise blue Nissan NRX parked just across the street. The motor rumbled as he turned the ignition, revving it slightly more than necessary, causing several heads to turn in his direction. He deftly waved as he jolted into traffic amidst loud honks from other vehicles doing their own gliding.

Rich, of course, and handsome. Married, no doubt. Or if not, a Latin lover playboy who would share his amorous nature with more than one mistress at a time.

She grinned, thinking of her own nature. Over the years she had developed a radar for men that had gotten her one or two comfortable positions as primary mistress for rich, powerful, and lonely men. She had been good at it but the little fiasco on Shell Island had caused a change in her outlook. Things would be different now and this time around she would be in control.

She had given it considerable thought and planning and had finally instigated her new initiative with the first call to Benny a couple of weeks ago.

"You weren't at the airport," he had said, his voice low and growly.

"No Benny, I wasn't. And I won't be coming back."

"You've been missing a long time. I had reluctantly assumed that was so," he said, his tone quickly changing to stoicism and reservation. It had always been his usual response when she did things he didn't approve of. He didn't sound like he had been worried though. And there was something else in his voice too: resignation. She hoped it was due to the strength and resolve in her own voice.

She had been sitting on the massive king-sized bed in her $600 per night boutique hotel room facing the ocean, the contents of the Dutchman's go-bag spread out on the bedspread. She had taken it out of the boat's hold when Frank had deposited her in Philipsburg. He had obviously assumed it was hers and since her own bags had been left at the villa on the island, it seemed natural that she would have one.

In the Princess Julianna Airport lounge, after taking a quick peek inside the bag, and while awaiting her flight home, she had begun concocting the first stages of her Natalie Grainger makeover.

"Frank suggested that you had likely abandoned the plane in Miami," Benny had continued.

"Hmmm," she mumbled. She wasn't going to acknowledge anything at this point, despite the fact that it was quite obvious where she had gotten off. However, she could have gone anywhere in the weeks since. She could be anywhere in the US or even abroad, though she vaguely thought Frank Daro may have flagged her passport in case he needed to know where she was.

"So, why are you calling Natalie? Do you need money, is that it?" His tone had raised slightly. He was hopeful.

"Actually Benny, quite the opposite," she had said. "So please go to your desk, pull out your little scratch pad, and listen carefully. You'll want to get it all down on paper, so you don't miss anything."

While outlining her plan that night with a bewildered Benny, she had fondled the eight stacks of fifty and one hundred-dollar bills, the passports

313

The Security

in several different names, and especially the blue ledger that had been carefully wrapped in waterproof plastic.

She explained to him that she currently had access to all of the Dutchman's accounts--five in all--spread across the globe. Although Diane likely had knowledge of them also, she felt confident the ledger she possessed was the only record of exactly how much money there was, and where it was. If the Dutchman had used a computer to keep track, there would have been no need for a handwritten ledger. No, she was sure the Dutchman had gone old school so no one could find his accounts.

The CIA and FBI would be slow to process all the items they would have found on the island, but it would take time, and without the ledger, considerable investigation. But they'd find them eventually.

The real reason for the call that night was that she needed Benny's help.

She outlined her plan succinctly and without interruption from Benneton. She suggested he take the fifteen million he had lost to Emma and the Dutchman, and she would take fifteen million for herself. They would leave the remainder for the CIA or FBI to find, likely the former since Diane was the insider and would know where to look, especially if Natalie aided that inevitable process. According to the ledger, what's left would amount to some ninety million American dollars. They would know that the Dutchman had amassed a large amount of money but they wouldn't know exactly how much without access to the ledger. She was banking on Diane not knowing the exact amount either. With a prize of millions, she felt confident the powers that be would think they had captured everything, and therefore, no one would chase them for the missing thirty million, if indeed, they even found out it had been skimmed off the top.

Natalie had no idea how to access the funds but she had all the bank locations, account numbers, amounts--and most importantly--the individual passwords, all neatly handwritten in the ledger.

Benny agreed to have his company's unscrupulous legal and finance departments figure out how to transfer funds without leaving a trace. Fifteen million would buy Benny's loyalty and silence. In return, she would not tell the local South Carolina authorities about his collusion in Emma's grand kidnapping scheme. It wasn't much of a threat she knew. After all, Frank and the CIA must have known about it all anyway. That's why he and Drew had met at the hotel that first day, ensuring that Natalie would unwittingly go along with the plan to ensnare the Dutchman.

Regardless, Benny agreed to have his people set up accounts for her, and then he would let her go. He didn't really need the money. And he didn't need her. He would establish a new mistress without much effort; money had a way of providing those luxuries. Eventually, he could file for divorce, once Emma's disappearance was acknowledged as permanent by the legal system. Then he would be a free agent, as he had intended right from the beginning. He had wanted Natalie back, sure. For a little while. But she knew he never intended to marry again, at least not to someone who played the role of perfect mistress. No, he would need someone more prominent, more trophy-like; another Emma, but more compliant. Natalie knew she could easily have stayed on as Benny's mistress--that had been the original plan--but that wasn't in the cards any longer.

Looking at her watch, and leaving some change on the table for her coffee, Natalie got up and strode across the street to the sparkling red Porsche 911 she had been renting. Her flight to the Caymans was leaving in four hours and she needed to pack her things. She patted her large purse which she now carried everywhere with her. Inside was the ledger, carefully wrapped in new plastic. Benny had been true to his word and her first meeting on Grand Cayman was with her newly appointed account manager. But it was the second meeting she was really looking forward to.

Chapter Sixty-Four

He could see her sitting on the stool next to the open windowed second floor bar. He could think of better places to meet on Grand Cayman than this silly pigeon-headed excuse for an island bar right at the port. But it was busy, being the place where all the transfer boats from visiting cruise ships deposited their multitudes of tourists three times a week.

She seemed even prettier than he remembered, more poised, more... together. Though the last time he'd seen her, she'd been disheveled and terrified. They had, however, spoken several times since then.

He looked at his watch and realized he was fifteen minutes early. Smiling, he walked in to the lower level and ascended the stairs to the balcony bar.

"Can I interest you in a swim with the stingrays, Miss?" he said as he came up behind her.

Natalie slowly turned and when she saw him, grinned. "You're early." She stood and they hugged, a little stiffly at first, then warming up to it.

"As are you," he said. "I gather we have both learned a little tradecraft over these past few months."

She cocked her head and squinted.

"Never mind," he said, sitting on a stool beside her and looked out at the view. "It's a beautiful day, I'm in beautiful company, and I feel like a beautiful drink; something with a plastic painted umbrella in it, I think."

Natalie smiled and motioned for the waitress to come and take his order. The view from the second floor was not terribly exciting: docks, plain white transfer ships, and scores of tourists milling about waiting for excursions. But the tropical breeze promised that sandy beaches and rollicking aqua blue waves weren't far away.

"I've seen our first mark," she said, pointing her head to a balding man at a table across the bar. He was sitting with a striking woman, both appeared to be in their late fifties.

"Daniel Shakton," her companion stated. "Retired judge, accomplished sailor, and all-around good old American boy."

"And his wife?" Natalie asked.

"Patricia Jeanine Shakton, former Texas state model, aspiring painter, and all-around good-ole trophy wife," he said smiling. "And she wants out."

"You've initiated contact already?" Natalie asked surprised.

The man patted her knee and stared at Natalie's eyes. "You said you were ready for this." He nodded his head at the couple across the bar. "And so are they. It's your first time, I realize, but don't forget, I've done this a few times before." He winked. "She's worth ten million to us."

Natalie looked at the couple, then back to her friend.

"You do have a way with words, you scoundrel," she said, then leaned in and kissed Drew Scanlon on the lips.

Half an hour later they left the bar, hand in hand. Natalie asked, "Is she pretty?"

"Who?"

"His mistress, you idiot."

Drew cocked his head and grinned. "Rule number one: never get involved with the security. They are so unpredictable."

They laughed as they stepped out onto Harbour Drive, turning left, heading into downtown Georgetown where they had a dinner reservation and a room for the evening.

As they passed by Cardinal Avenue, a man in a loud Hawaiian shirt sat in a black jeep, tinted windows rolled up. He had allowed the concession of the canvas roof to be rolled back to allow in fresh air but he didn't want to be seen. Unfortunately, he had travelled here many times and was known to many locals, as well as the people he was currently surveilling.

He had always thought Drew had enjoyed his undercover work a little too much. But the girl was a bit of a surprise. It didn't matter though. He wasn't sure how he was going to play this one out yet. He was CIA, and he was on American soil. Not much he could do officially. Unofficially though, the new team might just be useful.

So, Frank Daro would watch...and wait.

The End

A note from the author...

As an author who has chosen self-publishing as the best way to reach a broad market, on a continuous basis, it is imperative that I convince readers to take a few moments to write a review... or at the very least, rank this read from one to five.

Although this is not mandatory in order to enjoy reading books by myself or any other author, I can assure you that without your input, we authors sit in the dark, day after day, wondering if what we are creating actually has any merit.

Your few moments of gracious participation justifies months—even years—of pouring our souls into words.
We only need a few from you to make it all worthwhile.

If you are so inclined, please go to amazon and look up the title, then leave a star ranking... and if you are particularly moved, a short review. If you send me the link to your review, I will send you a copy of my bestselling "**New York Fried**!" FREE of charge (including shipping) in the format of your choice.

I, and every other author, am forever grateful for your participation.

Thank you!

Robert J. Morrow
editor@robertjmorrow.com
January 2019

PS: I answer all my emails.

Robert J. Morrow spent four decades in advertising, marketing, journalism, publishing, and real estate before becoming a full-time writer. His bestselling non-fiction books on real estate can be found at amazon.ca/com or robertjmorrow.com.

The Security is his second thriller novel. He lives with his life partner, Susan, in Southern Ontario.

If you enjoyed this book, please go to www.amazon.com and rate it (from 1-5). If you don't mind, also write a short review (good or bad) at Amazon. This is how self-published authors get known to other readers like you. Send us your review and we'll send you a FREE BOOK. books@SunaoPublishing.com

To see more books, go to www.RobertJMorrow.com. Join the mailing list and receive FREE BOOKS as well as deals on hot new releases.

FOLLOWING is an excerpt from **New York Fried**, Robert J. Morrow's bestselling debut novel and first in the Artichoke Hart Adventure series.

New York Fried

by Robert J. Morrow

Prologue

The scariest place in the world is also the quietest.

At least that's what Lieutenant Jeon Byung-Soon thought. He had been wandering through the slowly lightening dawn for about twenty minutes, the rest of his small platoon following behind. Every few feet, one of his men would pull at the wire fencing and another would prod the barbed wire above with the tip of his M4 assault rifle.

Beyond the fence was the most beautiful scenery the twenty-one-year-old Lieutenant had witnessed. He stopped and watched as a slow, creamy white fog drifted across the lowlands, filtering the sun's emerging morning light as it traced across tall grass and low shrubbery, its lazy entrails whispering around small trees and other outcroppings. Few if any humans had walked this land for over sixty years, leaving it to nature, which included rare and endangered tigers, amur leopards and Asiatic black bears. Lieutenant Jeon liked to stare out into the wilderness at times like this, just as night became day. He would let his eyes rest, eventually letting them defocus. It was a trick his father had taught him as a small child chasing crickets in the back yard of his home. Soon his eyes rested, focusing on nothing in particular but rather taking in the entire panoramic view as a whole. It was then that he could discern small movements in his peripheral vision, like a rare red-crowned crane stepping tentatively between the grasses, or a goat grazing lazily on the edge of a hill. And, of course, any stray humans attempting to cross the deserted landscape, seeking refuge on his side of reality.

A Seoul native, Lieutenant Jeon was patrol leader for a Republic of Korea platoon delegated with ensuring the Demilitarized Zone was secure and without breaches. Twice a day, Lieutenant Jeon and his camouflaged group of South Korean soldiers would trek alongside the eight-foot high fencing that marked the edge of the DMZ on the South Korean side. Two and a half miles distant was similar fencing creating the official edge of the Democratic People's Republic of Korea, better known as North Korea. Running the width in the center of the DMZ was the Military Demarcation Line (MDL), which was the actual political border running along the thirty-eighth parallel. According to the armistice established in 1953, troops from both sides were to retreat twenty-two hundred yards from the front line, thus creating this no-man's land in between.

There were a couple of villages within the border of the DMZ but not many people lived in either and those who did kept to the village proper for fear of being mistaken for the enemy by either side. Panmunjom, near the western coast, was home to the Joint Security Area (JSA) and was really the only place where humans actually congregated; mostly soldiers from both sides who spent hours staring at one another across a five-inch-wide concrete slab, which represented the border. Of late, there had been an abundance of tourists, which to Lieutenant Jeon's dismay, seemed to lessen the importance of what was actually happening here. Over a million soldiers were posted on either side, making the DMZ one of the world's most heavily fortified frontiers. All it would take is for one brazen tourist to skip over the concrete slab and it wouldn't be absurd to have that become the catalyst for starting World War III.

All Lieutenant Jeon wanted was to finish out the week and take leave to see his girlfriend less than 65 miles away in the South Korean capital and get away from the maddening solitude. He was an avid soccer player and the cacophony of shouting voices, thudding feet, and spirited after-game celebrations were like a magnet for his senses which had been numbed by the constant silence.

"Sir, we are ready to move on, Sir," Sergeant Park said, his Korean clipped and insistent. Lieutenant Jeon's mind quickly returned to the task at hand.

He brought his eyes back into focus, grasped his rifle tighter and, pointing the muzzle toward the ground, nodded his head for his men to move out.

Twenty minutes later, the terrain became steeper and Jeon knew they were approaching the last of three observation towers on their route.

"Sergeant, take Corporal Sung and go ahead to the tower," Jeon said, nodding toward the turn in the trail that he knew would lead them up the twenty steps built into the hill, ending at the tower that marked the turning point in their patrol. The Sergeant nodded and, together with the Corporal, disappeared around the corner.

Moments later, Lieutenant Jeon and the remainder of the platoon rounded the corner and saw the tower just ahead. Situated on a rise at the edge of a sloping cliff, it overlooked a lush green valley, dotted with small, ponds and mini-lakes. They purposefully climbed the steps and were almost at the observation level when Sergeant Park gestured at him animatedly, his arms swinging quickly, his eyes questioning.

"Lieutenant, Bob is not there," he said, his arms gesturing across the valley.

"What do you mean Sergeant?" Jeon said.

"I mean Bob has not emerged from the tower since we arrived Sir," Park replied. "And I see no others from the platoon in the immediate vicinity either."

"Let me see," Jeon said, impatiently jumping up the final steps and grabbing the younger man's binoculars.

He focused the lenses and gazed at the tower located approximately 1800 yards away, a little lower down the valley aside a clearing. He waited. And waited.

"You see, Sir?" Park said, his voice shrill.

"Perhaps he is taking a leak Sergeant," Jeon said, smiling. The platoon saw the same North Korean soldier every day, his binoculars raised in a similar fashion, aimed directly at them. Since they didn't know his name, they called him Bob.

"The others are not there either, Sir," Park continued.

Jeon surveyed the opposing tower, moving his focus up and down the tower's steps, then side to side, taking in the landscape to each side of the tower. There was no movement whatsoever. He thought for a moment.

"Sergeant Park, take three men and follow the trail to the rise," Jeon pointed in the direction of a hill that was the highest in the vicinity. The patrol didn't normally go that far as that part of the trail was designated to another patrol, but it was the highest peak for several miles. "Take your binoculars and see if you can locate the platoon."

Park nodded and turned, then quickly turned back, remembering to salute. Then motioning three others, he bounded down the steps and raced along the fence toward the hill.

Lieutenant Jeon continued to scan the lush area surrounding the tower, resting on the small pond to its left, and the clearing where the North Korean troops usually sat smoking cigarettes and cleaning their rifles. Bob was usually the only one at the tower and he never left unless relieved. It had been his habit for the months of observation Jeon and his platoon had been witness to. Jeon didn't really think Bob had disappeared behind a tree to take a leak; he had never done that before. If a North Korean soldier abandoned his post during a patrol, Jeon knew the others in his platoon would report his actions and the man would be immediately disciplined.

So where the hell was he?

"Sir!" Park jumped up the steps to the tower, his breathing fast and heavy. "I scoured the entire area, Sir. There is no sign of any platoon. Not only that but we didn't see smoke from the Dyang frontier either."

Jeon stared at him. The Dyang frontier was a nickname the troops had given to a camp post just beyond the fencing on the Northern side. It was known to be a place where several platoons met daily and, over raging barrel fires, smoked, talked and generally wasted time before heading back to or from their barren barracks deeper in territory. There was always a fire going, day and night, and as a result there was always a trail of smoke in the sky directly above its location.

"You are sure Sergeant Park?" the Lieutenant asked, knowing full well the Sergeant would not be mistaken.

"Yes Sir!" he confirmed. The other men were all looking at one another, blank expressions on their faces. Obviously they had no idea what to make of the mystery.

The Security

Neither did Lieutenant Jeon. In his two years patrolling the DMZ, this had never occurred before. He pulled at his lapel, searching for the communications switch that would connect him to his commanding officer in Panmunjeom.

Before he spoke into his tiny microphone, he stared one last time out into the wilderness, the green grasses glistening as the fog dissipated and the dawning sunlight filled in shadows throughout the lonesome scene. Silence pervaded, with only a light wind causing the low tree limbs to bristle.

Where the hell were all the Koreans?

Chapter One

The quiet was absolute. Outside the circle of light caused by the three-foot flames of the campfire, there was nothing but darkness. The high-canopied trees acted like insulation against the outside world and all they could see and hear were the orange and yellow flames and the crackling of the dried pine logs.

"If I threw a grenade in the middle of the fire, what would you do... dive for cover, or jump on top of the grenade?"

Frank Daro and Arthur Hart had been camping with their kids in upstate New York for nearly ten years. Pretty soon, the kids would be teens and have no desire to camp with them anymore. Then they'd need a fresh excuse to do what they were doing now: sitting around a roaring fire drinking beer, smoking expensive Cuban cigars, and discussing idiotic scenarios.

"I'm serious," Frank continued. "Would you jump on the fire, killing yourself but saving the kids, or would you save yourself and yell for the kids to do the same?"

"I'd kill you," Hart said.

"But I have the grenade."

"No, you just threw it in the fire."

Frank laughed. "You saying you wouldn't act on instinct? You've thought it through, right, I mean, something like this?"

"Frank, I've been your friend for what, a decade?" Hart said. He took a long swig of semi-cold beer and stared into the flames. "Of course I've thought about situations like that."

Frank's smile faded. "Ah, come on. Nothing's ever happened."

Hart's twelve-year-old son, Jamie, came out of the tent and ambled over to the fire. He grabbed a long stick he had previously carved into a point, slumped into one of the cheap beach chairs we'd lugged around for years and looked around for the marshmallows.

Frank tossed him one from the bag in his lap. It flew across the fire and landed in Jamie's lap. Hart glanced at Frank. He grinned.

"You moron," Hart said.

Jamie snickered and stuck the marshmallow on the end of his stick.

An hour later, the three kids were in the tents playing a game of Pictionary, an old standby that always occupied them well once they realized there was no TV, no computer, no video games, and definitely no smartphones. Both fathers agreed there would be no electronic gadgets after 11pm. If they had their way, they wouldn't bring them at all. But then, neither Frank or Hart could live more than an hour without their Androids, and hypocrites they weren't.

Frank could keep a fire going for hours, not huge but steady; the kind of fire you could roast weenies and marshmallows on, and then when it got a bit chilly, could be turned into a raging inferno with the twist of a stick. That was Frank's job, keeping the flame going while they finished off the twelve-pack.

Hart's job was setting up camp, unpacking groceries, cooking, washing up, and putting kids to bed. For almost a decade nothing much had changed and--despite Hart's ex-wife insisting that it was a ridiculous relationship (there was irony in that somewhere) --neither Frank nor he felt it should. Recently, the kids had taken over some of the chores but then he felt useless and usually told them to go take a hike…literally. Frank would just laugh and pass him another beer.

They weren't really drunk all the time; that wouldn't be good parenting. But from Friday night to Sunday night they were never completely sober. A dull, summertime haze is what they called it. The kids didn't mind, or at least wouldn't mention it until they were in their thirties and in therapy. And they hadn't started drinking themselves yet so they weren't feeling appropriately guilty, again, according to Hart's ex. He figured within a decade, they'd be bringing a twenty-four pack to accommodate the whole crew.

"You talk to General Wade lately?" Frank asked.

"Not since your last get together," Hart answered.

"He wants to hold a gathering," Frank said. "I suggested your place."

"Of course you did," Hart said.

"You'll find this one particularly interesting," Frank continued. "And personally gratifying."

Hart tried to make out Frank's eyes across the fire but the flames were too intense. His face was a mask of smoke and flickering light.

"Don't bullshit me," Hart said. "You're spying on someone, and just need a place to do it."

"You're spoiling the surprise," Frank muttered.

Hart groaned. After a few moments of silence he said, "I'll set it up with Al. He'll know what to do."

The Security

"Yeah, Al's good.

They were silent for a while, both thinking about kids, parenting, and gatherings organized by high-ranking military acquaintances.

"Hey Frank?" Hart said. The other man looked up at him finally. He noticed Frank's eyes were a little glazed. "When they come for you, you'll let me know, right?"

Frank guffawed. Hart knew he hadn't taken him seriously.

"Oh, and by-the-way," he continued. "If anyone ever does throw a grenade into our campsite, I'll expect *you* to dive on it."

Chapter Two

The restaurant was called *The Artichoke Hart*, not because the specialty is artichokes but because of his name.

Since Art Hart was difficult to trill off the tongue, he had grown up with monikers including *part fart* and, of course, *Art the Fart*. But sometime in his early teens a school friend had discovered the prickly fruit--her parents ran a grocery store--and he became *Artichoke*. Since he couldn't find anything disparaging other than the vegetable being mysterious and a little hard to swallow--which he thought was kinda cool anyway--it stuck.

Some twenty years later, his name was now associated, in subdued neon, with a barely viable, upscale casual dining establishment that arguably offered some of the best jazz in the Baltimore, Maryland area. He felt time had rounded him, physically and mentally, but knew he'd become even more prickly. Staying in shape was getting harder as he aged but he still exercised most days and kept his mass under two hundred pounds. He grinned recalling that some patrons told him he looked like Chef Gordon Ramsey without the hair. But since running a restaurant was not something he had ever aspired to do for a living, he was forced to hire Al Rocca.

Al was a former colleague of Frank's, but unlike the roguish, tough-guy persona Frank exemplified, Al was short, round and cuddly, in a brown bear kind of way. He would make some career-obsessed woman a tremendous wife someday, Hart thought. He was also the best chef Hart had ever met, despite having absolutely zero formal training. He was organized as hell too, which was good, because although Hart dabbled in cooking, he couldn't balance books if his life depended on it. Lately, that had become evident every two weeks when he sat down in his office and emptied his bank account via payroll checks and supplier invoice payments.

Things weren't all bad though. There was always the assurance that should someone have too much to drink, Al can easily double as the bouncer. Because Al used to be employed by the CIA.

"Frank called Friday," Al said, without looking at Hart as he strode into the restaurant early Monday morning. "Wants to do another one of his gatherings."

"He only told me yesterday," Hart said. "At the campfire."

Al smiled. He was wrapping cutlery in cloth napkins at the bar. He still didn't look up.

"He wishes to spare no expense," Al said.

"That's because the taxpayers will be footing the bill," Hart said, joining him at a barstool opposite. Hart knew Frank had already discussed his speakeasy with Al before laying it on him at the campsite. Telling him was a courtesy since Al did all the organizing and prepping. And besides, Frank knew Hart needed the income so why would he say no?

He grabbed a few recently washed cloth napkins and began folding them into triangles. "He's also expecting special guests, no doubt."

"No doubt," Al said. He finally looked up. "He wants us to record it."

"Of course he does."

"He didn't tell you anything?" Al asked.

"You know we never talk shop on campouts," Hart answered. Actually, Frank and Hart rarely talk shop at all. The less Hart knew about his best friend's life as Deputy Director of the CIA, the better.

"I've got a menu figured," Al said. "You want to have a look?"

Hart cocked his head sideways and smiled.

"Okay, just checking," he said, pulling away from the bar, leaving Hart to finish wrapping the cutlery. A moment later, he called from the kitchen.

"If you see Lazare, hold me back."

"Only if it gets me out of dishes detail," Hart yelled back. Al didn't answer but Hart heard pots clanking loudly as they were being racked. Daniel Richard Lazare was the current CIA Director -- Frank's boss. According to Al, Lazare stood for everything he eventually had come to hate about the Company.

Al Rocca looked like an Italian bricklayer, complete with the receding hairline and bulky forearms. He would be the owner of the *Hart* if he had the money and jokes that he would have called it *The Rock*, but since his ex got most of his money, it hadn't been an option. Hart had already solved his alimony problem by giving his ex the matrimonial home--Hart lived in a tiny apartment above the restaurant and strongly felt the kids shouldn't have to move--so most of his savings had gone into the first and last month's rent and a lot of leasehold improvements for the restaurant.

Al liked to cook…a lot. And he had read a couple of books on running a restaurant which made him more informed than Hart, so Hart made him Manager. He paid him enough to be a partner, though they'd never considered formalizing the arrangement. Al wasn't worried. Neither was Hart. They probably should be, Hart thought, since they never seemed to make a profit at the end of the month. But Al created some amazing dishes and

Hart hired some awesome bands. It was fun and the customers loved it. So far, their heads were above water. They were dog paddling but had yet to drown.

During the week Al and the staff handled supper easily most of the time which is why Hart played sommelier at his favorite spot at the bar whiling away the weekday evenings watching videos of new bands he was considering booking for the weekends. Occasionally, he'd get up and make the rounds, conversing genially at patron's tables. On Monday evenings, once a month, the doors closed at 3pm and he cooked for the staff and their spouses. It was costly, stressful for him, and they lost the evening dinner income, but it was his way of saying thanks for their running a four-star restaurant with very little help from the owner.

Prior to the *Artichoke Hart*, Al and Hart both had challenging careers and after a while they had both lost their jovial attitudes, their zest for life... and their wives. The *Hart* was therapy for both of them.

Ten years after leaving their paying jobs and starting the restaurant, they'd got their lives back. Except for the jobs…oh, and the wives. In Al's case, he was still trying. In Hart's, he felt like she had never really left. Spending time with his two children meant he had to stay in touch with her. He couldn't wait till they turned sixteen.

A moment later, Al came out to the bar again. "So who's the party for?" he asked.

"I'm sure General Wade has a new pet project," Hart said.

"Oh? Anything earth shattering?"

"He's Military Intelligence's liaison to the CIA," Hart said flatly. "Everything he does is earth shattering."

"So we can anticipate some of the postulators?" Al said

"If I know Frank, he's going to take advantage of the occasion and do a little schmoozing."

"I'd better get out the boxed wine, eh?"

Hart laughed. Frank arranged for important intelligence community functions to be held at the *Artichoke Hart* as often as he could, and he always wanted the booze to flow. Once any official festivities were done with and the reporters had left, everyone took advantage of the rare chance for field agents, analysts, politicians and influential business magnates to mingle. They drank, smoked cigars, and talked about things they really shouldn't be talking about in public. Occasionally Frank would invite people he was investigating or researching. Thus, the reason he often had them record the events.

"I'll help at the bar on this one," Hart said. Al's eyes narrowed. Hart grinned. "Don't worry, the tapes will be running, as they say. But you know what else they say: people tell bartenders things they wouldn't tell their therapists. Listening to drunken spooks is a great way to find out what's going on in the world."

Al returned to the kitchen.

Chapter Three

Although the *Artichoke Hart* prided itself on being upscale casual, this was Baltimore, not DC; people tended to be a touch more relaxed. At Company events, however, everyone was in their finery, and, depending upon their age, typically emulated Don Johnson's *Sonny Crocket* or his more recent television persona, *Hap Briggs*.

"Nice turnout," Hart said to Frank. He was dressed in a dark blue Armani pin stripe that Hart hadn't seen him in since the last event.

"Hmmm". They didn't make eye contact. Frank was distracted, or focused, depending upon your understanding of Frank's moods.

"Wine okay?"

He leered at Hart. "Just make sure there's one of the good bottles under the counter where I can reach it."

Hart smiled.

"Frank, I need you to introduce me to someone." Director Lazare had snuck up behind them, grasped Frank's elbow, and nudged him toward the center of the room where several strangers were gathered, talking animatedly. Lazare looked like an accountant, with receding hair, a paunch, and short, thick legs. He'd never been in the field and had ridden desk jobs in the quagmire of Washington legaldom before being appointed as top spook. He gave Hart a curt nod while leading Frank away. Lazare and Hart had a terse relationship, mostly because he didn't like that the *Hart* wasn't a CIA-owned facility.

Al came through the kitchen doors carrying fresh appetizers. When he saw Lazare standing with Frank and Hart, he quickly turned about and returned to the haven of the kitchen. The appetizers went back too.

Hart smiled again. Frank's events were so much fun.

Lazare had led Frank into the center of one gathering and was introducing him to the very attractive Latina woman General Wade had introduced during his initial informal speech at the beginning of the gathering. Hart guessed her to be in her late twenties. About five feet, seven inches, she had classic long black hair, a noticeably narrow waist and long legs, hidden well at the moment in a very stylish business pantsuit but accented stylishly with four-inch black heels. Her hair was tied back in a ponytail and for a moment Hart thought of other exotic young women he'd met over the years. If he hadn't heard General Wade call her one of America's brilliant young IT experts, he would have thought she was some Senator's aide.

Frank glanced at Hart who motioned with his head toward the table in the far corner, near the glass block wall that allowed a great deal of light into the room from DeQuincy Street. There were hidden microphones set in the centerpieces at every table but Hart could only engage one at a time. The recorders and ten monitors were in my office in the basement.

Frank could review the whole event from several angles afterwards, or he could sneak down to the office part way through and listen in on conversations he thought were important enough for eavesdropping.

Frank had paid for the entire system, including a security set-up that rivaled most banks. Bands often left their equipment overnight, so Hart liked the fact that the restaurant couldn't easily be broken into, though knowing Frank, the *Hart* could likely take a nuclear hit and come out of it intact.

"Who's the hottie?" Al said, returning with the appetizers and placing them on the table beside Hart.

"Lena Lopez Castillo," he said. "Wade says she's some kind of IT genius."

Al's one eyebrow rose questioningly. "In that outfit, she could be a Columbian drug runner and Wade would still be working the crowd with her."

"Wade can't be swayed by a good-looking woman," Hart said.

"Sure," said Al. "That's why his wife of thirty years left him and he has thousand-dollar call girls coming to his penthouse every weekend."

Hart laughed. According to the General, Ms. Lopez Castillo is about to unleash the next big thing," he said.

Al's head tilted sideways as he looked at Hart, then over at Ms. Lopez Castillo, then back to Hart. "I'm not even going there," he said.

Hart laughed again. Al could be the life of the party. Too bad he couldn't be let loose on the crowd.

"So why do Latinas always have two or three last names, anyway?" he asked.

"Maybe she kept her ex-husband's name and added it to hers," Hart offered.

"She's divorced?" Al said, his eyes roaming her body up and down.

"Doesn't look old enough to have passed puberty to me," Hart said.

"Geez, you're getting old. Or blind," Al said.

"I think she's with the greaseball," Hart said, nodding his head toward the skinny man standing just behind Ms. Lopez Castillo. He looked to be a similar age as her but with his shiny greased hair pulled back in a ponytail he looked a little like Leonardo DiCaprio in that Four Musketeers remake. The ponytail looked odd when he and Ms. Lopez Castillo were close together, making him seem a little effeminate somehow since they both adorned ponies and both wore pants. Hart did register, however, how easy it was to tell the male from the female, thanks to the young Ms. Lopez Castillo's curves.

"Jay Losano," Hart said. "Her security chief and partner."

"Mafia?" Al asked.

"He grew up in Vegas, has Italian ancestors, and likes poker," Hart said. "Of course he's mafia."

"Seems he's got Lazare eating out of his armpits," Al said. "Wonder if the old codger knows he's gay."

"Who's gay?"

"Your mafia dude," Al said. "Look at the way he stands."

Hart looked over and thought perhaps Losano's way of leaning on one foot, arm on opposite hip, and chin raised did look a little less than manly but even DiCaprio had questionable posing moments.

"What an idiot," Al said, shaking his head as he sidled back to the kitchen to retrieve more food. Hart wasn't sure if he meant Losano, Lazare, or both.

Hart watched Losano scribble something on the back of a calling card and hand it to Frank. He held the pen with the two middle fingers of his right hand and handed the card over with a little flip of his wrist. Hart still wasn't sure. He courted the prerequisite permanent five o'clock shadow, and he dressed very well, tailor made right down to the tapered white gino shirt with subdued frilly designs embossed on the chest. Okay, on second thought, maybe he was gay.

Frank looked down at the card, grinned, and lifted his gaze up to Hart. He gestured toward the kitchen door. Hart nodded and headed for the stairs that lead to his downstairs office.

To continue reading **New York Fried**, please visit either Amazon.com, or RobertJMorrow.com.

And don't forget to join the mailing list at RobertJMorrow.com to receive FREE books!

The Security

Made in the
USA
Columbia, SC